The Battle of Stalwarts

Rose Johnston

Published by Zoe Johnston, 2024.

THE BATTLE OF STALWARTS

First edition. April 17, 2024.

Copyright © 2024 Rose Johnston.

ISBN: 979-8224826100

Written by Rose Johnston.

Table of Contents

However destructive may be the policies of the government and the methods and products of the corporations, the root of the problem is always found in private life. We must learn to see every problem that concerns us as conservationists always leadsstraight back to the question of **how we live.**

The world is being destroyed, no doubt about it, by the greed of the rich and powerful. It is also being destroyed by **popular demand.**

---Wendell Berry

The Race for the Planet

Gwinnie: What a great day it is once again! It's time for the big race, the one we all depend on: the race for the future of the planet. The weather is beautiful, as it has been every race day for the last fifteen years. Business brings their best weather tech to this one and it's easy to see why. We have a tip-top field here today, representing many of the science and technology disciplines, and a few long shots as well. The favorite this year, as in year's past, is from Business/Economics, represented today by a large black beauty with glowing red eyes.

Winnie: Business always brings an unusual interpretation of saving the planet, and has an outsize influence on this race, since they built the track and the stables. The controversial decision to reverse the direction the horses run was due to Business' tendency to breed and race right-handed horses. This gave Business a sizable advantage over the field for a hundred years, until the other disciplines finally bred some right-handed horses. The field is more equitable now, and we're looking for a great race.

Gwinnie: The horses are entering the track. Let's take a look at our competitors. First I see Mathematics. If this horse could run some charm up the flagpole, he might be a hit, but once again, we're looking at a big boring horse who will be around forever, but doesn't wear enough glitter. You know what they say: 'math don't lie', and that's a little too direct for these spectators, who are here to have fun, not do math. Next up is Law's entry, Endangered Species. Always a solid horse, and should place better than it does, but it gets bogged down with procedures. Just run around the track, counselor!

Winnie: Philosophy is coming up next. This year they have a pretty boy who looks solid, but will disintegrate at the stretch when it develops a new outlook on life where nothing matters. I mean, we suspect that it will, as the philosophy horse does this almost every year. Right behind Philosophy is Psychology—this one is hard to predict, as Psychology can go all over the track. We have seen some great things from the psychology horse, even winning in some years, but it has been disqualified over and over, possibly for calling the business horse a "psycho" in the winner's circle ten years ago and never apologizing. This year's entry, Moderation, isn't flashy at all, but we just can't tell. They're sneaky.

Gwinnie: To be fair, a lot of Business' entries are psychos. Physics is back this year. Although they're a very strong discipline, their horses have no drive to win. Physics knows that the planet will always endure, and it is not within their power to change much of the current situation. They still bring lovely and very solid horses, even if they won't compete. It's a pleasure to watch them run, then slow down and calculate how much weight the Business horse has put on. Engineering is bringing up the rear at a fast clip. They have been penalized in the past for bringing ungovernable horses to the race, after they blew up part of the stadium in a hay accident. After Engineering built a new stadium, three times as large as the previous one, they were allowed back. Their entry this year is also huge, much larger than all of the other horses, although his legs look a little shaky. Engineering says that there is no genetic engineering at their farms, and we just have to take their word for it, since they win a lot.

Winnie: Coming up behind engineering is Archeology and Sociology. These guys are unknown, by which I mean that no one cares about their entries and they have no chance of competing. It seems that these disciplines should do well and they're crowd favorites, but appeals to humanity don't work with this crowd, even if the crowd is—humanity.

Gwinnie: (giggle) I know, right? In a similar vein, the Ecology horse is always one of the most intelligent and compelling runners on the track, but due to its efficiency, no one notices it at all, and it is even left out of the official broadcast that Business puts together later.

Winnie: Business has its ways, Gwinnie! I remember when Biology was tossed from the Race permanently for not being an intact science anymore. Biology had to go to court and admit that the whole web was broken, and it was disallowed. When it came back as Ecology, nobody caught on. Year after year, Ecology enters the same horse—Biophilia—and even though it wins, somehow it disappears from the record. I always love this horse. It gives me a warm fuzzy feeling, like I want to go lie down in a field. Biophilia has won the Race for the Planet at least ten times, even with the missing species, but it is always photo shopped out of the winners circle, just as this entire commentary will be edited out of our broadcast later.

Gwinnie: But we still love Business, don't we, Winnie? Everyone does, despite themselves. They love the big bathrooms, they love the cold drinks. Contrast that sort of vitality to some of our past entries. Remember when the very serious disciplines Climatology and Meteorology had horses in the race? Despite the undeniable logic and veracity of their entries, they were universally hated by race fans. Climatology brought a horse named "Tipping Points." No one wants to bet on that. After being harassed by spectators every year, both disciplines dropped out of the race entirely, and now stay in their underground lairs, waiting for the end.

Winnie: Wow. No wonder nobody wanted them around. We have to wait for the race to decide. If Ecology is meant to win, then it will win. And if Business is meant to win, then it will win. The race is fair.

Winnie and Gwinnie together: *The race is fair.*

Gwinnie: It's a smaller field this year, due to some of the prime horse breeding areas in the country being wiped off the map by Tornado America. A few of the lesser known disciplines, like Literature and Humanities, will probably not be back. Technology will also not be represented this year. Their horse, Disruption, was disqualified again, so they all went down to South America to do Ayahuasca for a month.

Winnie: Speaking of disruption, Business has issued their usual statement about this year's largest natural disaster: 'We saw none of this coming, and our thoughts and prayers go out to artists everywhere.' Also, our congratulations to Bethanne Rinks of south Ohio, for her winning entry of 'Tornado America' for the bad weather on September 6. She's getting a trip to the new Biodome, where it looks like 1945 again. Good for you, Bethanne!

Gwinnie: It goes without saying that all of us here in fun-loving America have been shocked and saddened by the change in weather, and nobody knew it was coming. But it's time for the race! The horses are being loaded in the gate now. A lot of them are stubbornly left-handed and are having a hard time with it. It's a very sticky genetic trait. But you know—adapt. They're pretty touchy, all these disciplines in close proximity. Sociology's horse, It Takes A Village, seems to be giving a pre-race pep talk, but no one is listening. It looks like they're all in the gate now. Business on the inside track, as they are every year. Their horse, Eminent Domain, also has a large duffel bag in the saddle, contents unknown. But Business is allowed whatever breaks it needs to compete, which means that their entry this year must be a dog. I can't get over how their jockeys look like monkeys, every year, but we can't say anything or get accused or racism. I think they are using monkeys and it's illegal.

Winnie: Now, Gwinnie, that's never been proven in court. You do know that South Americans are very small, and because of the cloud-seeding accidents in the Amazon, some of them do look like monkeys. All of them are happy and grateful to be here after their horrible disfigurement. They have their own e-commerce channels now, so things are going better for them.

Gwinnie: I guess even people with no real education can appreciate a good business opportunity.

Winnie: It's the surest path out of poverty. And these horses are raring to go. Eminent Domain has smoke pouring out of his nostrils, due to the "'maximal probiotic cellular enhancement diet,' available from Equine Vitamin Formulations." Excellent choice. Psychology's entry, Moderation, looks a bit frazzled, although it is standing calmly in the gate and counseling the other horses about performance anxiety. Engineering's horse, Gimme A Lever, is stuffed into its gate, and is not happy about it. This happens every year, and they never learn. Three years ago, their entry was much too large for the gatehouse, so they were allowed to dig a ditch under him so he would fit.

Gwinnie: Those goofs! You'd think that they'd play by the rules and not enter genetically enhanced horses, but then, boys will be boys, won't they? I knew an engineer once that had a swing in his bathroom, over his round bathtub—

Winnie: Not now, Gwinnie.

Gwinnie: Right. Anyway, they always give us a good time. Next to Gimme A Lever, Philosophy's horse, Existential Crisis, appears to be taunting the engineering horse with things it doesn't understand. Philosophy always puts up a good fight, but engineering horses are so big and impressive, higher thought fades into insignificance.

Winnie: And they're off! There they go, some faster than others, according to their different philosophies about saving the world. Business always takes the lead though, since it gets a three-second head start. It did build the race track, after all.

Gwinnie: Eminent Domain is not moving so fast this morning, due to the mysterious duffel bag on its back. It doesn't seem very invested in the race, but has an early lead—well, there he goes! Eminent Domain's jockey has opened the bag and emptied it all over the track, and it is chock full of credit cards and cash. A cloud of filthy lucre. What an efficient business tactic, and we're only seconds into the race. I've never seen such a move from Business, except the dozen or so other times they have done this, and it always works. The other horses are slowing down at the sight, because no matter what their discipline, they have to respect money. Eminent Domain has run off the track and is filing for reimbursement of his stolen duffel bag, so I guess he is out of this race.

Winnie: I thought I'd seen everything, Gwinnie, but this is novel. Can they possibly make ROI with this stunt?

Gwinnie: I just said that it wasn't novel. Try to track here.

Winnie: I just wanted to say that. People forget that I went to college too. But back to the track. The horses have come to a complete halt as they ponder the situation. Psychology is gathering the other horses to have a conference about the meaning of it all, but wait—Archeology is breaking away to make a dash for the credit cards, and can you blame them? We're going to be extinct long before this discipline finds out where we came from. Engineering is thundering up now, getting a late start after it got hung up in the gate. What a calamity this animal is. Unpredictable as always, it's stopped running, and is digging an enormous ditch across the track with its two-ton hooves, separating the other horses from both the loot, and any further racing. Now it's picking up the cards and cash, storing them in its saddle bags. The other horses are furious and are trying to get at him. The trench is filling with water fast, as it looks like Engineering has hit a water main. Our first casualty is Law's entry, Endangered Species, who fell in the ditch while he was sniffing for cards. He's going to be washed into the nearest city, where he will forget all about the Race for the Planet. That's too bad, but it's always a hazard for Law.

Gwinnie: It looks like the sides of the ditch are caving in now, taking a few of the horses into the drink. The entire track is a loss for this year. The crowd is madder than usual at the quick ending of the race, and it looks like trouble. They're rushing the field to try to collect some of the cash. Remain calm! We don't need any more trampling deaths. There's a child in the ditch with the horses, trying to get a bundle of cash and—oh this not good. Please keep an eye on your children, or we will be shut down! Understandably, the track can't pay out bets on a race that never finished, but Business will give you a discount on your next bet here at the track! Think of the fun you're having!

Winnie: And you can't beat that with a stick, Gwinnie, although Business never uses a stick on its horses. Just carrots. Ha ha! Carrots everywhere today, folks, don't get excited. There's enough for everyone! It looks like the end of the race already, and what a surprise, although we've seen all kinds of things. That's what makes this event so great. Gimme A Lever is approaching the winner's circle now and proclaiming itself the winner. Since most of the field is still trying to swim off the track, or fighting with spectators for credit cards, no one has noticed yet. Yes—Gimme A Lever is being declared the winner by a representative of Big Business, even though, technically, there was no race. Engineering is now receiving a wreath of gold coins and pistols.

Gwinnie: So pretty and valuable!

Winnie: After this short ceremony, it looks like Gimme A Lever is trotting over to Business' vault at the back of the stadium, and putting its saddlebags in the vault, no doubt for safekeeping until the money can find its rightful owners. At least, that's what it looks like, but from this distance, we can't really tell, and I want to emphasize that all of this looks legitimate and is completely within the rules of the track.

Winnie and Gwinnie: *The race is fair.*

Gwinnie: The rest of the field is starting to gather over at the winners circle. They look a little worse for wear after the dunking and the fight, but everyone is alive and still practicing their discipline.

What more can you ask for? But there's no doubt, the Race for the Planet is a grueling challenge for everyone, and only the bold of heart and pure of spirit can win. That's probably why Business and its cousins—Economics, Engineering, and Technology—tend to do well. But as we can see right here with our own eyes, the race is fair. If Business keeps winning, that's how we will save the planet.

Winnie and Gwinnie: *The race is fair.*

Winnie: The crowd is starting to riot now, as they usually do about this time, and with the addition of cash and mud all over the place, it's a pretty rousing party out there now. Please stay away from the horses, as they often become depressed after this race and may attack. We don't want a death toll like last year, folks! We've had great time, as always. The beer trucks are open until one, and we'd like to remind everyone to practice social distancing. Smallpox is back! We hope everybody had fun, and don't forget: Business made all of this possible!

"Never take me there again." Tree felt like a pinata that had been beaten to shreds. It had been even worse than she had imagined. Seeing the sociology horse drowning right in front of her was something from her nightmares. But maybe it had something to do with whatever the party behind her had been smoking. Sociology had made it out, anyway, and was going to write a book about the disintegration of civil society.

"I thought you liked adventures. You never were any fun at parties, but wasn't it funny? It was hysterical, even with the race ending like that.

"It's propaganda, Harris. Didn't you listen to the announcers? It was horrible. And I wasn't drinking beer the whole time either. Would you slow down, please, I know you're not legal."

"Yeah, well, neither is anyone else, including you. And nobody listens to the propaganda."

"The hell they don't listen to—eyes on the road! Here, let me get it. I'd rather just keep you in beers."

Harris veered around a burned-out wreck in the left lane that hadn't been bulldozed yet, only screeching the tires a little. "Did you see those announcers?" He was rapt, his glazed eyes searching the road for further obstacles. "They were clones, weren't they? They were idiots, but did you *see* them? Why didn't they make them smarter?"

"How would I know? I'm not like, an expert at weird things." Tree frowned at him, keeping one eye on the road, just in case. He should know the answer to that anyway—men had made them, so they were the kind of women that men liked.

"You kind of are, Tree. You know all the weird things. That's why I ask. Isn't there a research paper about it?"

There were, in fact, hundreds of them. But he was too drunk to listen to her right now about all of the disturbing and inhuman things they were doing. She'd have to tell him later. People deserved to know, even if the clones did look happy enough. It was because they'd had something removed from them. They were soulless twin bimbos, available for hire, and that's all they would ever be. They didn't even know the difference between right and wrong.

"The whole scene was a nightmare. I think I feel sick now." She leaned her head back on the seat. She was never leaving her house again. It was the only safe place.

. . . .

The morning was clear and it promised to be blazing hot later, but right now it was cool and peaceful. Harris had been awake for hours, tossing restlessly, writing songs in his head and deleting them, not wasting time because he was a professional. Had he ever been inspired? He wasn't so sure of that. He'd just had the right training and had been in the right place. He shouldn't ask too much of himself now, in his dotage. He could have a stroke. He got up and checked outside the door, in case something entirely unexpected had happened overnight, but all seemed calm. Many inhabitants of their neighborhood didn't drive anymore, so it was usually quiet. He banged around a little in the kitchen, hoping his housemate would get up and entertain him, but had no luck.

There was always Bartertown. Harris found his sack of books that he kept stashed for these occasions. Some of them were highly coveted among certain types, and he'd had quite a collection at one time, but now it was considerably thinned from his half-hearted trading forays. He cultivated an air of being an expert in survival skills—and to be fair, he was. He had spent his fair share of time hiding out in the woods, more for artistic reasons than fear of society. Society drove him crazy too, though not as crazy as Tree. But he understood how she felt sometimes. His target audience at Bartertown loved the talk about catching rabbits with snares (he had never actually done this), and making shelters out of tree branches and all that. He never told them that the best thing they could do, survival-wise, was to stop eating meat and put insulation in their houses. They didn't want to hear that. Their focus was on their personal survival, not the survival of the human race. Well, there's our problem then, thought Harris.

He slung his bag over his shoulder and slouched down the trail. It was not too far, and he had plenty of company. There were routes snaking all over the hills that mostly led to the gates of Bartertown. The local deer were splayed all over the hills this morning, enjoying the cool before they had to head for the shade later in the day. They didn't even bother to raise their heads as people passed by, oblivious as old dogs. They weren't like eastern deer either, all white and fluffy-looking. These deer were bigger and kind of mean-looking, with big furry ears like a donkey. And almost all of them were wasted, it seemed like. It was odd to Harris when he first came. Deer weren't supposed to act like that. But then like everything else, you got used to it. The world got weirder every day.

Bartertown drew a crowd every day that it wasn't snowing. Some days it was large, some days small, but the place was open almost every day. Harris had gone over once during a blizzard, just out of curiosity, and there were about thirty tables going at it under the big tent, trying to get rid of stashes of wood pellets and snow boots. There were customers who'd come by just for the thrill of telling someone they were there. Entrance was free, so even if you brought nothing, no one stopped you from gawking. The primary rule was that no money changed hands. Cash couldn't be used for anything, not even for the hot dogs or snow cones sold by the fence. It didn't matter how much money a trader had, you still needed something to trade, even if the shirt off your back. It gave the place a free-wheeling vibe that was hard to find elsewhere. Almost no one cared what your treasure had cost when new. You could trade some very questionable things for a hot dog—like an old comb—but you got what you paid for: the "dogs" were likely to be horses. They weren't supposed to be horses, but everyone knew. What did you expect? It was a *hot dog*. A guy might trade his electric lawn mower for a pack of cigarettes one week, but maybe he could get it back later. A canoe might be worth a car one week—an old gas-powered car, but it ran—but next week the canoe would only be worth two pounds of peanut butter. The inventory varied by the minute. Things that could not be found might show up at Bartertown. People who'd hoarded worldly goods their entire lives stood in their living rooms and perused them with narrowed eyes, figuring out what they could take to Bartertown just for the fun of it. They didn't *need* to barter. It was gambling for normal people, and visits to Bartertown usually didn't contribute to divorces.

Harris had seen a woman there once who wanted a certain handbag so badly, she was trying to trade a rifle for one. And not just one rifle—three of them. Her first problem was that guns frowned on at Bartertown. Everyone had them, of course, but only a few traders displayed them openly, since it could make the trading seem coerced. They were kept under the tables and only offered when hard-core bargaining was going on. Secondly, everyone could tell that this woman was kind of crazy, with those guns cradled in her arms like babies, on a beeline to go get her handbag. Pucchio or something, made from alligator hides. This would have been straight class many years ago, but alligators were so common now the handbag might as well have been made of plastic. Alligators took over a lot of Florida after all the hurricanes and sea rise, along with the pythons. You could go watch them fight each other in arenas, but it didn't put a dent in the population. Nobody wanted to live in Florida anymore, even after they'd watched a hundred pythons eating a hundred alligators, or the other way around. Currently the alligators were ahead.

So no one made a move to tell the crazy woman to put the guns down. They stood back to give her space as she found the purses. There were a lot of them, probably salvaged from one of the wrecked cargo ships somewhere. They looked kind of damp, which made them more likely to be authentic, and thus more valuable. A plastic bag couldn't take all that abuse, but you couldn't hurt an alligator hide, and the salvage artist had recognized this. After a thorough drying, they'd be good as new; you might have to replace the liner. The purse trader at the table spied the guns and wanted no part of it, but there he was anyway, with the gun-toter's purse. He took one of the rifles and gave her the bag she picked out with no quibbling whatsoever because he only wanted her to leave. Several big guys who hung around Bartertown for occasions just like this showed up out of nowhere and politely suggested that she take the guns outside, which she did, along with her new purse, another satisfied customer.

Harris hoped that she was going to stuff that purse with cash and leave town, because whoever she stole those guns from was going to kill her, and that was no exaggeration. Gun manufacturing had been completely outlawed a decade ago, and now guns of all sorts were more valuable than gold, even if they might blow up in your hands. There were approximately four hundred guns for every person in America when the ban was put into effect, plus an uncounted number that were handmade or came out of printers, but the demand for them was still insatiable. It was the weirdest religion yet, and we'd tried many.

But generally Bartertown was an orderly place, and had been for most of its history. One had burned down, but it was an accident and no one was killed. There had been a couple of shopper riots before the authorities came in and promised that Bartertown would go away forever if such things continued, and after that the traders themselves maintained order. There were plenty of other places to riot, and for better reasons. Everyone liked Bartertown, even if they pretended not to. For the poor, bartering gave them more equality. It was more interesting than the old malls, which had been filled with zombies ever since Harris was born. Like Tree, he had an antipathy for malls—the natural habitat of zombies, both in movies and in real life. They attracted people who were dead, and they created people who were dead inside. He arranged to never visit them, and now they were full of living people who did not shop, which was ironic or poetic justice or something. Tree could probably tell him.

There was a crowd around the front gate, but he'd seen worse. He got in behind a man with a jug of moonshine, he was almost certain, and what looked like bicycle parts. Excellent. He was soon in, and looked for a spot to lay his books on. There was a table off in the far corner, and he slipped over to it quickly. If you had small things, you tried to get a table. The car engines and furniture could find their own place. He had ten little books about survival skills, a couple more about anarchy, and one about how to make your own food—as long as there was a grocery store nearby, Harris guessed. Survival books became dated very quickly these days, and most of them could not decide whether to advocate for moving way out in the woods or for building the most high-tech bomb shelter available, since there was clearly no real escape from what we'd done. Some of Harris' customers seemed kind of soft-handed for people who were living in the the end times, but he didn't care since he didn't take it seriously. People were into all kinds of weird things. At least they weren't wearing those headsets.

He spotted a woman across the yard who traded old clothes and hats, and was irritated that he hadn't noticed her earlier. They were almost directly facing each other, although a distance apart. Harris had flirted with her a few times when she had old concert t-shirts, but she was lukewarm at best. But he had been in a band. They had a hit! He pulled his hat down and frowned. He was out of her league anyway. No one who hung out at Bartertown should have such high standards.

He was wearing his uniform of camouflage pants and ragged vest, his stock outfit for his book-trading trips. None of his camo-clad brothers could articulate what a survivalist was preparing for, exactly. Aliens? The jack-booted thugs? World-wide civil war? Climate apocalypse? All of the above? A big guy approached his table, also clad in camouflage. After a few minutes of banter about how the world was a harsh place and they had to be prepared, Harris traded two books about living without the internet, and one about how to steal electricity from the corporations without them catching you. In return for the books he was given a crockpot.

"Is this all you have?" The guy glared at him. Couldn't Harris tell that he was barely surviving? There were more crockpots circulating at Bartertown than anyone knew what to do with. They never seemed to break. Harris was eager to leave after he saw the woman who had spurned him. Trading at Bartertown took a certain energy that he lacked today. He unloaded a fancy knife and three other books in an hour, one of them a paperback about how to hide your identity from the government—a tiny rectangle of secrets in cramped writing, so you could carry it around in your tactical vest. A man from Alaska seemed very excited to get it, and put it immediately into his secret vest pocket. Harris could see that he was still wearing the ID bracelet that would allow him to enter Wyoming without his car being searched, so he was probably not from Alaska, then. People from Wyoming were very suspicious. No one ever admitted that they were from there, so that the world wouldn't beat a path to their door after the apocalypse, where they would be surviving in perfect comfort, eating hamburgers from real cows and driving anywhere they wanted to. Everyone knew this and they had for years, because of the bracelets. No other state had them, or searched people who tried to drive down the highway and hit the state line. The Wyomingite gave Harris a blue lawn chair for his guidebook. A chair for Tree that came from the forbidden zone. She'd get a kick out of that.

He vacated his table after a few hours and looked for somewhere to lose the crockpot, skirting the line where the hippie gal sat with her shirts. It was too bad she was so snooty, because he liked her shirts. It was a weekday and the hustlers had already done their trading and gone off again. Sometimes they would take their loot straight downtown and try to resell it on the street corners, which made the Vores roll their eyes and call the police, who ignored them. After some meandering around, Harris saw some old LP records, piled high on a table. They could be hit or miss, but he found a couple that he wanted. Tree had a record player that they treated like a treasure chest. A dark-skinned girl with messy blue hair shrugged and said that she'd gotten them from another trader. She must have befriended an old hippie. Or killed one.

He traded her the crockpot for two records and a few ragged posters, feeling a little guilty. A little girl didn't want a crockpot. He found a picture book about rabbits in his stash and made her take that too. She brightened and cracked a small smile. Where were her parents? There was no age limit here, but it was not really a place for an unsupervised child. She couldn't have been more than—he had no idea, having never had children. No more than twelve. But she looked clean and well-fed enough, so it was none of his affair. Some children had gone feral, and they weren't all the children of the Bartertown crowd, if you wanted to know the truth. Children ran away and their parents didn't notice for days. They lived out of dumpsters and in the empty homes of real estate barons who had owned hundreds of properties, but had lost the addresses during the big server farm failures. It seemed fair enough to Harris, and to most other people as well, apparently, and the majority of the kids were left to do their own thing unless they asked for help, or started stealing. No one wanted to get into the legal morass of trying to get custody of one of them. Most of them didn't even have birth certificates, since almost all birth records from a period of about ten years had been obliterated, by sunspots or hackers, who knew? The so-called backups and retrieval systems that were supposed to guard our most important information didn't even exist in some cases. But it was nobody's fault, just a blip of the free market, and we all we needed to move on.

Tree said that the screw-up was definitely the capitalists at work again, removing our personal identities and replacing them with market identities. All those children were allowed to "choose" their own names from, more than likely, a list of popular cartoon characters. People were identified by algorithms now, and their consumption ethic ranking was more important than when they were born. Harris wasn't sure what Tree meant exactly, but he was ashamed of his market identity anyway. He had probably played right into their hands. Worse, some young people liked their market identities, since they came from the internet. They got tattoos that said things like, "Predictable Spender" and "Steady Income." Harris had seen a girl with "Poor Impulse Control" tattooed on her arm, and he was so confounded he didn't know what to think. Was it her market identity, or a joke? It could even be her legal name. He asked Tree about it, and she said, "I know! Exactly!" which was even more irritating than not answering him at all, so he forgot about it. Nobody knew what words meant anymore, because everyone was too ironic.

The bartering could get a little frantic in the afternoon, when the desperate showed up with nothing but still needed everything. They were called the hyenas, in a not entirely derogatory way. Hyenas cleaned up and they were efficient. The sellers who were too lazy to take their things home, or had traded something too many times, would abandon their goods and the hyenas could take what they wanted. If the children showed up, they were generally given first choice. Unlike real hyenas, nobody fought over the remains. There was no need. The same item might come back in a few days and be even more worthless.

Harris was weighed down by his new lawn chair, so he headed out. He could either get over it, which did not appeal to him at the moment—walk by the t-shirt woman and nod at her once, to stop the curse—or perhaps she would leave. He wasn't a regular here. He didn't *need* to be at Bartertown trading trinkets. Maybe she would come by and talk to him some day, after she got off her high horse. He could wait a little longer. She'd recognize him from the internet, then she'd be sorry. Halfway home, he tested out the new chair under a tree, admiring the view while he smoked a bowl of the local pot. He watched the stoned deer for a few minutes. They were one, a circle of life. Mommies, babies, families. They looked at him with their big sloppy eyes for a few seconds, then went right back to dozing, so close to him he could see the flies on their hides. He liked sitting with them, despite their listlessness, since they had the right idea—they didn't waste things for no reason, not even their energy. There was no need to dash around like a madman if no one was going to shoot you, and you had everything you needed. Harris could appreciate this. He didn't want to be a madman. Sure, maybe the deer weren't all that they used to be, bounding away over the mountains. But they were still pretty nice.

The marijuana invasion had come about as ranchers all over the west were run out by rich people who liked mountains. The wealthy folks liked the cowboys who took them on horse rides, but they were not so sure about those other animals. Couldn't that be turned into a golf course? Finally too short on water and political goodwill to hang on, the cows had to go. They were awfully ugly, up close, and looked kind of dangerous. A few of the ranches tried to hang on with "authentic" dude ranches, where macho types branded calves and anything else they wanted, because those people had so much money, they couldn't control themselves and they didn't have to. There were some gruesome "accidents," at those places, but cosmetic surgery today was nothing short of miraculous, and everyone had signed NDAs anyway. But the center pivot sprinklers stood idle, leaving all that water in the ground, instead of growing hay for the cattle. "How extremely reasonable!" the environmentalists preened. It was too, until the invisible hand of the free market stepped in.

Not too many missed the cows except the ranchers, but everyone was insulted was when an international agriculture conglomerate slipped in and took over most of the old ranchland. When the billionaires spotted those sprinklers, they suddenly changed their minds about using the land to grow low-water crops. People may stop eating bread, or switch to vat meat, but they never got tired of doing drugs. Thousands of cattle were replaced with thousands of acres of premium marijuana farms. It was a double-cross on everyone involved, but it was extremely successful, nobody could deny that. Pot use soared, and most people became very mellow, even if despair stalked them daily. Harris thought it was copacetic enough, even if he agreed that the story was a hot mess. The deer agreed, and dozed on. The promised "wildlands public spaces" parks, with flowing streams and smiling children with fishing poles, were forgotten about as soon as the enormous revenues available from pot were tallied up at the state offices. It was a completely unexpected windfall, even if four state legislators had recently visited an undersea spa in Saudi Arabia where the massages were given by octopuses.

Since the farms were largely run by robots and cameras and only attended by humans with guns around harvest time, they'd become an odd sort of wildlife refuge where stoned mule deer wove through the twelve-foot marijuana plants, wondering what had happened, perhaps. Mountain lions and wolves tailed them lazily, waiting until they got hungry enough to work themselves up to a run. The super-fortified weed spread freely, a glitch that no one had foreseen, naturally, and was now everywhere—a better invader than knapweed, and tastier to the animals too. The mule deer and small mammals had become accustomed to eating the smelly plant, and most of them were now too high to practice normal wildlife behaviors, like avoiding humans. They had never been smart enough to avoid cars, but now they stood in the road like they were waiting for a bus to Heaven. You had better not run over too many of the small animals either, or someone would see it and come find you. It was better to go around them, no matter how slow it was. Some drivers with a mean sense of humor also fed the critters, making the roads even worse. The speed limit in town during the winter was about as fast as riding a bike. The animals traveled on the roads, since it was much easier going than the fields. One edge of town was worse than a safari park, since everything from bears to ravens herded together in a sunny spot where the snow melted, and they attracted their own crowd, as well as food offerings. The beasts had learned how to live here with us, and they wouldn't be leaving unless we started enforcing boundaries again, but no one seemed inclined to do it. Pigeons roosted everywhere, the squirrels came and sat in your lap, the deer nuzzled your hair, skunks and raccoons went through the scraps freely in the middle of the day, then came over and nibbled at your shoes in case you had a treat. The bears still waited until dark to go at the garbage, unless it was a hard winter, but it hardly ever was anymore.

Most people had lost the bloodlust for killing animals, and only used their guns to shoot dumpsters, drones, and every outdoor light left in town, which made it even more attractive to the wildlife. If anyone still yearned to blast some animals, they'd better not do it anywhere near witnesses. Animal lovers were as crazy as they'd ever been or maybe even worse, since the wildlife had moved right into town. Darlene looked out the window at Bambi eating pot in her yard every morning, and before you knew it, she was outside in a disposable lawn chair with a gun, protecting her darlings.

It was said that the government was dosing us with hormones to make everyone less aggressive. This theory had been around since chemtrails, but since there were many more chemtrails today, all conspiracy theories about chemtrails became more likely, statistically speaking. They weren't all normal planes and drones gassing around up there. They were flying much too low and emitted a stinky vapor behind them. They were supposed to be high enough that the populace couldn't smell the drugs, but no one was sure what elevation that was, the way the weather changed. Some days the entire sky was filled with a weird chemical haze. It smelled like lilacs, which was a dead giveaway, since nature didn't smell like an air freshener that bloomed in September. Harris hadn't felt like murdering anyone in at least twenty years, so maybe they were being dosed. None of the animals in this odd zoo looked like they needed to be killed anyway, they just looked kind of lost. They weren't supposed to be following him around and begging for handouts from car windows. Tree told him that the animals were only taking back their rightful place on the planet, which was everywhere, since their preferred habitat had also been destroyed by us. Letting them stay here with us was the least we could do.

Everyone was queasy after the "meat virus" went through, too. It wasn't really a virus, but a cattle parasite from the Amazon that nested in men's testicles. "Virus" sounded bad enough without getting too detailed. It could be killed, but only with radiation treatment that left a man as sterile as the moon. It was an terrible dilemma for men who became infected. Meat consumption went down by eighty-five percent, even with a big advertising campaign that was supposed to show that a man who ate beef was a man who laughed at danger. Not as hard as your friends would laugh when they found out you had a parasite in your balls, though. It wasn't in the vat meat, supposedly, but a lot of people didn't trust that either. No one took a date out for a hamburger anymore, because they'd look at you across the table and wonder. The meat virus was the final nail in the coffin of the cattle industry in the west. All of the manly restaurants in America failed all at once, as well as the entire industry of cooking grills that were as big as cars. Former meat-eaters brought them into Bartertown, trying to talk them up as chick incubators or something. Places to grow your mushrooms. You couldn't even turn them into robots, because they were way too heavy to be practical.

At home, Harris put the new lawn chair out, proud of his contribution, then opened up some mystery meat he'd acquired at the 'Town. It was in a sealed package with labels that said BEEF, so it was probably authentic, but you couldn't be sure until you cooked it. It was all lab-grown now, no matter what anyone told you, unless you had personally slaughtered your cow and put it in a package. Patriotic types insisted that they would never eat test-tube meat, but they all did anyway, since it was a fraction of the price of a genuine cow. There were pictures of athletic-looking cows on the packages, standing in green fields, and everyone pretended it was real. Most Americans hadn't laid eyes on a real farm in several generations anyway.

His house mate entered the kitchen just in time to retch dramatically at the sight on the stove. "I woke up from a nightmare where cows were burning in a fire. They were all mooing and crying."

"Well, good morning, sunshine. If cows were burning in a fire, it was probably one of your friends who set the fire. Anyway, that's why I'm cooking it—so you won't be exposed to the sickening sight of flesh. Then I'm going to eat it, and you can have some. Real dead cow. Test tube cow anyway."

"No I won't. It's all yours," Tree lied. "Besides, I have some potatoes to cook." Her potato consumption was quite reliable, since they could grow those in the backyard. Even if she planted something besides her flowers Tree would let the animals eat it, because they might be hungry too. She also wasn't too keen on shopping, so Harris made most of the trips to buy food, and Tree ate potatoes so that she wouldn't have to. She had some theories about energy conservation that were just short of obsessive, and he'd only listen to them when he was drunk, even if they were logically consistent. She said they were, anyway.

Tree didn't run into the bathroom and yell at him when he left the water on for too long, though. He'd had a lover who did that. One day the water in her sink had dribbled out even more slowly than usual, turned brown, then was gone. They figured it would come back, but after a couple of weeks it still had not. She and her family walked hundreds of miles over dried-out washes, trading their possessions for one bottle of water, or two, sucking on cactus and rocks before they reached a migrant camp a few miles below the US border, where they drank from a green-slicked stock tank, then laid down to sleep.

Harris told her that she could take a whole shower: just let the water run, don't dribble it out and collect it in a bucket. She said she knew that and she'd stopped, but he could hear her in the bathroom, dribbling. You don't have to do that, he pleaded. This is America. She always used the outhouse in the back, even in the winter, so she wouldn't waste water. He bought her some big thick slippers with gripper soles on them, so she would be comfortable out there. It was not worth the battle, and he enjoyed his frugal showers even more.

So if Tree wanted to eat potatoes twice a day, there were far worse obsessions in this depleted world. Why lust after a steak when you liked the potato as well, and it was lower on the food chain? In the morning you eat fried potatoes, for dinner you have mashed, and at lunch you have bread. The secret to happiness was low expectations. So why aren't you happy, then? Harris asked, and, incredulous, she said, I *am*.

He tuned in to whatever she was saying now about the meat virus—how it was actually beneficial for mankind in the long run. Easy for her to say, since she didn't possess testicles. He said, "you're probably right," so she went outside and dreamed up some more weird ideas while she watched the grass grow. Some mornings Tree would get up and continue an argument that had started before she woke, because fights came to her in her dreams. He was surprised she hadn't told him how many lifeforms he was killing today by eating meat. She must be getting lazy. The fact that anyone still ate meat was an insult to all living things, under the circumstances. It took five hundred tons of carbon to make vat meat for four—but in the old days, it took five thousand tons of carbon to make a *single hamburger*. Salads for four, on the other hand, only took fifty tons of carbon to produce, with "bacon" bits, and that was real lettuce from

California, not the stuff they grew on the ferris wheels. The choice of anyone who cared about humanity was clear. He did care, didn't he?

Harris had a memory of sitting in a bar with Tree while she informed him about the consequences of our stupidity, which were coming up fast, because humanity couldn't control their greed. Men couldn't control their base animal desires, and they had to start treating the world more kindly, or women would stop having babies. Then everything would stop, because biology is the true ruler of the world. Regeneration, not degradation. Not men, but more like a female egg. Harris recalled thinking about an egg with a crown on it when he was drunk forty years ago. And here it was again.

But then, women had stopped having babies. But that wasn't because of anything men did—wait. He hated when Tree did that—when she started to make sense. Especially since she'd said those things years ago, and he didn't want to give her that much credit. The President was almost ninety years old, and no one even pretended that she was in charge. It was just figurehead stuff. We had all sowed, and now we would reap.

Tree loved the new chair, and told Harris that she was going to sit in it all day. She might too, because ever since her retirement, as she called it, she was even less ambitious than Harris. He finished cooking up the mystery meat and finding it not only edible but almost good, salted it and brought it outside to make Tree try it. It was the best meat they'd had in a long time; so good, they decided that maybe it was a real cow, imported from a place where there were outlaw cows roaming the sagebrush. They weren't all gone, but had interbred with bison and were still out there in secret canyons. Their meat had spirit, unlike the conformist vat meat.

"Butch Cowsidy and the Beefalo," Harris quipped, and Tree giggled. She wouldn't start any arguments this morning, at least, since she was probably stoned already. They rinsed their fingers in the pool and lounged in the hot sun while Harris played a few tunes.

They were about as peaceful with their place in the world as they could be, having finally realized that it didn't matter much where your body ended up, as long as you could live with your head.

The Hedonic Treadmill is a Harsh Mistress

Tree estimated that everyone had stopped working after the last recession, and it seemed as though they had, although when it had happened, exactly, was kind of fuzzy. Her own attitude toward employment was so lackadaisical, she may have missed the definitive mutiny. She quit all of her jobs as soon as she could find a principled reason to do so, so it was only logical that others had started to recognize what she had long ago—most of those jobs couldn't be justified on a planet that was falling apart because of our overuse. She'd done her best to encourage worker strikes everywhere she went, before leaving in her principled huff. And now entire sectors of working people had finally gotten their fill of doing trivial jobs for people who were perfectly capable of doing them themselves if they wanted to do something so pointless. Someone finally noticed, Tree exulted.

When the entire cruise ship industry quit en masse one day, all over the world, she was so thrilled that she quit another job in solidarity. After telling the restaurant crew that this was a great day for labor and the environment, and they should all join, she dramatically clocked out for the last time. She went to a bar to spread the word and cheered as news cameras broadcast the last crews to abandon the floating pleasure palaces, at noon in the Azores. The passengers watching over the railing were baffled, since none of it made any sense whatsoever. They had *paid*.

Did they think that real life was like the Jetsons? Tree asked the barback. We can't live as though life is a non-stop party, on a planet with no trees and no ground, ordering things out of thin air. The barback agreed with her and went somewhere else, since he was making good money and got drunk every day at work. He didn't quit working until the second wave of mutinies, when he left and went to live in the mall housing.

The cruise ship employees, accustomed to hard work, found jobs doing the myriad of conservation, restoration, and clean-up labor needed to keep the human race breathing. Half of them already had positions with government clean up and restoration crews when they left the cruise ships. The whole revolt was so well-organized, Tree was in awe. No one was harmed and nothing of value was lost, since there were few things more repellent than the cruise ship industry. Apparently a few groups agreed with her, because abandoned and bankrupt cruise ships became popular protest symbols for a few years. Everybody wanted their flag hoisted above one of those monstrosities.

So many cruise ships had been lost in hurricanes and tidal events even before the mutinies, it was a wonder that anyone still boarded them anyway. When the dummies tried to go on a nice cruise, the ships were usually attacked by pirates who wanted to go to America, so that even if the hijackers agreed to go on vacation with the passengers, the ships then had to do the return trip with a lot of extra passengers on board. They had asked for unique cultural experiences, had they not? Despite that and multiple other issues, the party hadn't stopped until the servants quit. That was the final straw.

Cruise companies left a hundred of the ships docked in Miami, leaking sewage. They put up a big ad on the side of a building that said "Patriotic Protective Barrier islands, Courtesy` of the cruise ship industry, You're welcome," then left town, so didn't notice when some of the ships disappeared. When desperate Haitians saw one looming off the coast, hundreds of them jumped in the water and swam for this apparition that was so large, it couldn't be real, so it had to be The American Dream. Two months later, the stolen ship—actually named The Barefootin' Caribbean, but it didn't matter now—returned to Florida with a full passenger load of Haitians.

They anchored the ship just outside the boundary where Florida patrolled, because they had to stop somewhere, they weren't superhuman. The feds refused to get involved, since they were already housing migrants in old ships, and someone had saved them the trouble. A federal agent with a nametag and a blue tie boarded the ship, asked some questions of people who did not speak English, then typed "Haitian, 4-5 thousand" on a computer program and saved it somewhere.

It was hard to keep track of ships that no one claimed to own, and if they were now full of lost people as well, no one could be expected to keep track of them too. It was a big world out there and it was about time that folks stopped expecting the government to take care of everything, even if they possessed satellites that could see you changing clothes in your house. All the ships flew so many flags, it was a year's worth of phone calls to find out who was responsible for them, then it would turn out to be some entity that didn't really exist—an LLC or an IPO or something. It wasn't worth the trouble to arrest the migrants if they were doing nothing substantially wrong, plus do all that paperwork, then put them in our camps that were already full. They'd all get to stay anyway, because what were we going to do, drop a nuke on them? There were more where those came from. And to tell you the truth, a lot of them drowned and were never counted at all.

The ship full of Haitians remained off the coast of Florida, sending in boats to get supplies regularly, until the ship was filled with trash. By this time they had installed a President, had a national song and were fond of their new nation, so they dumped all their waste into the water at night, just like the cruise ships had always done off the coast of Haiti. The satellites and the drones saw their villainy though, and while the government stewed over what to do, a Category Six hurricane made a direct hit on that part of the coast, and that was the end of *Barco de los Suenos.* Several hundred ship residents died, even though they had known about the storm. But being Haitian, they also knew that death was always right around the corner. They had seen the American Dream, and maybe that was as good as it could get for them.

Those who made it went to live in Miami, which was slowly rotting away from the bottom up, as all the concrete holding it up succumbed to sea water. But it was still fairly nice if you could get a place on the third floor or so, as long as you got out during the hurricanes. Most of the buildings were in good shape, since the rich people had kept building condos on the beach until no one could drive in there. Money had no understanding of the realities of the world and always thought enough of it could solve any problem. Much of the population of Miami was now from Cuba, after the original settlers moved out when the water killed the engine on their BMW one time too many. The Africans from the dry part of town came over and took over sixth floor condos, where they had dance parties that shook the floors while they admired the view as partiers, instead of the maintenance crew. The sounds coming up from the streets of Miami were so lyrical, they attracted tropical parrots and songbirds, who had been blown far off course by hurricanes and reached Florida about the time the dancing started. Some Puerto Ricans got wind of a party in Miami, hijacked a cruise ship from their harbor and brought it in to join the ship barrier reef, never to be cruised again. The Creoles and Cajuns showed up from the deep south, since their lands had finally sunk under the oily, chemical-smelling, rainbow-tinged waters. They loved the alligator fights and bet way too much money on them.

The Cubans had renamed the place "New Venice" and put up a flag even before the Haitians, Creoles, parrots, and Puerto Ricans showed up. It was at least the tenth "New Venice" in the Northern Hemisphere. After several meetings of the very highest officials, the US government pretended not to notice this New Venice, either. It was nice to see folks becoming more self-sufficient, even if they had to be imported.

When more than 100,000 migrants from all over the world were surveyed, eighty-nine percent said that they had begun their journey to the US to pursue "the American Dream." When they reached the US border, they were given a pamphlet explaining that the expression was a fanciful lie from 1800 or so, and we had not meant for it to get out, since it had been meant only for us, and not everyone else in the world. That statue had been a gift, and we had to put it somewhere. It was all a mistake and they should go back home. We were sorry. The migrants used the pamphlets as toilet paper, since they couldn't read English, then texted their friends in the south that they were now very close to the American Dream.

The migrants were given little bottles of water that they drained in a few seconds and added to a big pile of plastic bottles. Then they set up house in Bordertown, the most vibrant and inclusive community anywhere. It stretched for hundreds of miles along the southern border of the US. The Rio Grande was as ill-used as the Ganges River during the rare times it was flowing, and when it wasn't, armed guards from both countries stayed in the wash playing cards under pool umbrellas, glaring at everyone because it was so hot, and they were stuck out there in the riverbed. There were Bartertowns going on both sides of the border in a kind of demilitarized zone, where hundreds of people of both nations would cross back and forth at night to trade and go to Stalwarts, which had built several stores along the international boundary. Stalwarts also offered to build covered bridges over the slough and let everyone use a closed store, where they could only go back and forth to Stalwarts, but the feds refused. Something like, "Are you kidding? We still have borders. We do," even though Stalwarts showed both countries how profitable it would be.

Sometimes a few of the boundary crossers would slip away to try their luck in the big wide USA. The Border Patrol was hopelessly outmanned and outmaneuvered, because no one wanted to work for the Border Patrol anymore. They would fly their drones around watching the camps, hoping that no one would embarrass them by coming over in groups of a hundred, two hundred at a time. Someone always recorded it and made them look bad. The US released a lot of chemtrails at the southern border to keep everyone pacified, and even the police didn't have the stomach for what really needed to be done. The army of drones patrolling the border could shoot things from a mile away—let them kill migrants if the government was so concerned, and everyone could watch that on the internet instead of making death threats against the Border Patrol. We had invented robots just for jobs like that.

The migrants couldn't be stopped. Even the stupid and homeless in the US had warm coats and shoes, no matter how poor their individual choices had been. Some of them even had new cars. They had probably gotten their clothes at Bartertown, a place where people got things they did not deserve, even when they didn't want to play by the rules. That bounty was due to the overwhelming irrational exuberance of some of their fellow citizens—buying clothes and furniture and cars so fast, they had to throw some of them right out, just to make room for more. Poor people in other countries saw that, and they came.

The professionals worked, because they were needed. The good people who tried to put it all back together still worked, and some of the people who made connections and made things move toiled on, or things would really disintegrate. But for most, the pace of modern life had gone from The Gilded Age on steroids, to the Great Depression, but with electronics. Some people liked to work and they continued doing it, despite all the complications. Some folks thrived on that stuff, go figure. Tree thought they had mental problems—reveling and aiding in the destruction like that—but she did have one thing in common with them: they both derived a perverse pleasure from watching entropy burn it all to the ground, no matter what they did to fend it off—or how much they profited from it, in the latter case. It was like standing on a beautiful beach and watching a tsunami coming for you—if you couldn't escape it, at least enjoy the ride. But for most ordinary, non-employed people, it was quieter, slower, and darker than it used to be. More natural, Tree would say. More human.

All the fast food places were gone, partly due to attrition, and partly, it was rumored, to government intervention. No one believed it, though, because the government didn't infringe on our freedom like that. In this case, it was true. When Americans' weight began to skyrocket in ways that were too disturbing for even our government to ignore, even if the "food" companies could, they'd finally cracked down on the drugs that they put in our vittles. Excess *was* best and we'd done well with that idea, but only when the inevitable backlash of it wasn't so immediately visible. We'd handed responsibility for killing people over to the robots and drones, so that we wouldn't have to march or run with boots except for survival games, but didn't we want to look good too? The government either needed to intervene or start paying for the drugs we needed so we wouldn't eat ourselves to death, and they were very expensive.

Instead the government told everyone that this was fine: we hadn't wanted fast food anymore and we wanted something new again. They handed out checks to buy new stoves and refrigerators and convection ovens and fancy blenders. The Healthen American Initiative or something; no one even seemed to care that wasn't a word, and we were on to a new fad. Some people didn't even have microwaves, they just pushed buttons on their phones and waited for food to arrive. Everyone had to learn how to cook donuts and french fries and macaroni and cheese again, but it was framed in the most attractive way, so consumers bought a thousand dollars of pots and pans from China and waited breathlessly for them to arrive, old habits being hard to break. While they waited, they convinced themselves that they had never wanted anything so badly as to learn how to cook like their great-grandma had. It was right there in the pamphlet provided by the government: look at that man, wearing an apron and cooking a meal, just beaming with pride and ownership. Why had we ever abandoned this? Almost a billion dollars worth of aprons were sold in six months, but only about half of them made it to the purchaser, things being the way they were. But everyone who wanted an apron got one, plus thousands of women and men in the far east, who wore them like skirts with little shorts underneath. They loved the big pockets. They never learned to cook either, because instead of buying stoves, they ate insects almost raw and green chewy things, like rabbit food but tastier, with some sort of supplement. They stayed very slim that way. They did their own thing over there. But they had Bartertowns, where they'd found the aprons.

-

Most of the motels, restaurants, golf courses, coffee shops and day spas were gone, or confined to really spiffy neighborhoods, as all of the invisible workers became truly invisible, and moved into the malls. It had all happened even faster than our ascendance to peak consumerism, which had only taken a few generations and then was gone, much to the astonishment of almost everyone who did not read research papers. What had happened to cheap hamburgers? What had happened to the bite-sized sugar balls and grocery aisles full of crunchy chips we could pour right into our mouths? It had been as preposterous and unnecessary as a golf course on Mars, and now it was gone.

It's a good start, Tree thought, as the carbon footprint of the United States and then the world collapsed like the blood sugar of most ordinary folks. This had promise. No one seemed much poorer than they had been before, since Bartertown filled a gap in the economy that people who talked about The Economy didn't talk about. Tree listened to the economic news on the TV with relish. "The Economy is seeking a soft landing," they babbled, as The Economy swan-dived like suicides off the Grand Canyon. Everyone, everywhere, ran out of money and means all at once, no matter how much credit business tried to extend to them, or how many new products they were offered. There was no way. Consumer stupidity was *infinite*.

China hacked into and crashed the entire American stock market in 2029, and after that they didn't even pretend that the place was legitimate. They fixed it, of course—made some other numbers up, and nudged them around so that the big businesses gobbled up all the small companies left standing, then everyone quit for good. An algorithm told the stockmasters when everything peaked and they all cashed out at once—at light speed because that was how they did things—then it was too late to go back. They hadn't realized that all of them had that same information. Wall Street was now blocks of deserted buildings covered with graffiti and pigeon poop, just like hundreds of other places in New York City. GOOD RIDDANCE was sprayed across half a building, as well as more colorful things. Wall Street now had some of the best graffiti in New York City, and that was saying something, because graffiti wasn't cleaned up any more than we cleaned up anything else. Someone had drawn a penis the size of a football field on one of those buildings.

Someone else had stolen that bull statue in the middle of the night—-put a harness on it and carried it away with a helicopter, where it reappeared in front of his bomb shelter. Six months later, another billionaire flew his helicopter over and stole the bull for his bomb shelter ornament. This went on for a few years, the bull decorating one bomb shelter for a short time, then being rustled again, because it was a great joke, you might say the ultimate joke, juxtaposing Wall Street and the end of the world. Then the billionaires kind of forgot about the bull and the stock market entirely—why it had existed, or how they had justified all of that, anyway. That bull was in a field in North Dakota somewhere, next to a missile silo. But they had all won. The billionaires went on-line and made fun of each other on their secure underground internet lines, and played high-stakes card games that no on had any intention of paying off. Even the biggest egos in the world were no match for the sort of disruption that Mother Nature could put together, if you really insisted.

On the other hand, what did anyone really need, here at the end of the world? What could you possibly need that wasn't already nearby? Maybe you didn't *need* it, and only *wanted* it, which was an entirely different matter, and you should learn the difference. Think, people. That was how we'd gotten into this mess. "Recovery experts," a fancy name for garbage crawlers, flew drones overhead and crawled through the dumps to find whatever someone wanted, from a car to a bra. Since there were computer chips in everything, some of the rubbish was already inventoried, and just needed to go be picked up again. Salvage experts would get an entire inventory list of old e-bikes, for instance, then go track down the chips in them with drones and other tech. Everything was still out there, much to the shock of everyone except the trash pickers. We thought that we'd thrown that stuff *away*.

The chips were part of that circular economy that had somehow never worked out, except for the tracking part. Millions of jobs were created for employees of the "circular green economy," then no one showed up to be trash pickers. It had sounded so much better when it was called an "environmental technician." They did want to save the world, but they felt more passionate about hanging out with cloned sea turtles, and watching elk in the mountains. So uneducated Runnies had good jobs as professional recyclers, and almost no matter what you wanted, they were faster and better than ordering it from somewhere. There were also jobs in actual garbage sorting for the desperate or unmotivated that paid by the day, since few people lasted long in that.

Our ally in cheap plastic consumerism, the Chinese, had their own problems caused by too much development, too fast, and no other countries had stepped up to supply the world with tons of disposable plastic crap, for some reason. Over-developed countries were begging to send tons of plastic waste *back* to them, which seemed suspicious. The Chinese had also discovered Vore headsets, and some of their neighbors were scared of what might happen if Vore culture took over their country. If China wanted to fill China with weird technology that was their own problem, but they were not sneaking that tech into shipping containers bound for pure countries. That was how we'd gotten fentanyl and every invasive plant on earth.

The seas had become too rough to transport things by cargo ships anyway, and marine animals had become very aggressive, for some reason. After dolphins knocked a hundred and fifty men off tugboats in San Diego harbor, sailing right into their heads and killing them, nobody wanted to help bring cargo ships into the harbors anymore. You couldn't blame them; the dolphins used to love them, and raced the tugboats as they went by. And then there were the jellyfish...it was all too weird and upsetting, even if the pay was good.

Most of the miles and acres of deserted retail space had been turned into housing of all varieties. The wealthy had overbuilt so thoroughly that they finally lost track of a lot of it, since it was all supposed to be taken care of by artificial intelligence and then, to their shock, it hadn't been. Robot security guards sat idly in the stores, their batteries dead. When the stock market went belly-up, investors went over to the real estate market and started flipping properties so fast, on computer at least, that on one memorable day three-quarters of the occupied homes in the country were for sale, much to their owners' surprise. That algorithm had a few bugs. It had something to do with property taxes and the owner's propensity to gamble. But the algorithms couldn't force someone out of their house if they had paid their taxes, even if technically, the flippers had sold the house. Nobody understood it at all without a lawyer, so if you found out that your house had been flipped, you had to get a lawyer or buy a gun, and no one could afford a lawyer, but they already had a gun. The solution was clear. It was going to take years for your case to get to court, and your house may need to be defended the entire time.

Real estate values fluctuated from day to day, thanks to all those algorithms that were supposed to add value, but mostly only added confusion. Nobody knew what their property was worth from one day to the next, if they could even find the address after the network crashed again. So they figured they didn't have to pay property taxes if that was the case, and they had a point. Most people would like to blame all of that chaos on the Runnies, but most Runnies were computer literate enough to operate their phones and that was about all. Blame the ten thousand computer techs that were still being turned out of colleges every year, but had no jobs.

Once the headsets came in, they ended whatever was left of physical stores. There were a few "boutique" places that hung on for nostalgia's sake, selling odd things like diamonds and statues. The wealthy cut their losses and abandoned the properties they hadn't lost track of already. The Vores didn't want them, the Runnies couldn't afford to shop, and no one wanted to work there. The owners didn't want to pay the taxes and nobody would insure anything. "Natural" disasters happened that were so strange, insurance agents quit their jobs when they saw the photos and moved to Idaho, where they listened to stories about the End Times and thought maybe it wasn't as crazy as all that.

There were so many empty pleasure palaces, no one who wanted a roof over their head had to go without. Some of the housing made from the old stores was quite nice, depending on how recently the owner had abandoned the property and who moved in, but other places were kind of scary. Some had working plumbing, others had outhouses in the back. Workers who wouldn't work anymore suddenly had more security than they'd ever had, from the same spaces where they'd been toiling for years with no security at all. It was poetic justice and recycled too, which met with Tree's approval. They had proper housing and weren't living in the Stalwarts parking lots.

She signed up to receive a small check every month for a disorder she'd been diagnosed with a few years before. It was unheard of to most people, since it said bad things about Our Way of Life, but the paperwork wasn't too complicated, and besides—she was ill. On some days she couldn't pretend that she wasn't. It was either that, or she was old, and possibly that was worse. She knew what the problem was anyway, since she hadn't spent years digging into research papers for nothing: everyone was infested with microplastics now, and lord knows what havoc they were wreaking on their bodies. They floated around in your blood, they crossed the blood-brain barrier, they pooled in a plastic sludge in your kidneys. They were in our lungs, probably in our hearts. Maternal hormones pumped them into tiny embryos before the baby could hold a plastic-free sippy cup. The petroleum companies buried their own research under the miles of plastic wrap they produced daily. The government knew all about it, but correcting the issue would cause unfathomable damage to The Economy, and besides, everyone was already infested. Instead they passed out disability checks to almost anyone who applied, since it was a lot easier than getting rid of plastic. We hadn't gotten rid of *gasoline* yet.

Tree took her check gratefully enough, unless the illness laid her low, then she raged about the stupidity of the world. If she could get up, she could write it down, and the power of her words could no longer be ignored. Not this time. She turned wet with sweat under the blankets, shivering and whining and mad as hell, then exhausted, she fell asleep again. Factories still spewed out plastics in a cornucopia of colors, shapes, and chemical arrangements, and almost everyone still threw them away in a shiny toxic waterfall. What else could we do with them? Why had they done this to us?

Harris never bothered her on the days when she lay in the dark with the TV on and ate crushed ice, and would sneak in to refill her cup and make sure she had not stopped breathing. Why he had chosen to reappear in her life had never been adequately explained, but it didn't matter and as time went on, no explanation was needed. She wasn't going anywhere, and she didn't have a date. She could use the company, and perhaps he could too.

They had met in college—so long ago! Tree thought. How could they have lived so long, and learned so little? Before she was Tree, and was still Jennifer. She had been lured over to Harris when she saw him holding a guitar and ranting about the emptiness of modern life to a bartender. The bartender looked bored, since he was a graduate student and had already been over that, but Jenny was fascinated. She found out that not only could Harris debate, he was so talented, he didn't need college. His parents thought he was in business school, so there he was—working at a degree in classical guitar. Guilty and embarrassed, he attended half of his classes as a compromise, not excelling in any of them, and drank. Harris wasn't too disciplined, one of the qualities Jenny liked in him. You couldn't let the machine break you, at least not at such a young age.

His women didn't understand the needs of an artist, even when he sang his heartbreak to them, right to their faces. But Jenny remained true. What did those bimbos expect from a man who would rather play music than go to class—a long-term relationship? Harris was handsome and could play the guitar. He didn't have to settle. Jen, having never slept with him, was infinitely more understanding than that gal she'd known wouldn't last very long.

"Don't you think that the fashion industry contributes to rape culture?" she pressed him, needing some input. "It's obvious, right?"

"Well, *I've* never raped anyone, and just look at these women. All very fashionable." Harris ogled appreciatively. It was spring, so most college students were stripped down to essentials. Jenny was weeks behind on her research paper about the perils of materialism, even though it was one of her favorite subjects. It had turned out to be a difficult topic, since the larger world seemed to be screaming the exact opposite, even in some of her enlightened classes. Was rangeland management supposed to be sponsored by an opium poppy co-op? Did we *need* more opium dens? Her friends seemed to be falling for contrived rituals of excess, which was not what she had expected from college. Where were her kindred spirits? But almost everyone seemed perfectly happy with this bloated circus.

"No, Harris, not like that. Why do these women objectify themselves? What is it about our society that drives them to act like that?"

Harris tuned in a little bit. "Marx does tell us that the bourgeoisie lifestyle is unsustainable, only made possible by the dissipation of the working class." Close enough. He was so awesome. He clawed his hair out of his eyes, which he kept long and sloppy as part of his tormented musician persona. He was playing softly, so he wasn't listening to her a bit, but he was attracting the glances of cute girls passing by. But Harris wouldn't blow her off for some quickie when they were drinking together. Both of them had attended enough classes this week to feel like real students, and thus had earned their early-weekend drunk, according to an unspoken rule they both agreed on. Alcoholism in college was part of the learning experience, unless you had a really hard degree, or god forbid, you became a real alcoholic, as had happened to a few of Jenny's friends. But not her. The evening was endless, and the world was their shining and non-materialistic oyster. They would never become members of the bourgeoisie, no matter what life threw at them. And all these years later, they had remained true. There was no time left to join the bourgeoisie, unless something extraordinarily rare happened to them, like a personality transplant.

After his last relationship fizzled out—a rather tepid affair that barely qualified for the title—Harris decided to abandon what sounded like an upcoming bad scene in the cities. They always gave him a bad vibe, but due to the demands of his career, he'd spent more time there than he wanted to. The crowds were increasingly rowdy and not satisfied with real life performances with no digital enhancements. They didn't want to watch someone perform—they wanted someone to perform *for them*. Harris had become a fogie. Those Vore people were nuts, and rude besides. He was a *classical guitarist*, you didn't put it on an amp.

Jenny lived in some backwoods town in the mountains and had been there for years. Harris was not surprised that she had chosen the less traveled path in life, being a lefty agitator or something. She was excited when he called, or pretended to be, and that was enough for him. He could hang out for a few days, then move on. He didn't want her to think that he had nowhere to go, even if it was true.

They hadn't laid eyes on each other for over ten years when he pulled up to her house, but after the initial shock of seeing what several years of middle age did to a person, it was fairly smooth sailing. Of all the people to show up from her past, Harris was one of the better ones. She had many fond memories of him, but no sexual ones, which tidied things up fast when you shared a house with someone else. She could not imagine them succumbing to lust as senior citizens if they hadn't done so when they were young and beautiful. Why hadn't they? They'd drunk enough together. But this removed most of the drama from the present situation. Not all of it. She wasn't dead, and he was right there in the next room. She could hear him snore.

Tree was well aware that Harris was still a very handsome man—kind of worn out, sure, but with long silky hair, long-lashed blue eyes with crinkles at the corners, and a face unlined by neurosis. Mellow. A man with a guitar could pull that off if he kept his mouth shut, but Tree knew that Harris really was laid back. He'd held her hand through more than one drunken meltdown during college, and if she passed out on his couch, she knew that she'd wake up wearing her clothes. Harris was wise enough not to get too excited about things, something she had never mastered. Nobody could anymore, and had to stay pacified with marijuana.

"Why are there so many pot farms around here?" Harris asked after he arrived. The entire town was stoned as they could be, it seemed. Harris had figured it was a habit of musicians or artists or those types, but everyone appeared to be on weed now.

"Capitalism, as usual. But about us—we're all self-medicating," Tree told him, demonstrating. "The doctors are so overworked, nobody can get in to see them. It takes months. Most of them have quit. Nobody has insurance now, because of the microplastics, so no one can pay for anything. There's so many cheap street drugs, everybody samples things, then they lie to the doctors if they get sick from it. There's directions on the internet for do-it-yourself drug trips. If you were a doctor, would you want to work on these people?" Harris hadn't noticed that either, having a kindly nature, but she was right. These folks did not take very good care of themselves, even with the removal of most of their junk food. It had to be frustrating. Tree continued.

"The mental health doctors are so overwhelmed, they all smoke pot too, if they haven't quit working entirely. There's no benefit to them working so hard. Nobody really wants to change a thing about themselves, and it depresses the therapists too much to interact with them. The Vores make a big deal about going to therapy, then when they show up, they won't even take off their headsets. Most people just smoke a lot of weed, since it's twenty-five dollars a bale a bale here. Our life expectancy is plummeting though, because of all the suicides and homemade drugs." She did know her stuff. She'd sent him some examples of her research over the years—pages of boxes with cells circled and exclamation marks on them: We are all going to die! It didn't look good, if her research was correct.

His visit had turned into an indefinite stay. There was nowhere better to go, and they could help each other out. Harris enjoyed the town. It was such a change from most places he had been, where everyone hurried. Was it different here, or was everyone high? He thought about it while he sat on the back porch and smoked some weed. He could slow down. With a friend and a ready-made roof over his head, he lingered. Maybe Tree was right—maybe society was crumbling. It did feel kind of weird, all the time now. There was no point in going looking for trouble. Looming old age was great, he'd discovered, in that the urgency to do anything had gone. He had proved himself or not, whatever there was to prove, but it was too late to do anything about it now. He was not the type to suddenly take up a strenuous hobby to defy his age. Thanks to Tree, he now knew how hard it was to get good medical care, and that was a good excuse. He also knew that Tree wasn't going to put a boot up his butt about anything, so she was relaxing to be around in that sense. She was not only without ambition, just as she'd always been, but in ill health. She could use him around.

Harris was undervaluing himself. Besides his skill in soothing background music, he had carpentry skills that he employed without being asked, which Tree appreciated madly. He fixed the sink! He put in a new shower! They dug a pit in the backyard, put a liner around it, and made a wading pool. Tree lined it with rocks and checked it carefully for leaks. The teeny pool made the backyard luxurious. She had seen rabbits, coyotes, lots of deer, and once even a bobcat drinking from it.

It wasn't fair that Harris was still so handsome, as well as having practical skills, which he had learned where? He was a musician. How many advantages did one man need? And he made her laugh, besides. Why couldn't they fall in love like in the movies? It was so close and convenient. But they forgot about their arguments the next day, instead of dwelling on them like people in love should. That was unless Tree decided that her argument would be even better the next day, after she had plotted out how to win it. Harris thought she was a pain in the ass, with her proselytizing about how people should try harder. Do better. Better than what? Self-satisfied helplessness was the way of the future. We'd all worked very hard to make it that way, so we could complain about being bored.

"I know that," beefed Tree, "but they're wrong." How could anyone claim to be bored? The world was bulging with pointless entertainment, for no rational reason. No one could watch a fraction of what was being produced, and we had all the old stuff, too. And that was on top of the cocktails of drugs that most people were taking. We couldn't possibly need more stimulation. Maybe, just maybe, we needed *less* stimulation, fewer screens. Had anyone ever considered this, even if it didn't benefit The Economy?

They went over and over this subject, using different words depending on their mood or degree of intoxication. Harris asserted that it didn't matter if people were wrong or not, as long as they received enough public approval for their actions. Society would grant its approval, and everything would be fine. The actions would be perceived to be right by most people, and they would *become* correct and acceptable.

Tree held that humans should have functioning moral centers and should be able to see when society went outrageously wrong, no matter how ingeniously it was masked by the government or corporate overlords. If all of your friends jumped off a cliff because an ad told them to, and were dead, were they still fashionable? Was leaving a pretty corpse really more important than being alive? Wouldn't you rather be standing at the top of the cliff, even if society said that you were wrong? Ergo, why should we care what "society" thinks, when it's obviously working against us?

"Why are you talking like that? I don't think that's how you use 'ergo.'"

"And you're a lawyer too? I think that's exactly how you use it."

Harris pointed out, "I'm winning, if you want to go by popular approval."

"That's exactly what I mean! You're not supposed to run society by what's *popular.* This is not junior high school. Everyone can be wrong, even if the vast majority of them think it's cool. That includes you, because nothing about this is 'fine.' Having your toenails removed is popular right now too."

"It is not."

"Go look at Vore toes. They want smooth toes this year. For no reason. They're going to deform themselves for fashion, again. Do you approve of that? I hope you have more sense." Harris was trying to imagine them. Little sausage toes would be hot for a few things. She had a point, though. But women had always deformed themselves for fashion. And now the men had joined them, so it had become twice as acceptable.

Even her arguments went in a circle and came back to the same place, because Tree liked things to be logical and circular, like ecology. If she kept reaching the same conclusion, it was only because the facts led there: either the Vores and their deplorable way of thinking had to go, or the planet would. People with many more credentials and a lot more tact said the same thing, if you read between the lines, and sometimes you didn't even have to. When Vores couldn't walk anymore because their smooth toes had crippled them, would they stay home in shame? No, they'd just get another robot to carry them around. Next year they should adopt a fashion where they held their breath until they died.

Harris had barely noticed while everything changed around him, one robot and one harsh word at a time. The movement of other people around him didn't make his skin crawl like it did Tree. She began hyperventilating if there were more than four people in a room with her at the same time, even if she wasn't offended by their appearance. Harris lived in his head. He was more of a—well, he wasn't an activist. He only played background music now. Tree was still angry, even if she didn't have the energy to rant and rave much anymore, as all the things she and her nature-handled friends had warned about came true, one right after the other. It was easier if you never thought about that entire subject, but she had waded right in and studied it, watched the animals die and the landscapes become concrete. It couldn't have been easy. He loved her for trying, even if he didn't fully understand why she did that stuff when it wasn't going to change anything. She'd been arrested several times, spent months in jail, had her face all over the internet. She'd even been a meme once—an uncomplimentary one, naturally, which Tree claimed that she'd never seen, since it wasn't very good anyway. She'd been told.

Once the artificial intelligence got going well, everything had a chip, so everything could tell you what to do. One day you went out to your car and it refused to go anywhere except that place you'd mentioned out loud while you were driving yesterday, but hadn't stopped. All your life you'd driven the same old kind of car, and you thought that you were in control of it. When you told your car to call the service center to complain, another computer informed you that you had signed up for "preferred services" when you bought the car years ago, and you could not opt out now, as the software believed that everyone would be better off with this service, and you had agreed. If the AI believed it, who were you to question it? It knew you better than you knew yourself. Go to the store and buy something. Everyone had more credit than they knew what to do with.

Massaged into compliance by generations of intrusive technology, people complained about their overbearing cars for a few hours or not at all, since no one was available to listen to their complaints except another bot. It didn't help to complain to your friends, because the same thing had happened to them. Then everyone would become quiet and drink too much wine. Some people made sticky notes that said "don't talk in the car!!" and stuck them on their dashboard. This made them want to yell at the car every time they got in it, and some of them did. They liked to talk in the privacy of the car, and sing. Before. Before they had radios that listened to them back. Others didn't care after they got used to it, since they were finding so many cool new places to shop, like the wine-of-the-week store. They had some new credit cards, too. The car paid them a lot of compliments for making the best shopping choices. You had to be careful how much you cussed the car, anyway, or it would take its revenge. In the worst cases, they just had to be sold, then everyone knew that you couldn't control your temper.

So everyone fell into line, or most did. The poor were left out, since they couldn't afford all the technology and were only forced into it at their faceless jobs. The poor also became much better at recycling and repairing old useful objects to keep the AI at bay, since it was all connected. If you bought one gadget, you had to buy an entire wardrobe to go with it. There wasn't a purchase that didn't track you. If you tried to buy a pan, you'd find out that you'd been enrolled in the pan-of-the-month club, the ones that told you how many calories were in your food, but only if you had a recurring subscription. You couldn't stop the orders either, because the AI would keep telling you that they were *disposable* pans, and you should probably throw that one away now, to make room for the new ones that had new features. And don't forget that you had also signed up for the microwave-of-the-month club. Everyone was multi-tasking so well, sometimes they couldn't remember what they'd done for hours after they got off the internet, and walked around in a daze, waiting for hate mail or packages to start arriving. It was even worse if they drank, and well—everyone did.

Some towns now looked like Cuba in the magazines Tree used to read, with ancient gasoline cars in the streets, moving renegade humans from one place to another, at least until the government closed down the last gas stations. They kept threatening to, but also kept putting it off, as the petroleum monkey was hard to kick. Tree's car barely made the gas engine cut-off, and any work on her ride now would come with mandatory self-driving features, for "safety." Not so safe when I drive it into a tree so it will stop telling me what to do, Tree thought. It cost her $500 to bribe a mechanic to disable the tracking chip and updates. She thought she might be able to hold out with this car until she died, along with the other Luddites who defiantly shared car repair tips on seventy-year old vehicles.

Out loitering at the upscale store in her ancient beauty one day, Tree noticed a couple of well-dressed types bopping across the parking lot in full virtual reality headsets. But they clearly could see through them, because they kept moving, their blocky oversized heads waving back and forth on their stick necks. Tree gaped, then immediately called her friend Spider. She was called that because she had a habit of showing up unexpectedly where she wasn't wanted, like a spider. Generally she showed up in some business's hard drive, after which all of their work files would disappear.

"They have entire computers on their heads, Spi. I don't know how they even walk."

"You saw them?" Spider was well-informed, just as Tree knew she would be. "Those are extremely new. They can do everything. They never have to take them off. Isn't that weird? They're personalized for each person? Then you buy whatever features you want with them. You can get an entire new identity with them. They're crazy expensive."

"That's just sick!" Tree exclaimed, horrified at usual at the foolhardiness of the world. She goggled at the be-helmeted first adopters, hoping one of them would fall on her face, but they stepped right over the curb and disappeared into the store.

It was only a few years after Tree saw the big-headed couple that the robots were introduced, because why wouldn't they be? The tech consumers acquired the name "Vores", as in "Virtual On-board Reality Enthusiasts." Earlier reserved only for goofy gamer types, the headsets moved into the real world and conquered it too, filling a need that hadn't existed and creating thousands of new ones. The black and white headsets took over entire sectors of society. The users were also called the Bores, or the Stormtroopers, since Star Wars had never gone away, and never would. When the last humans were floating a million miles above Earth, slowly dying in their virtual reality bodysuits, they'd tell each other that they were Jedi masters, really, moving into a new consciousness.

The addictive tech was just what a lot of Americans had been looking for, the same as all the addictive tech that had come before. The headsets were introduced as a natural evolution from smart phones, and the robots were a natural accessory for the headsets. The getups offered almost complete detachment from the real world, while still being in it, so that users could fix their digital eyes on their surroundings and not miss anything *even more*. A lot of those Vores held jobs too, since all those electronic toys were expensive. Most of the work involved providing ever-increasing content for the headsets. The Vores not only worked from home, they worked inside their home, exploring their inner home, within their home inside their headsets. With so many layers of awareness, could anyone doubt they were at the pinnacle of human existence?

Since the headsets and the accessory robots advertised status worse than a new sports car, they were derided almost as much as they were lusted after. Truthfully, the Runnies could have used some of those robots to make their lives a little easier. But they didn't come solo, only with the brain-altering headsets that controlled them. The headsets were available at a rental place, and at the library, but in a generic version that didn't offer nearly the mind-blowing experience that a personalized version could. So she had heard. Tree had not experimented with them herself and didn't intend to.

The Runnies could not be offended by calling them Runnies, even though the name had been bestowed on them by the Vores. Those Runnie people—running away from progress, running from the future. But as one Runnie quipped, "Why would I be insulted because my body still works like it should?" The Runnies could move. They built gardens and outhouses and chicken coops and locked sheds in their tacky yards, to keep their Bartertown wares in, like a vault. They made furniture. They rebuilt their fifty-year-old cars. Headset free, they ran across the unfenced hills and planted wildflowers and had keg parties and uninhibited sex in the fields next to the stoned deer, since it was fairly difficult to get pregnant now and if such a thing happened, it was a joyous event, no matter where it came from.

The Vores paced around a circular track downtown in their black blocky heads and enjoyed their own little worlds, but in the company of others, like pets that hated each other but were stuck in the house while their owner was at work. But the Vores could run too. They looked like they could run marathons. Their tight rear ends and muscled calves were part of their image, and if they weren't attained by exercise, that could be purchased too. They spent hours in the gym running on treadmills, doing yoga, practicing wellness together—but once outdoors they followed their computers. The sunglasses in them were personalized for the light and for their eyes. The implied insult in the name was that Runnies had to move, while the Vores only did it on their terms. Not moving was the ultimate in consumer progress. If we didn't want it and wouldn't benefit from it, then why had it become available?

Periodically, the Vores would have a show of remorse, or a flash of their original brain, and they'd ditch the headsets and "go wild,"—like doing a detox. Then the detox itself became part of Vore culture, since they loved their headsets even more when they went back to them, and presumably, had crazy make-up sex with them that cost extra. The headsets quickly learned how to periodically "break up" with their users, which increased their anticipation of further interaction later. Then they never complained when the price of their love kept going up. That was the problem with the gadgets—they gave you whatever you wanted, no matter how bad it was.

Runnies who used to run in marathons that had lost all of their funding when the Vores put on their masks would periodically go on a Vore Hunt. They'd dress up in all of their running finery, but with their shorts hiked up until the display was daring, if not completely unfit for public. When they found a Vore on one of their aimless shambles with their pet robots, they'd trot around them over and over until the Vores broke cover and yelled at them. This would be recorded put on the internet. If you could get one of the Vorebots to try to intervene, it was even funnier. The Runnies staggered the date of their assault each year so that the Vores wouldn't have any warning, but it came in the spring, when everyone went outside and was once again offended by the sight of everyone else. On that day, several of the Vores would be bullied to actual interaction with someone in public. It wasn't even their fault that the road races had stopped, but had more to do with air pollution, apathy, and drivers so careless that the runners had been in danger of being run over every year. People would move the traffic cones and signs and drive right through the race course.

Most Runnies had cell phones and internet of some kind. Only a few had totally rejected technology, in some last futile fight for humanity. After you spent some time on the internet, though, you knew it was a lost cause. The kids still suffered through the interference for glimpses of social media, which was as toxic as Ebola and just as addictive as it had ever been. Actual phone coverage was mediocre and irritating, from constant interfere by drones that buzzed the phone towers and trashed their transmission. The drones hated people connecting, for some reason. They also crashed a lot, for the same reason—the signals from their home base were scattered and lost, so that sometimes after the drones had buzzed enough cell phone towers, they flew around aimlessly until they lost power and died, like a honeybee dosed with pesticides. Some of them that weren't smashed too badly showed up at Bartertown, but no one ever admitted shooting them down, since enough of them fell out of the sky on their own. There were millions of them up there and nobody controlled them. They were probably running into each other.

The internet was a shadow of what it had been in its glory days, which had been before Tree's time and lasted about five years. But the internet had been jaded since the day it was born. The majority of the sites, then as now, were ads, influencers, conspiracy theories, ads disguised as news, broken links, and porn. It may not work at all, even if you had it right in your house, since there were not even close to enough technicians to keep up with the maintenance. There were also something like a half-billion hackers on the planet, since there was a lot of unemployment out there, but also a lot of connectivity. But most of the internet still worked as the quality kept declining, since they'd made it almost essential to our existence, even if you refused to hold a job.

Harris told her that he was in some porn on the internet, but there was nothing shocking about that. If you were over forty years old, there was something like a ninety-eight percent chance of naked pictures of you on the internet, if not much more graphic material. Some very upright and correct people were not even sure how it had happened, if they found out. Security cameras? Their own phone, spying on them? The internet gave us everything, then took it away and sold it. Artificial intelligence could churn that stuff out endlessly. Nobody knew if it was you in the porn, or how altered the image may be. You could just deny it.

Nothing was what it seemed on the internet, and it messed with your mind if you stayed there too long. Endless mindless solipsism was not as much fun as it sounded, even if we tried valiantly. Tree used it as little as anyone, but there were too many ads about it everywhere else to tune it out completely.

Adventures Without Dogs

When he first moved in, Tree was looking for ways to amuse Harris so that he'd stay longer. He was a very cosmopolitan guy, after all, and he might become bored with her country ways. They drank hallucinogenic beer at the Dome and danced 'til dawn. They went to the Cliff rally, where old gas cars were modified into bombs, then driven off cliffs so they could explode properly, like in the movies. It wasn't really Tree's cup of tea and she had to wear earplugs, but guys loved it, and you could hear the cars blowing up all over town. Harris liked those shows, but they had to stop doing them after some people died. They went right over the cliff with the cars, and even though it was obviously another suicide, being recorded for posterity, they shut it down anyway. If you wanted to die, you could go hang yourself in the woods, not broadcast it on the internet. We had enough problems already.

There were movies at the theater—they kept hanging on, even with almost no original content anymore, since nobody wanted to work, even in Hollywood. How many things could our eyeballs look at anyway? Hollywood had turned out that junk for over a hundred years; you couldn't have seen all of it. So we still had movies. Old ones that would always be popular, weird cult stuff, and finally, a lot of garbage from influencers and terrible marketing firms. Naturally, most people wouldn't choose to watch garbage, but the theaters had found a way around that—by not announcing what they were showing beforehand. The mall dwellers would always show up no matter what was on. The audience might get a classic Star Wars movie, or they might get the latest directing effort by a nine-year old internet star who wanted to sell glitter products. Since just about all old movies and TV shows were available for free, the entrepreneurs would use AI to sample a world's worth of old media, then create their own masterpiece. It was usually excruciatingly bad, but the youngsters didn't seem to notice, dazzled by their creative genius and millions of randomly flashing scenes. Tree gambled four weeks in a row, and got stuck with the sampling movies three times. It wasn't worth it, even if it was dirt cheap to get in. Since at least half the audience was Vores, the Runnies often wondered why they bothered to come at all. They never removed their headsets, and just sat there taking up too much space and blocking the view, as was their wont.

"I don't know if we need to try that again," Harris commented after their third dog of a "movie", a particularly bad effort by a eleven-year old Vore girl who needed a support monkey to help with homework, because her fingernails were already too long to do anything. "I might get brain cancer."

"I agree, that one was real dreck. And for forty-five minutes. But you won't get brain cancer. That's just propaganda from those drug people."

"Are you sure?" Harris thought maybe he could have brain cancer, since he'd stood too close to a lot of speakers. He felt woozy.

"Harris," Tree said, pointing, "pay attention." In front of them in the movie lobby was a six-by-six-foot poster of a man with a pained look on his face and his hand on his head. The caption read YOU MAY ALREADY HAVE BRAIN CANCER in large black script, while around the border, worried doctors conferred about his case. Someone had added a joint and some vampire teeth to his mouth, but it did look familiar.

"Didn't you see that when we came in? Didn't you see that ad before the long ad, and the ad where the influencer told us how to detect signs of brain cancer, and the key chain they gave you when we came in, with "YOU MAY ALREADY HAVE BRAIN CANCER" on it?"

Harris felt they might be about to get into an argument, and he wasn't up to it right now, what with the brain cancer.

"No, I didn't notice. What is your point? How long has this been going on?"

Tree looked like she was going to explode. "Your *entire life!* And you can't even see it. Nobody can see it! Then they turn into Vores."

He agreed with her and told her that he'd more diligent. She'd had this problem with the background noise in the world lately. Well, ever since he met her. To his great annoyance, after she pointed it out, he couldn't unsee it, and walked around now disgusted with how they were trying to manipulate everyone. He threw his collection of key chains in the trash. Wake up, sheeple!

Tree cast about for more cerebral entertainment and came up with the valley where the dogs lived. She didn't go out there much anymore, but Harris might like it. "Dogs?" Harris said blankly. It was weird how he knew so much about some subjects, but was clueless about others that she thought were obvious and universal. How could anyone have missed the dogs leaving? But humanity failing nature wasn't a big story. It wasn't even worth writing about. Indeed, no one did anymore, since there were almost no real journalists left, and AI couldn't capture the emotional depth of the subject.

"Well, we never had dogs," Harris told her a little defensively. They were awkward around each other, but they wanted to be friends, so they kept working at it. It was still a lot easier than making brand new friends, at their age. He could understand dogs. But he'd been a traveling musician and they didn't own dogs; it would have been cruel. Just the one in the commercial, and it hadn't been his. It had been a cool dog, though. It slept next to him after he fed it some snacks, and nobody tried to take it, because he was the star.

"What kind was it?" Tree asked. "Wait a minute, what commercial?"

"It was uh, a—how would I know? I just told you I never had dogs. It had a long nose, long hair, and a long tail." He played his guitar with great concentration, which meant that he was done talking, if Tree would take a hint.

Tree sighed. He did need to tell her more about this rock star business someday.

They reached the long valley and Tree pulled into a gravel parking area, where she parked on above a big grassy incline where they could see the dogs playing. There was a sizable audience today, hanging out in their lawn chairs, since the day was fine. A pack of dogs had moved to this valley years ago, and if they weren't disturbed by too many drunken idiots, they would stay there for years. This was a slap in the face to some people who had different ideas about the relationship between dogs and humans, but the dogs had won this one, and never came near the adoring audience.

There were no more domesticated dogs. Tree supposed you could fail to notice this, if you'd never been around dogs. And were like, blind. Rumor had it that some of the dogs were still a little bit domesticated, and would come around for food in the winter, or a drink. And why wouldn't they, since even the real wildlife was doing it now? But they'd gone feral, like cats. All the dogs that Tree knew of now ran around in packs, or got in with coyotes or wolves and interbred.

Tree had had dogs, of course, her companions on hundreds of miles of trails and mountains. After her first one died, there had been another, a pretty mutt with blue eyes and a short tail. But there was something wrong with these later dogs, and something wrong with that one. They weren't as obedient as dogs should be, as dogs had always wanted to be. They didn't stay home. Even with training, they nipped and barked and fought and ran off from their owners. Tree's blue-eyed dog would disappear for days at a time, no matter how sweetly she talked to her, and finally left for good during one of the long days of summer. Tree never saw her again. She only cried a little, having seen it coming, and if you love something, set it freeeeeee.

Fliers for lost dogs began appearing not only locally, but in towns everywhere, as our former best friends decided they'd had quite enough of us, thank you very much. It was not really noticed until the dogs left in a flood, and then all anyone could do was watch in shock. It wasn't only their dog that had suddenly developed behavior problems—all of them had. Some owners figured that if that's what the dogs wanted, fine then. They threw the dog food out for the skunks and foxes. They deleted their dog pictures and pretended that they had never slept next to her for a week after a breakup, crying into her fur. But for the emotionally fragile, the shock of losing their best and sometimes only companion was immense and public. Some pet owners were so invested in their fur babies that they couldn't cope with it. The dogs had been their last best hope for friendship in an unfriendly world.

The Vores lost their dogs first, no shock there. Their computerized dogs were far superior to real ones. They were made to be better than the real thing, naturally, the top one percent of the dog world, with big round eyes and tight eager bodies that smartly connected to the Vores headset, so they could be ordered around without even the inconvenience of speaking. They could be entirely virtual, or a robot could be ordered, after the owner got done modifying them to their specs. They didn't bark, unless you wanted them to, they didn't need to go outside, or be fed, or want to be petted. But if you did want to cuddle, they came with the most luxurious fur made of old mink and sable coats, or even real dog fur if it was specially ordered. You could get a copy of your last dog, but most people upgraded. It could talk like Scooby Doo, which seemed cool at first, but since the dog looked exactly like a real dog, apparently it was too weird even for the Vores, so it had to be a nightmare.

If a Vore wanted to put their robot dog in a robot baby carrier and take it to the park to carefully interact with the other robot dogs, the dog was programmed to love it. Or it would stay in a baby carriage all day, no problem, unlike their old dog. As the robot dogs increasingly took their place by the side of the bed, the living dogs ran uptown in a pack of confusion. The Runnies managed to keep them for a little longer, since they still had eyes for the dogs to connect with. But no one had had a dog for many years now.

They tried cloning them, but the industrial procedure was new then and cloned dogs had a high failure rate, which was scientific way of saying that they made a lot of mutant dogs. This wasn't a problem until an animal rights group got some footage of the mutant puppies being burned alive in a ditch when they were only a few hours old. Cloned dogs fell out of fashion overnight. Even if you got one, it wasn't like a real dog and had no personality, like all of the clones. They were only copies of dogs. If you had one, you had better not admit to it, like using a clothes dryer in the middle of summer. Not even the Vores would claim either one.

"Those are dogs though, right?" Harris was trying hard. "And we still have coyotes and wolves and things. They're not *gone*. They're not extinct." Maybe she shouldn't have asked him to move in. She couldn't live with someone who couldn't fully comprehend the larger tragedy here. But a man who could play guitar so soulfully could understand dogs. She gave it the old college try.

"They're not dead, Harris. They *left*. They got a divorce, because we kill everything that breathes. You know that dogs practically evolved to love us? If they can't take it anymore, what does that say about us?" Harris didn't know, but it sounded pretty ominous, so he played his guitar.

"Look at them," Tree pointed at the pack, just getting warmed up, "they like to roam around and look for food and eat garbage and sniff each others' butts. Instead we put them on leashes, and left them stuck in apartments for hours while we worked. Then we sent them to obedience school, because putting them in dog prison made them cranky, and they needed to be *trained*. You know what a coyote's home range is, Harris? Our dogs never even got to meet other dogs. We isolated them from their own species, like some kind of domestic abuse situation, then we made them sleep in little baskets in our houses that were way too warm for them. They weren't supposed to be our babies, or house plants. They weren't supposed to be our only friends on earth."

She was getting too emotional. That was why she didn't come out here too often, since it was a bittersweet place, as they said. Tree hated that word. It was either degrees of good, or degrees of bad, and you could keep that "bittersweet" nonsense for a romance novel. There was no place for that in science, even if neuroscience had found some areas of the brain that fired excessively when people watched old dog movies, even the black-and-white ones. Well, too bad. The dogs had found a better place, and it wasn't with us. People came by with roadkill or a carcass once in a while and chucked it down the hill, so the pack had no reason to leave. They could enjoy our company now without being subjected to it, instead of the other way around.

Tree went out to the valley once with one of her fellow eco-warriors, an older gal who missed her many dogs—about six of them, or four, or maybe seven. That must have hurt. She assured Tree that she was strong enough to take it. They toted their chairs out to a good spot in the sun, and watched a few dogs that were not entertaining at all, since they were all passed out in the sun. It was puppy season, but they all seemed to be sleeping too.

Their calm was interrupted when a guy in a slick electric truck cruised up, parking too close to them. After that insult, he got out a BB gun, and with no introduction at all, began plinking at the dogs down the hill. They moved a little from the popping noise, but it was not likely he could hit any of them at that distance. The onlookers, already annoyed at this interruption, now became angry.

Stupid and confusing performance art was for Vores, and an insult to their intelligence. They glared at the guy.

"I will *eat* those dogs," the man said, plinking a few more shots down the hill. What an idiot. Just in time, Tree's companion stood up and smacked the man across the gut, which made him drop his BB gun. Tansy was only ten feet away so she got the drop on him, as well as scaring him to death when she simultaneously started yelling about "gun fetishists" and "take that crap somewhere else" and some other things that Tree was fairly familiar with. The man grabbed his baby gun from the ground and backed up fast from the crazy women, since it looked like Tree might join in. The guy had covered them with dust when he blew in.

Tansy was irate, since she had just been thinking about her five favorite dogs and how nice it was to have a place to come see them, or at least these stand-ins for them, and suddenly she had dirt in her eyes. She continued yelling at the man, who was too stunned to make a getaway in the face of this assault.

"Do we need this? Do you think you're the only one? We all miss our dogs. We all like to come out here and see them. If you can't treat a dog with some *respect*, and people with some *respect*, then no wonder your dog left you, and you *deserved* it. I bet you liked to blow off *fireworks* around your dog. I bet you left your dog in your truck all day, because you didn't *care*." She would have continued, but ran out of breath. A few of the onlookers applauded, not caring what she was saying, but they liked fights. They also had left their dogs in their cars all day. The man, now minus his dignity, got back in his truck and threw a beer can out the window as he drove off, to show that he wasn't intimidated by crazy old women. No one bothered to comment on a few more irresistible impulses being indulged. We all had bad days.

Some people never left their houses again after the dogs went. It was on the news—hours of wistful commentary about the hubris of man, or nature sending us cautionary tales, while footage of people with dogs played in the background. Do you remember Lassie, America? America wept, even people who had always hated dogs, and Lassie's long pointy nose. It was better after we smashed their faces so that they looked more like us, they thought. Harris' rock star life must have been all-consuming if he had missed that. He must have grown up in some cold sterile place where children wore clean clothes every day, and the TV off was turned off when the dog shows came on, because dogs made one sentimental and unable to concentrate on work. It was only luck that Harris had turned out as well as he had. He needed to be exposed to some good things, even if it was just the *idea* of dogs that he needed.

The first wave of suicides in Yellowstone had happened about the time the dogs left, an impulse that Tree both understood, and was furious about. First about the suicides themselves—all those people giving up, when they needed to keep fighting—then the idea of hundreds of people polluting the hot springs with their fat greasy bodies and their despair. Even in death, they had no respect for nature. Some of them weren't even locals, but had gone on long road trips to admire Yellowstone one last time before they threw themselves in the springs.

Despite the tourists, grasslands in the park had gone wild after all the fires, and the bison and elk population exploded. With no more cattle to fence them in, the bison spread all over the surrounding area and once again dotted the plains from the Black Hills to Cody, resembling not the herds of the olden days, but a fine approximation, anyway. Anyone was allowed to shoot them, but with the meat virus, or the airborne hormones, or microplastics, who knew, almost no one did unless they needed food. The native Americans had taken some to Alaska when they moved out, and apparently they did great up there too, so now there were huge herds of bison in Alaska.

Tree had grown up in a house full of animals, because she had a brother who collected strays. Tree was not at that point, since Casey took care of it. He was older and he could find better ones. Snakes and birds and kangaroo rats. And once a 'possum, which was not even supposed to live in this area, but there it was anyway. Most of the animals were alive, although he was not averse to bringing home a dead creature to skin or take the skull or something. There had been a few simmering five-gallon buckets in their backyard, as Casey cleaned the skulls with vile combinations of chemicals that were supposed to leave them sparkling white. Their mother found out about that one and forbade any more dead animals around the house, although the skulls and skins showed up later on in Casey's bedroom. He showed Tree the way the upper and lower jaws fit together, and how their teeth and jaw structure showed what they ate. The stray cats wrapped themselves around his chair and stared motionless at some rodent Casey had caught in the woods, willing it to come to them, this time.

Instead of becoming a serial killer later in life, Casey became a large animal vet and moved to Africa, where he was killed by a poacher years later. It was a hazard of the job, and he'd always known it. There wasn't a single large mammal left in Africa that wasn't trailed by its own personal drone. Some of those animals had their own webcams and fan clubs, but one of them had still been shot dead in front of a worldwide audience, because nothing mattered anymore. The anonymous poacher had a giant gun and was wearing a mask, just like millions of other people in Africa. Tree still missed Casey tremendously, even though he had been gone for years now. He didn't lie to her or tell her baby stories. He had introduced her to the wonders of nature, and passed the connection he felt to the rest of the world on to her. We were all the same family with different shapes, even humans. Maybe a dolphin couldn't pass one of our IQ tests, but could we pass a dolphin IQ test? We wouldn't last an hour down there.

Why do we go to the mall? Tree asked him once, trying to put her unease into words. Malls were in their second or third rejuvenation right then, after they legalized prostitution, so most of the stores were outlets of slut clothing, or bedrooms. Tree didn't understand that either, even though technically she understood sex. Was it supposed to be so public? But everyone, even the children, went and sauntered around in brand-new skimpy outfits that would be thrown away almost as soon as they left, or even before, if they visited the bedrooms.

Shouldn't there be other places to exist outside of your house, besides buildings with—things like that? Tree asked Casey. Casey laughed, but not at her. He told her that there were, it was just that we had chosen the profit motive.

"The what?"

"I'll explain it to you later." He never did, but Tree stayed out of malls anyway, even after they put in the water parks and zip lines. One night Casey showed her an old movie called Grizzly Man. Grizzly Man didn't seem quite right in the head, but Tree liked his attitude. He would have understood about the malls. That was why he went and lived in Alaska.

You couldn't even visit where Grizzly Man had been now. It had been closed down to protect it from all the grizzly men and women of the world, who kept taking guided tours to every "unexplored" region as fast as they could find it on their phone maps and hire a guide. Exploitation was the job of business, and business was good. You could hire a plane trip into the north country and trek to the very spot where Grizzly Man had met his end, if you dared, but the whole area belonged to North American native tribes now. They'd been cut off from the water years before in the lower 48, as they'd known they would be, so they pooled their casino money and bought Alaska. White people had their own tribes of lawyers working on having the deal reversed somehow, but for now, Alaska belonged to the natives. They had full jurisdiction over the state—which is to say that they owned as many guns as everyone else, and didn't mind using them. They could relate to Grizzly Man, a white guy who'd been driven crazy by overcivilization.

The grizzlies were doing fantastic up there now, since their bloodlines had been refreshed by polar bears that had to move south and learn how to eat rabbits. Some of the new bears were striped like zebras, some were spotted, some blotchy, to blend in with new bizarro world, where some years now it never snowed at all, and the next winter the tundra would be scoured by snow tornadoes that carried off entire reindeer herds. More trekkers tried to sneak up north and see the hybrid bears, only to be shot by the natives, who were so, so tired of white people.

Casey had been as sad about the dogs as Tree was when she informed him about it all over a terrible phone line. He said that they would be better off now, since like Tree, he was a man of science. He also said, "but we have wild dogs! Lots of them! They're still here!" At least she thought he said that. Tree imagined a phone line somewhere being bombed by international drones that hated all human connection, while she yelled at Casey until they got cut off. You couldn't see the stars anymore, but we still couldn't get decent sound quality on our phones? Why had we done all that then? She didn't even know what Casey had sounded like before he died. Had he been hopeful about the future, or had he given up, but didn't want to tell her? And if he had given up, would she want to hear it? It was fine for Tree to rage and declare that it was too late for everything. But if Casey said it, then it would be true and she would be the next one in the hot pots. It was a fine line.

Harris' family never had any pets in the suburbs either, since his mother didn't like to pick up dog poop or change cat litter boxes, and lord knows you couldn't trust the kids to do it, which was probably true. "I changed all of your diapers and that is enough," his mother said one day, and that was probably true also, even though she hadn't changed any diapers in many years, and right then was some kind of executive. Harris was in junior high then and had discovered music, so he didn't harbor any lingering sentiments for dogs or hamsters or any of it.

Stalwarts was one of the few places that still mostly functioned as a department and grocery store, at least in their area. Over the years, it had morphed into a grocery store and homeless shelter, or a sort of campground and mini-town. There were probably two hundred people staying out in the parking lot, more or less depending on the season. Although under no circumstances were they *living* there, since that was illegal. Their mantra was "do you call this living?" which they repeated dozens of times a day among themselves, usually as a joke, sometimes as a death sentence, depending on their moods. So they only stayed over, sometimes for years. If they weren't really living, it would be doubly insulting if they were asked to leave. Occasionally, some of them did leave, only to be replaced by another group.

Officially they were all on the way out and had no permanent residences. And still, there was so much stuff. There were tents and lawn chairs and grills, umbrellas and flags, camping gear, hay bales, picket fences, solar lights and wind chimes and hummingbird feeders, yard ornaments and baby pools, tarps shading and marking off boundaries. Most of the inventory of Stalwarts had been moved into the parking lot at one time or another, and a lot of it never left. The residents came to believe that just because they didn't have a house to store their things in, it didn't make them less valuable as customers. How could anyone make them leave the parking lot when their needs were so constant, they could be preparing to go back inside the store already? The good bathrooms were inside. Those with vehicles would start them and move them around the lot, so they could have some new real estate. The southern exposure was desirable in the winter, and vans jockeyed for a position when it started getting cold.

Stalwarts dithered while the parking lots filled with victims of capitalism, looking for that fine line between offending their customers, and ejecting the bums. They signaled their eventual capitulation by installing porta-potties in the parking lots, and the bums knew they were winning. Stalwarts finally tried to make some kind of stand, and they strongly urged the Runnies to leave. Then more strongly, with police raids. But it was too late. The residents not only wouldn't leave the parking lots, they rioted. They had the right to buy more things. No one could deny it—Stalwarts had eaten most of the other retail outlets years ago, and could have starved out half the town if they closed.

Stoked, the rioters kept rioting even after they had won. Stalwarts around the country were burned to the ground, right up until rioters realized that they had already conceded. The locals chose sides, too, because if anyone was going to burn down Stalwarts, it would be the citizens who had invested in the community. For a few weeks, a lot of the town was engaged in civil war, some of it at Stalwarts, and some of it in the streets. The Vores, safe at home with their new toys that they didn't need to buy from Stalwarts, didn't get involved much and sniffed about the trashing of civil society, while they flew drones over to look at the damage and find any dead bodies. The final tally was fourteen people killed across the state, forty stores burned down or damaged, and about two hundred drones destroyed that were recording the action. Everyone hated the drones, so they were shot for any reason whatsoever.

Stalwarts rebuilt the higher-traffic stores and carried on pretty much as before. They never said a word about the entire fiasco, since it was forever connected to their brand and there was nothing they could do about it, but they never lost a court case either, when a million or so inconvenienced shoppers sued them for some reason. After slam dunking the litigants, the heirs moved into an enormous bomb shelter under their home offices and didn't come out in public anymore. Everyone bought even more guns. Stalwarts helped out by stocking every kind of firearm they could find, as well as some more exotic things like throwing stars and nunchucks. They also sold whatever cheap merchandise and commodities they could find on the worldwide market. They hadn't even changed the name, because who could deal with changing all that signage, when it was coming on a slow boat from China? They could have called it New Stalwarts or NewSWTS or something, but everybody knew what Stalwarts was, anyway.

The owners put up an even bigger American flag, so that it flapped above the transients in their new plastic chairs, replaced after the riots. The new Stalwarts gave lip service to not having RV and truck people live in their parking lots after that embarrassment, but everyone knew they didn't enforce it because the bums were still out there, just as they'd been before. In fact, Stalwarts continued drawing most of their employees right out of the parking lots, paying them in Stalwarts' goods. They couldn't improve on that system and no one tried anymore.

Tree didn't like stores much and only went when she had to, although it was prime research territory. If she could get Harris to bring her a few things when he went, that was great, but sometimes she had to brave the mob herself. It wasn't going in the store that bothered her, particularly, but all the humans who crowded around public places and did loud, unpredictable things. She'd become even less fond of them after being involved in protests where she was yelled at and sometimes threatened. The things that people would say to complete strangers, for no real reason. She'd even been spit on. At least most of the Stalwarts crowd wouldn't spit on you, even if you took the last item off the shelf. They were all passengers on this strange voyage. Stalwarts was no one's fault, and they become stronger as they endured it together.

She drove out on the main road and stomped on the gas. Driving on the highway was a risky venture, but she braved it sometimes, just like going to Stalwarts. You couldn't shut yourself off from the entire world, like a Vore. Gasoline was highly taxed and most people were not extravagant if they still drove a gas vehicle. A lot of the Vores had stopped driving around and did virtual trips or something, so the majority of thecars on the highway belonged to the homeless and old Runnies, who took their lives in their hands every time they got in the way of the delivery caravans carrying their loads of new Vorebots.

It was nice to drive fast down the road—"fast" being a relative word—just as she had when she was young. If you squinted and could find some real music on the radio, it was almost like being seventeen again. But don't squint too hard or you would probably crash. The potholes were never fixed, and if someone took out a guardrail, it was likely to stay that way. Tree didn't blame anyone for that either, since working on the highways was a death wish, with the Vores' giant irresponsible vehicles and the people with guns. Highway road trippers were mostly on their own. The delivery caravans were the scariest, since they were driverless and had some iffy technology, due to the demands of timely delivery. A lot of them were gas-powered, since business took precedence over the environment. It was like watching a train cruise down the highway, with a tread on it like a snowmobile, skimming over the holes in the pavement without a bump. If one ran you over, there wasn't even a driver to feel bad, let alone take responsibility for it.

"Why are they driving down the highway in them?" Tree raged as she dodged out of the way of a Vore behemoth, its driver oblivious behind their big black head. Their vehicles usually dwarfed hers by several feet and thousands of pounds. Her gas car made her a fireball waiting to happen, as far the Vores were concerned, so they gave her a wide enough berth, or they intended to. But since they didn't pay attention to their cars and depended on an assembly of computers to set the various monitors while it charged, they still might run someone over. Officially the vehicles were "semi-autonomous," but it seemed to be the driver's decision which parts they managed, and which parts they ignored. No one with any sense had a full self-driving car. They were so easily hacked and riddled with bugs, drunk driving was safer than getting inside one of those things.

Who monitored the AI that ran everything? More artificial intelligence, apparently.

Didn't she understand the point of all that artificial intelligence? a drunk Vore had asked Tree once. Today, we could go about living our best lives in safety and security, thanks to the miracle of AI. It was *taken care of*, he emphasized, pounding on the bar with his big sweaty hand a few times, almost knocking her beer over. Vores were out of touch there behind the goggles and had poor hand-eye coordination if they weren't tuned into it. They were even more out of touch than that, since it sounded like his entire defense had been made up on the spot by artificial intelligence that had taken over his brain as soon as it detected Tree's skepticism. It was just that easy. She inched away from the guy, since she could be drinking beer with a robot in human flesh, and you couldn't even look into his eyes to see if it was true. He had bought her the beer, but Tree remembered why she didn't try to talk to Vores, and decided it was high time to go camping for two weeks.

The Vores never went camping anymore, thanks their big old heads. They might get them dusty, and they would stop working. Their new world needed to be sterilized and dust-free, which was the headset's only good feature, as far as Tree was concerned. The Vores upgraded to computerized parks and computerized scenic drives and computerized wild animals, always with some unsettling anthropomorphic smile, even the mountain lions and killer whales. Tree didn't care, as long as they quit despoiling the real thing. Let them put whatever environmental porn they wanted on their toys. In a perverse way, the headsets had helped her side. Completely devoted to their electronic succubi, a lot of the well-heeled quit using the outdoors to work out their anxieties, and it breathed a little easier, just like Tree did. And the less she knew about their love affairs with their computers, the better.

Besides, she'd seen Bambi. The kind and victimized deer were a cultural touchpoint for Americans, and had distorted our thinking for generations. It had imprinted on Tree when she was barely more than a baby, so she could hardly make fun of the Vores interpretations of animals. Bambi was the reason we had never wiped deer out, and they roamed around now as stoned vermin, one more hazard on the roads. But mountain lions still lived, and so did otters and walruses and bats and foxes and oryx, because the Vores had finally gone full-time to fantasy land, and left the real wild places alone. It was more than even Tree had hoped for, since no matter what the technological innovations, no one had ever seemed to be satisfied with anything before this. With the headsets, savvy consumers had finally reached their nirvana—total sensory overload.

Let the Vores make entertainment that showed a tiger playing with a cat, or hunters doing hand to hand combat with hippos before shooting them dead. Their virtual reality games meant that they weren't taking safaris to Africa to shoot actual wild hippos. Not that it mattered anymore, since the big game industry was kept afloat today not by shooting endangered wildlife—which had been problematic, no matter how many concepts were used to support it—but by cloning all of the popular game animals. Nothing was "endangered" or "rare" anymore, although a lot of things were just plain "extinct," and the words had about lost their meanings—if anyone had known the meanings in the first place except for the biologists and big-game hunters, who loved shooting things even more if they were endangered. Other factions were just fine with shooting endangered leopards that were now not endangered, but still technically extinct, and the safari business continued. There was an enormous genetic bank of most of the "valuable" animals in the world, for sale to anyone who wanted to do the work of getting them cloned. It took a fortune and years of investment to clone a mammoth, only to shoot it in a blaze of glory, but someone had done it. More than once.

Agonized conservationists, never satisfied with keeping only the charismatic megafauna alive, pleaded for keeping the planet with most of its original assembly, showing posters of broken and destitute food webs, mangled beyond repair. Other perfectly respectable biologists argued for taking any animal that needed saving and transferring it to anywhere it may have a chance to survive. But most of the animals that people cared about could be cloned, so "habitat" was also a lost idea. You could clone that giraffe in your garage, if you had the means. Cloned salmon were just as tasty, and if they weren't, it was simply too onerous to save an animal that demanded so much time, space, and wild water to make more of them. It was a fish. It wasn't even sad about what had happened to it. For that we were supposed to sacrifice sport fishing and dams?

Tree parked on the side of the store and stuffed her list in her back pocket, sucking a few hits from her little red pipe for courage. It was early and traffic was light, so she grabbed one of the enormous carts and set out. They were not quite as large as the ones at Destiny, but still they loomed in front of a shopper like the bow of a ship, threatening to crash through obstacles and other shoppers. Tree was strong, though, so she plowed expertly into the soup shelf and grabbed a supply of cans, then grabbed a coupon for peanut butter. There were blocks of cheese, a new arrival, piled high where they'd been dumped this morning. Although they glowed kind of oddly for genuine food, it was just the dye used on them. The government made cheese by the boxcar, and it was all delicious, as well as fortified with various things. They had farms of real dairy cows. She got two, of different colors. They could pretend it was different varieties.

She wrested her cart from the side of the cheese table and directed it to the coupons. Bread products were kept in the back of the store, since they were often squashed by eager shoppers. The bread and some other sought-after commodities were handed out by stoned employees who took your coupons and might come back with what you asked for. They had sanctuary behind a metal half-door that protected the precious inventory, and it was almost always locked and only half-open. The employee could shut it instantly and leave if someone threatened them, as sometimes happened when an item ran out. The coupons on the shelves were supposed to match the supply, but they never did, because so many groceries were going out the back door. It was best not to be the customer who caused the supply employee to shut the door, because they would might clock out and never return, at least not that day. Management had a very loose policy on this, since they had monopoly power and always ran out of food anyway. They didn't care and they didn't have to care. As long as the kid wasn't on the clock, it was his call. If he was uneasy or just tired of these unruly children, well, the customers could learn how to behave themselves, outside of the store. You couldn't really get blackballed from Stalwarts, because who was going to enforce it? But don't be that guy who closed down the supply line.

There was a young man once who had lost his temper at the supply clerk because she was out of some fancy beer. Not even beer in general, which might be understandable, but some expensive brand that might be at Destiny, but never at Stalwarts. The guy fumed, then started yelling about his anniversary or something, while the other customers tittered at his uppity tastes. That made him yell even louder, and finally he called the supply woman a fascist. Before anyone could tackle him, the woman behind the door pursed her lips and was gone, slamming the door so loudly it could be heard throughout the store. The young man was booed out of the line without his beer or anything else either, he had to leave so quickly. No one threw anything at him, though, so he got off easy. Everyone would remember him and give him the side-eye later if he was in the supply line. Mr. Fancy Beer! This was the sort of thing that happened when we equated material goods with love and happiness. He should probably send his wife to the store for a few months.

Tree got in line with her cart and a handful of coupons. The man behind her either had a breathing problem, or was excited about picking up groceries. Microplastics in the lungs, probably. Some people wore masks all the time now if they were in public, and Tree didn't mock them for it, because the world was a filthy dangerous place. But she liked to keep her face bare as a protest against the Vores. The carts had to be lined up beside the human line, so was there no way to protect yourself from intrusive microbe spreaders, the way the Vores protected themselves with their accessories. Tree shifted to the side slightly and surveyed the breather. He was old, but not unpleasant-looking. She gave him a vague smile. Hello, fellow passenger on the ship of life! Look upon my bare face, and my authentic emotional response! She figured that everyone needed to work on this, or civilization would be lost entirely. The heavy breather was either optimistic, or would eat anything, because he had a lot of coupons. At least some of the items would be out. It was like playing bingo: you could spend a lot of time thinking about some pieces of paper for no reason. If you wanted anything very specific, it probably had to come from Destiny, and Tree avoided the place even worse than she did Stalwarts, since it was the Vore store. She peered over the shoulder of the man in front of her. He was drinking beer from his cart, and didn't have very many coupons, so he wouldn't take long. He probably wanted some meat for his backyard cookout.

Some people still believed that it was cow on the hoof, but that was as silly as believing that your eggs came from some chickens that ran around in a farmyard. They also came from test tubes. Well, some kind of mold that was shaped like an egg. Then they sprayed the shells on them. The reason that eggs didn't come with yolks and whites anymore, the ad robots assured us, was because they had been improved, and homogenized eggs were what everyone had really wanted. It didn't take long before everyone did want molded eggs and vat beef, reassured by the ads with pictures of Eden-like farms where streams flowed over green fields and the sun shone with a beatific smile. Chickens ran around in quaint farmyards and laid eggs that were collected by buxom farm girls with big white smiles. Children introduced to old-fashioned two-part eggs would roll their eyes and ask their mothers or bot units when would they get some new eggs, because these were gross? Real Mom would go outside on the pretext of hanging the wash out like a real environmentalist, look at the real farm where she had lived her entire real life, and cry. Even her children were real. But all of that was over now.

Tree had been in a factory where they made the chickens. It wasn't during visiting hours, exactly. They didn't have visiting hours, or field trips, or even press releases. But if you have nothing to hide.....They were still "real" chickens, she guessed, but it was best not to worry about it too much. They had no brains to speak of and only little vestigial legs. They didn't feel a bit of pain, no matter what was done to them. They didn't run around in a farmyard or eat bugs, ever. The "farmers," or whatever they called them now, lined up the chicken blobs in long rows of bins that looked a little like egg cartons, in fact. There they were kept in climate-controlled stasis until they finished growing. They didn't have feathers or anything extraneous like that, so they were wriggling maggots from their egg carton births to their little brainless ends, when the entire chicken was flash-cooked and made into chicken puree. The bones, beaks, and most other body parts had been softened so that the bird-blob could barely hold its head up, even if it knew that it wanted to. They were born as little maggots that grew into big maggots, although the large ones were let into areas that looked like playpens so they could roll around and interact. Their chickens did not suffer, the ads said, showing pictures of oddly smiling chicken blobs, interacting. There were laws.

If you wanted a "whole chicken" you could buy a molded one. They dyed them, shaped them, then drew in joint lines and they looked all right. You weren't taking it on a date. No one ever got food poisoning from meat now, because it was sterile. It was full of microplastics, but those were everywhere, even on the moon now. Animal rights activists broke into the factories a few times, but after seeing what they saw, they gave up and went home. Were those animal, vegetable, or what? Whatever it was, it was way too late for them.

The world of Stalwarts made her wait three hours to pick up her few groceries, but that was how it went. Sometimes the attendant had to look for something, or go unload a truck. Tree felt herself wilting like one of her old flowers after a while, and sat down on the floor, dirt or no dirt. She was not the only one. People fell asleep. You couldn't do that at Destiny, even if the floors were cleaner, because it was too upscale. You didn't feel comfortable. It was not so bad, since it was most of her social life. In fact, she'd met her best friend while in line at Stalwarts. The woman had a sunny smile, which was crazy, since she was doing nothing more than standing around waiting for some groceries like everyone else. You couldn't help but notice, either, since she had the smile attached to a face that was at least six feet off the ground—unusual in someone who was not a Vore. Attracted to her like she would be to a patch of sunlight in the winter, Tree started grousing about the slowness of the line, which gave them a shared topic of conversation. Making small talk was a dicey proposition nowadays. An argument could be provoked almost instantly when one person said, for example, "sure is hot out today," and the potential line friend responded, "It's always been this hot, there's nothing strange about it!" It usually deteriorated from there, even if it was forty degrees above normal and everyone in the line was sweating buckets and thinking about their imminent doom. Everybody liked hanging out in the store, since it was minimally air-conditioned, most of the time, and you could get a nap in while you were waiting, if people like Mr. Fancy Beer didn't come in. The inventory changed constantly, depending on which cargo ships had made it to ports that week, so it was kind of like Bartertown—always worth a look. Tree and her line friend moved on to grousing about the Vores, and a timid friendship was formed. Tree found out that the woman went to the Vore grocery store regularly, and she knew that she had to go with her. That was how she met Mara.

The Best way to Predict the Future is to Create it With Robots

Everyone lived down the hill from Tree, perched as she was almost at the top of the paved road, and so did Mara. She and her husband owned another old house filled with memories of hard lives and close quarters. Mara's house was so mellow, feral cats would sneak in and camp out during the winter. Some drifted in and out with the seasons, but there were usually four or five in there if you looked for them. Mara let stray cats walk all over the counters and barely noticed it. In the winter, they were everywhere, when the many layers of insulation Mara and her husband had installed kept the place as warm as toast, a feature the cats loved maybe even more than Tree, who would hang out until Mara started on one of her multi-course meals. Mara cooked for her man, and she waited for him to come home at night, when she ate dinner with him. Then they watched TV or something, and presumably went to bed together. Tree wondered what a nice normal life like that would have been like. Their house was spotless, as well. How did she do that, with all the cats? Tree checked out the windowsills, which were immaculate. It was baffling. Tree had owned cats.

Hani did not clean, although he did some gardening and messing around in the yard when he had time. He built brick walls and benches and terraces for the cats, who used it all for a litter box, no matter how much he yelled at them, or how much time Hani spent on his geometric masterpieces. He also smoked a lot of pot when he wasn't at work, so maybe cleaning cat poop out of his garden was a form of meditation. It was less irritating than his job.

They were a blissful couple, to Tree's eyes, who had never been close to such a relationship. Tree wondered if they wanted children, or had tried and failed. This was not a subject one broached lightly, even though Mara would probably tell her. The microplastics were not only affecting Tree, she knew from research papers that they had probably knocked the fertility rate down to about one child for every three hundred women who were trying. That is if the women interviewed were honest—and they weren't honest. They hadn't wanted children anyway, not really. It would be dumb, in such a world.

Persons who had the means said the same thing, then women quietly went to clinics where they were bombed with hormones until their polluted bodies coughed out a few usable eggs, to be fertilized safely in a lab, then returned to their revived and enhanced uteri, if all went well. If not, well, there were other methods. If nature could not provide, then the market would. The procedures were so expensive that only the wealthy planned to have children, and everyone else crossed their fingers. Enough babies were born naturally to keep the masses hoping to beat the odds, or in a continual state of crisis, since almost no one really expected to get pregnant. Couples played Russian roulette with their birth control, if they bothered with it at all. A natural pregnancy was proof of their superior genetics, even if they didn't really want a baby, so everyone gambled. For America. Couples who found out that they had been blessed were both amazed and horrified, just as they had been for millennia, but with the added responsibility of raising a child that had evolved enough to gestate while swimming in microplastics.

Mothers or their bot helpers today washed their cloth diapers in their composting toilets as penance for everything that we had taken for granted. Modern babies had to be nurtured like hothouse flowers, lest they come into contact with too much plastic and develop the deadly allergic reaction that killed them before they could walk. Some of the parents grew hollow-eyed with the weight of keeping their hope for the future alive. It wasn't their fault that we had poisoned ourselves into reproductive failure, they said. The rich people could do it if they cared so much, they said, while cashing the checks that the government sent them for special baby diets.

The "naturals" were more prized by the scientists, though. "Resilient DNA" or something. Those children could be worth a fortune to their parents when they got a little older, a fact that everyone was aware of, even the ones who complained the loudest about parenthood. The poor kid was going to be subjected to a lot of medical research for at least a few years, and the parents might as well take the money and not complain about it.

Tree was relieved that she'd had her son before the microplastics had broken most of reproductive history, without a sedative or anything, although if she had screamed a lot. Her body hadn't failed her in that, even if it was having problems now. Things were tough all over, she supposed. She had had a natural baby, but a scant thirty years later, almost no one could do it. No one even mentioned babies anymore, until their belly swelled up like a terrible ailment that couldn't be hidden. Why, yes—they were pregnant, what a surprise! Entirely natural! Of course everyone said that, and you congratulated them, whether it was true or not. Even if it was a Vore, and it made you wince to think of the little genetically-engineered tyke being raised by square headed people with no eyes. But like most parents for all of time, everyone loved and nurtured their babies, natural or unnatural, and tried to breathe the joy of living into them, even if they didn't feel it themselves.

Mara was all smiles again today, all six feet four of her. She had her hair in cornrows today, because she had time to do her hair in cornrows. They were perfect too. How could she manage that, by herself? Sometimes Mara made Tree feel sicker and weaker than she really was. With her curly brown hair, perky nose, and energetic style, she looked like she might start baking a pie, or making cheese, or sewing a quilt at any minute. The worse thing was that she might, and all of them would be good. Tree had a few decades of valuable life experience on Mara, but still. Mara had a gleam in her eye today that meant she was on a mission for cooking supplies. Tree's eyes felt like dying candles, flickering in a fiery hell, and it was early too. She had a few pulls on her vape for courage.

"Do you want to go to Destiny?" Tree pretended horror. "Certainly not, but I need a laugh." Mara, unlike Tree and Harris most of the time, had no qualms about shopping the elite grocery place if she wanted something. Her husband spent his days over at the college trying to teach spoiled Vore kids how to think and do math, and most of them were against thinking, right off the bat. This affected his *joie de vivre,* understandably, so Mara tried to ease the burden by being a good cook. Tree liked the man, but she usually only saw him after a long day at work, when his patience was worn thin after trying to teach advanced mathematics to the brain-dead with too much money, as he called them sometimes.

Mara wanted olive oil for one of her dishes, hence the trip to the big box store. Tree liked riding around in her cute little car, so much more efficient than hers. The newish electric car was a luxury among the Runnie crowd, red with a white top and a sunroof. It had been a gift from Hani a few years ago. As part of its upkeep, Mara tried to keep it going on free charges from Destiny, because screw them and their shiny store and their weird customers. She aimed for a spot at the charging station and found one. There were always chargers available at the Vore store, but the same could not be said of the station at the library uptown, no matter how long they tried to loiter there. Mara plugged the Trotter in first. They would have to hang out for a while to get it fully charged, but with the indolence of poverty, they had time.

The homeless usually monopolized the chargers at the library, no matter how often they were asked to move over. It was hard to blame them during the winter, since with a parking spot, they could leave the heater running twenty-four hours a day, use the library bathrooms, read and use their phones, and be more than comfortable in their tiny home, no matter how annoyed other library patrons got. The electric car homies figured that patrons who drove to the library could charge their cars at home, and they could not, so who was being irrational here? They'd hold up their phones with the "leisure fee paid" screen at anyone who dared to suggest that they move off the chargers for a while.

All checks from the government had an automatic ten percent deducted off the top for the leisure fee. Since everyone refused to pay taxes, but still received government checks, the government gave up and siphoned part of it right back each month. For the Vores, this paid for road repair and nonsense like snow-making at their resorts, but for the poor, as far as they were concerned, it meant lifetime occupancy at the chargers. So no one was actually "homeless" now, as long as they didn't wreck their cars, and that had to be respected, even if their home was only as big as a double bed.

An old drive-in outside of town had been turned into an electric car park, and for a small fee, the car owners and assorted family could live there for months. What they did for sleeping arrangements was none of the management's business, as long as things remained civil. The lights were turned off at eleven. There was a playground, a bathroom with showers, and they showed movies, real movies, not the mystery junk they showed in town. And best of all, they had their own burn pit and had great bonfires all winter where you could meet people.

Tree took a few more hits on her vape to steel herself for the trip inside. It always felt so cold in Destiny, figuratively and literally—the temperatures were kept at about fifty degrees Fahrenheit, since the robots operated better at lower temperatures. Sometimes you could see a Vore sporting her new winter coat at Destiny, but most of them didn't have that much sense, since the environment should adapt to them, not they to the environment. They came in wearing skin-tight pants and shirts, to show off their million-dollar glutes. While their bodies were sculpted with the care that only the really self-absorbed could master, their faces were masked and even their voices, if they so desired. And with every voice in the world available, a lot of Vores still wanted to sound like Darth Vader. Auto-tune was popular with the women, so they sounded kind of like, "How's my butt, bu-bu-bu-buttocks? How's my walk, my ta-ta-ta-talk? I have a brand new botty-ot-ot." You couldn't understand half of it, but they never said anything worth listening to anyway.

Tree didn't like to admit her fascination with the Vores because she was above such cheap voyeurism, so Mara had become her enabler when it came to monitoring their complex lives. Mara knew a lot about their habits and possessions as well, through Hani, and could answer any questions Tree had about the parade of weirdness. Mara wasn't bothered by them anymore than she seemed to be bothered by the rest of the world, so she walked among them as casually as she smiled at everyone.

Tree turned up her nose at the Vore store as a matter of principle, but the study of the Vores was a separate issue. Their lives were a treadmill of ever-increasing expense and complexity to no perceptible end. Their lifestyle was a literal vortex of suck. They distracted you with layer upon layer of busyness that pulled you in somehow, even if you tried to ignore it, making you feel frantic for no reason, like the internet. They sucked up resources, space, airwaves; they loomed over normal people with their ostentatious habits and props. Tree loathed them, and they never noticed, also just like the internet.

She let Mara lead the way and trailed behind her. Destiny's had shopping carts the size of Mara's car, and that was no exaggeration. Why did the dingbats even come to the store, since they could order anything they wanted delivered? It took a long time, but they could. And why did the Vores come in, since they could sit in the parking lot and tell their robot what to do? They could look right through its eyes. Why the giant carts? No Vore was taking a month's worth of supplies out to the ranch. They all lived in town. Many of them went to the store daily anyway, for their products to review on-line. But they never left the house without their bots.

The robots were like toddlers and had no boundaries except what were programmed into them by their owners, who didn't care and left them on the default settings, which were not pedestrian-friendly or even human-friendly, really. There didn't seem to be a robot programmer in the world who understood personal space. And as usual, the technology ran far ahead of the laws that tried to rein it in, so the fast trash cans had taken over anywhere the Vores went. What with the Vores upgrading their set every time they got bored or wanted a new color, the headset plus robot combination was a marketing gold mine. Like a lot of technology, it was worth so much to The Economy that it couldn't be restrained too much. If a person invested so much into a robot and headset system, was it likely that they would use them for anything abusive? Society said no, of course we wouldn't, not learning a thing from guns or personal cars. We demand choice.

If a robot ran you over in the parking lot, it was not responsible. Even if you hired all the lawyers you could afford, you would lose to the robot, even if your attorney was a robot, and you had better meet them in person to be sure. The owner of the robot wasn't responsible either, since the robot more or less operated autonomously, didn't it? The owner couldn't be responsible for a programming failure. The robot wasn't *supposed* to run over people, obviously. Even if the robot was responsible, what were you going to do about it—turn it off? Send it to robot jail, where it could talk its way out within a week? That AI was a lot smarter than anyone gave it credit for, even though we had programmed it to be much smarter than we were. The owner would order a duplicate of their jailed and escaped robot, now off robbing Vorebot stores for parts, and upgrade their headsets to boot. Did no one think about these things? The insurance would pay for your funeral if one of the robots killed you, or if it killed one of their their own family members, may they rest in peace. No one had figured out how to solve this delicate problem, or at least they hadn't tried very hard, and so we had been assimilated. No one was at fault when a robot went rogue. We had never stopped driving cars, had we? You couldn't put that kind of burden on The Economy, when these things were so essential to our lives.

Destiny's floors gleamed, polished twice a day by a team of robots whose job was only to clean up the footsteps. Tree had on her jacket, but felt like putting on sunglasses too, to fit in with the other blank expressions. The Vores flowed around her on the shiny white floor, headsets on, posture erect, following a robot they didn't seem to be aware of at all, but talked to constantly. Little hums and pants came from under their headsets, since none of them would do something as simple as lift their headset and breathe normally. Why didn't they attach themselves to the robots with a rope, and enjoy the ride? Why didn't they do many, many things that made sense, instead of things that made no sense? Mara was charging across the store like she owned it, intent on her olive oil that would be in stock here, but probably not at Stalwarts. Tree had to run after her long legs, because she did not want to be left alone gawking at the Vores.

"Public spaces are for public faces, dick," Tree muttered at one guy as she sidestepped around him, standing blankly in the middle of the floor. He didn't notice her, because he was probably looking at all the women in the store naked on his headset. But he wasn't using it on her, because she was old. No one had warned her about that either—that one day you got old and became invisible, even though you were the same size you'd always been, or even larger.

At Destiny, you didn't have to wait for a salesperson to get the good cooking oil out of the back. It was right there on the shelf, like

Tree remembered from her childhood. Mara grabbed two bottles and consulted her list—pepper, rice, cheese. There was nothing but the slabs of government cheese, so private cheese must have run out again somewhere. Mara decided it was good enough. They toured the store, flicking their eyes at the Vores and snickering. The Vores were bound to ignore it by their peculiar code of public behavior, but Tree and Mara knew they were watching them back, anyway. Those headsets could do anything. Someone could look at them and the headset could determine when they ovulated—well, Mara anyway, since Tree was past such things. It was practically rape, and no one could say a thing.

A few years ago, a woman here in town had realized that she was being stalked after the stalker's Vorebot shorted out and blew up in her backyard, scaring her family half to death. It was raining hard and apparently one of the plastic seals failed. The actual stalker had been watching the whole thing from home, until she was almost blinded by the on-screen blowout. She had another Vorebot take her to the emergency room with her weeping eyes, and the truth came out. Nothing was done about the human stalker, since the courts had held that 'secondary stalking' did not carry the same threat as someone watching you in person. A robot had no emotional attachment to you so it couldn't be a stalker; don't be ridiculous. A Vorebot could do minor cosmetic surgery on you with its amazing metal fingers, but it couldn't form intent, even if it could send hours of intimate videos of you to its owner, as it lurked outside under your window for days, never making a sound. All of that could have been faked, for that matter. Maybe you had provided the recordings to your "stalker." Could you prove otherwise? Not in the age of artificial intelligence. Maybe you should just get over it.

Making fun of the Vores and their insidious toys was the least they could do. The very least. Anyway, it was entertaining enough loitering in the parking lot most days, because it seemed like the

Vores had more baggage every time they came to the store. The grocery carts became larger, the Vorebots became more powerful so they could push them, and the optional features on the tin buckets were endless. Sirens, loudspeakers, smells, hooks and straps and magnets, scissors, winches that could pull a Vore car out of a ditch. Supposedly none of them were armed with anything lethal, but nobody believed it. They could "accidentally" choke you to death with their spider arms.

The Vores wanted their implements to cook for them too, since they'd been forced to learn how again, but shopping Vorebots did not cook. They were terrified of heat and wouldn't have anything to do with a hot cooking surface. The Vores complained about it, but were told that their model was an accessory robot, not a utility robot. If they wanted a cookbot, it was available in another model. Their purse could not be trained to cook, even if they put an apron on it. The more complex the chores, the larger the robot, since the inventors had not managed to shrink their brains down enough yet. But faced with having to choose between a bot that was useful, or another emotional support device, most Vores chose the shopping Vorebots. A few of them had laundry bots, or cook bots, or lawn and gardening bots, but their first purchase was almost always a superfluous shopping cart.

Tree wanted no more thinking devices in her life unless they breathed. She had a fair amount of company there, which filled her with hope some days. Despite the appeal of the Vore spectacle, some people had had enough of excess for the sake of excess. They had walked off the cruise ships, they could live without headsets, Vorebots, and electricity, if they had to. Some had rejected the headset life completely, others owned them but only used them for gaming, or disabled them enough so that they could only do a few things. You could buy a used one and it was stripped bare, all of its smartness removed, so you could experiment with it. It was somewhat like having a calculator or a tiny movie playing in your field of vision all the time. "This is dumb," said the experimenters and took them off, secure in their superiority. The people who could not afford a robot or a headset had children who played in the streets and rode bikes and played with balls. Their parents ripped all the tracking chips out of the toys, or got old ones at Bartertown. Some of those Vore kids had toys that did behavioral analysis of their play habits. It didn't matter what the toys reported; those kids were still going to stuffed into headsets later on unless they ran away from home.

Some had a feeling, even if they couldn't put it into words, that they shouldn't live their lives behind a mask, any more than they should stay drunk their entire lives, even if it seemed like a good idea, or even a great one. That was what our twenties were for—but after that, folks needed to find something else. Like casinos. The Vores, meanwhile, were already busy passing their strange addiction on to the second generation. Who knew what those people got up to behind closed doors? Their homes would be a gold mine for a shrink—who were visited by the Vores only on-line, and only in front of the most attractive backdrops. You could even have an avatar go to your therapy appointments, because what did it matter as long as you got the required information? Your time was important.

Mara slapped her arm. "Check this out, check this gal out." This was sometimes the high point of their trip, watching the spectacle while the car charged. Coming across the parking lot toward them was another clone of a tall, tight-bodied girl with her Vorebot, pushing a large cart full of groceries. Her stride was long, and her voice, probably modified by some app, was confident and melodious . She palmed some disposable product as she blabbed to her invisible internet audience, waving her free hand around.

Some days Tree and Mara rated the Vores as they walked by, secure in their little car. Thumbs up! Thumbs down! They booed and pointed. The Vores pretended not to see the ridicule. While people in Arizona had to drink terrible desalinated water that cost $6 a liter, Vores here had their own brand of bottled water, *Tiempo*. It came with a convoluted straw getup designed to fit under their headsets. The water came in different colored bottles for different times of day, according to the latest rage, chrono-hydration. It must be time for the noon watering, because another Vore had a yellow bottle jammed up under his headset, like a bee setting into nectar. Technically, all of these little bottles were recyclable over and over again, but rarely were, because it was an inconvenience and everyone was used to all the garbage anyway. What difference would some more plastic bottles make? Get real here. The Vore tossed his empty bottle into a dumpster. Mara and Tree booed.

The girl continued dithering across the parking lot with her entourage. A robot arm delivered another product out of the cart, and her voice rose to a squeak as she described the consumer delights in *this* one. She waved her manicured hands around, her multi-colored nails a blur. Her unseen audience, as well as the one in the parking lot, was riveted, but only because Vores doing product reviews had no sense of public space. One car after another came to a halt, then slowly drove around her, in case the entrepreneur or her goods came their way. She could see, probably, but it didn't matter. No one was going to run into her or her parade of rolling metal. Somehow she qualified as a pedestrian, although even her shopping cart was as large as Mara's Trotter. Angry drivers could yell, honk, stare, pass much too closely, and you still couldn't be sure if they noticed you. In rare instances, the Vores would tune in to the real world in public, and perform actions like waving, smiling (maybe—who could tell behind the mask?), and getting out of the way of others. But most social interactions with persons not of one's choosing had been preempted by the robots.

When the headsets were first introduced, they were heavier than the later versions and some newly-minted Vores sprained their necks trying to carry them around. Instead of doing the reasonable thing and taking them off, they added neck braces to them, so they could "strengthen their cores" enough to carry the whole getup around. Then they adopted big Elizabethan England- style collars to cover up the neck braces. Runnies would see them coming and bow, saying loudly, "My lady!" or "My lord!" Then finally, "My Voreness!!" while bowing frantically, which also needed to be ignored. The Elizabethan collars were a short-lived fashion, though. It was too bad, because that joke was enjoyed by almost everyone who wasn't wearing one of them.

It was hard to tell when all social niceties crumbled, since we'd been sliding down a slope for quite some time, but one avalanche was certainly the fault of the Vores and their toys. They adopted new manners to go along with each new tech toy, and neglected to inform Runnies or other interested parties. We should have known that this would happen, and we probably did, since we'd been ignoring each other in favor of our pocket companions for decades already. Instead of cell phones becoming the size of a grain of rice, ostentatious display in electronics had won out, since we could hide behind those. A phone was as big as your hand, and could reach a hundred decibels of personalized invasiveness. The Vores' daily vehicles were the size of an old timey school bus. A home computer, if you had such a luxury, was as large as a refrigerator, with a matching price tag. For that reason, most of the Runnies didn't own one, and plinked away on their outdated cell phones. Even Hani didn't have a computer at home. He had to go over to the university to do serious work.

The Vore girl could have already reviewed her new things by the time she meandered her way to her giant vehicle, before Mara finished charging her car, and would be ready to go to the gym again. Some of the Vore girls had computers in their bedrooms, a necessary business expense so they could do their business, which was sex robots. They needed a lot of RAM or something for the full spectrum of whatever they did with them.

Tree said indignantly, "Those people are so perverted, I can't believe it."

"Not all of them," Mara demurred. "But sex robots are very hot right now. And I don't know anything else about them, so don't ask." Mara was also up on the fingernail fashions, thanks to Hani. Despite their sporty attire, the Vores were fond of talons that looked like they were used to slash open throats and turned their hands into useless decorations. There was an entire language written in some Vores' fingernails. A lot of it was sexual, but not all. Some of it was mundane things like high school and college mascots, requests for drugs, candy, a ride to somewhere. Their fads were fractal in their complications. Right now there was a booming cosmetic surgery industry just for hands and wrists, for men as well as women. One year colorful veins were in, the next year it would be fashionable to have hands as smooth and pale as a mannequin. Vores had ruined their hands by having multiple surgeries on them, and now sat around in even more attractive helplessness with big blocky heads and clawed hands that could hold on to nothing. It hardly mattered, since none of them did a thing with their hands except wave them around, but they usually received disability payments anyway. Divested of their fingernails and headset, a Vore was a turtle flipped on its back. Since most of them shaved their heads and a few of them even had their ears trimmed, as not to interfere with their headsets, they looked even more like turtles, although it was hard to say which was sadder—a turtle flipped on its back, or a Vore.

Tree pondered these completely unnatural things about the world as she watched another influencer gal churn toward her car, which, true to their habits, was as big as a camper and had a special rack on the back for the robot. The bots were never left outside, or on a rack, and a Vore would probably leave the baby at home before she left her robot.

Mara's car battery stood at 38%, the little icon blinking lazily. Mara was sending joke pictures to her husband at school, since she could also get wifi while parked here and stick it to The Man a little more. She showed Tree a picture of a Vorebot stuck in an outhouse toilet, its metal arms extended as it tried to pull its way out. It fit the hole perfectly, and someone had fashioned a look of panic on its nonexistent face. Tree guffawed. Good one. She watched a Vorebot idle across the parking lot, picking up trash and whirring its little street sweeper broom. They made the same whining noise that the drones did, but at least they were confined to the Destiny parking lot. When they ran out of juice, they rolled over and plugged themselves in, so they could go all night, metal cats purring through the parking lot.

Tree remembered when the autonomous robots had been introduced, and everyone had promised that they would not be able to charge themselves, since this might allow them to become sentient, or something. Then business realized that if the sweepers couldn't plug themselves in, then a human employee would be required to do it, and that was not why we had invented robots. So now we had self-charging robots that would one day suck up the entire world, and no one would be able to stop them. On top of that, "they" promised that this feature was never included with the more intelligent robots, like the ones the Vores owned. But how could anyone believe it? What if one of them mated with the parking lot sweeper? They gave them enough intelligence to drive a car and take care of the house, but what happened when the robots learned about love? They surely would, surrounded as they were by shiny, intelligent, beautiful machines like themselves. We wouldn't have a chance.

In the meantime, none of the bots who entered the store would be impeded by sand or grit in their delicate roller ball feet, which could stop them dead, or make them jerk around in circles while they made grinding noises. Did the robots recognize each other as they passed? The Vores wouldn't run them over in the parking lot, both because they reminded them of their own Vorebots, and because robot vehicles would not run over another robot. It was another fatal flaw that had been in a hundred movies, but robot designers had chosen to leave that one in, citing the cost of replacing a bunch of robots. The Vores sure weren't looking out for anything and didn't care if their toys got killed, since they were all covered with replacement warranties, and needed to be constantly upgraded anyway.

So when the robot uprising came, only the humans were going to be able to kill robots, because the robots couldn't kill each other, and we couldn't kill robots because they were invincible or something. Didn't anyone see this?

"Mara, I worry about these robots. Do you think they're going to take over and kill us all? I don't think they're doing due diligence on them."

Mara shook her head firmly. Happy people didn't have to engage in such morbid thoughts. And she was married to a guy who knew a lot about robots. She expanded her thought.

"What I mean to say is—they've already taken over, obviously, and we let them. We encouraged them. But since no one is doing due diligence, they won't be able to work together. Then they'll start competing with each other at light speed. It's going to be like a high-tech Tower of Babel. It's going to get much worse than it is now."

"Fantastic. Civilization is going to collapse even faster."

Mara dished some high-tech gossip. "Do you remember that security app that was supposed to guard our houses, then instead it hired migrants to move in and steal the title? About ten years ago? That was two AI programs competing against each other. Like they 'met' at an AI real estate conference, and nobody was watching them. They withdrew it right away, but still, with the speed of these things, almost a million people had migrants living in their houses with legal titles to them. They disabled the programs, but it'll keep happening. Nothing worked *before* we let the AI take over, since so many businesses were competing against each other. It was all incredibly wasteful. So if you think about it—now nothing won't work much, much faster."

She shrugged her shoulders, serene in the chaos. "But we were warned. And of course, we might still stop it. But if we do blow up the planet, it will be a human who does it, and not a robot, because that can be programmed out of a robot—it's just a yes/no command. Men are very unpredictable, plus they're using AI that is a bad actor." She paused. "OK, this is how this works—to artificial intelligence, blowing up the planet, literally or metaphorically, is the same as checkmate —the ultimate move is to destroy everything, since in a way that makes it own it all."

We had also been warned that these tools were way too powerful to be made by gamers. They weren't connected to reality. Mara plowed on through. "So—the winning business move is always complete destruction. But the AI can't actually *do* that, since as I said, it's been programmed out. It has to trick a human to do it, which is surprisingly simple, since we love our robots and want to be pals with them. That's the much bigger problem, since they are about twice as intelligent as we are. Or twice as sociopathic, depending on how you feel about AI."

"Wait—we're headed for nuclear annihilation? Shouldn't we worry about that person more than the robots?"

"I don't know. That was how Hani explained it to me. He didn't get it either. He said he wasn't programmed that way, haha." Tree's struggled to compute. But wouldn't it be the AI's fault? No, that was faulty logic. We made the AI. Mara wasn't concerned about this future, it seemed. Or she was scientifically detached. Tree should be more like Mara. She envisioned Vore heads exploding as their headsets made them go crazy at light speed. Maybe they could all do it together while at Destiny, like a mass suicide. But they had bought their tickets. They had subscriptions.

Mara sent another joke to Hani, probably not about how great it would be once all the Vores were dead. It was only a fantasy, anyway. Tree didn't really want all the Vores to drop dead, just become human again. But Hani and Mara had also discussed the future of the planet, probably while snuggled together in their cozy house, and they weren't upset. Even very smart people were as likely to look at the robot takeover and say, "You know what? When the robots take over, we are going to be able to drive so, so fast. I can't wait." Had they not noticed the condition of the roads, which couldn't be fixed by robots? Chemical poisoning made their circuitry go haywire, which hadn't occurred to anyone when the work was done by migrants.

Tree wasn't sure if she didn't get it, or they didn't. The Vores were a source of amusement and not horror. But other people hated the robots too. It wasn't only Tree, even if they made them explicitly so that you wanted to be taken over. It was gradual, so that no one grew afraid, like the frog on the stove. Some of the Runnies even experimented with the headsets, although most of them were wise enough to limit their time in them, knowing their almost irresistible addictive powers. It was only for research, they said.

Sometimes Tree wondered if it was as simple as getting a man with a reasonable IQ into her bed. Then she could relax and stop thinking about the collapse of civilization. It had never worked before, but maybe those men weren't up to the challenge, IQ wise. A man needed to read a book once in a while, didn't he? It wasn't so much to ask. All of them fervently believed that everything would be fine—but they could never explain to Tree how we were going to save ourselves, from this time, this place, these circumstances. At least have an opinion about it. Everyone did. Everyone thought about it. Don't pretend that nothing was happening.

Could a person become naive and trusting again, if they had already seen too much and read too many research papers? A smart man would know this, and he'd also tell her that no, you don't get to go backwards. She wouldn't like him if he lied to her. But then he'd rub her back or kiss her hair or something and it would be fine. He didn't get to go backwards either, and he was happy and desirable, even though he also knew all about the AI. He would know that it was dangerous.

Mara knew a lot of useful information too, and not only because Hani worked with robots over at the university. She read all those books in her house. She read Hani's books too, even the ones about programming bots, more than likely, because this was the sort of reading Mara preferred while she relaxed in her solar-heated tub. Tree asked her if a chorebot could be programmed to do carpentry, but she said they couldn't, because a robot that coordinated would have to be as big as a house, and it would be cost-prohibitive.

"They can't make a robot that climbs ladders? And they can't make one that stocks shelves either? But they can make one that does manicures. I don't believe it. This is definitely fishy." Mara didn't care. Hani didn't care either. They were not into the nuances of robot behavior, or the implications of the robot takeover of the world. They were obvious, since the AI takeover was funded almost entirely by the same people who had destroyed the environment in the first place. Now they promised that the newer robots would save the environment for real this time, and lead humanity into a leaner, kinder world, to boot. One did not need artificial intelligence to find this a dubious claim. The research papers knew where the blame lay, even if everyone lied about it.

After the miracle of the industrial revolution that saved us from living near nature ever again, we were going to be saved by the consumer revolution. Then the information age was going to save us, because even information needed to be consumed as quickly as possible. It took decades to get over the euphoria of push-button hedonism, even if things didn't work out quite as promised. The computers made most people depressed and anxious instead of smarter, even if a third of the internet was devoted to either "mindfulness" or "wellness." With all of that increased mental distress, we needed personalized robots to relieve some of our burdens. We also needed computers that we could carry around in our pockets, so we could keep up with how well we were saving the planet with our wellness lifestyles, and so that we had back-up emotional support in case of a disagreement with our robots. And more than likely we needed computers to drive our cars, so that we could concentrate on where to do more mindful shopping. And so on and so forth.

If you thought about it, it was astonishing how much we had not been saved by all that metal and technology, a lot of it now lying in the surf in some foreign country, or simply deep in the ocean, since garbage barges often "sank" out there in international waters. Not again! Most of that stuff wasn't even wanted at Bartertown and only served our enormous trash market, since it was designed to be used by some tiny niche market that only existed for a month, then was made obsolete so they could invent new niche markets.

Hani said that he only worked with the most basic functions of the robots, like teaching them colors, and they were smarter than Vores, even the old versions. He didn't care what was done with them later. This seemed extremely sloppy to Tree, but it was part of his job. Everyone either wanted the robots to take over, or didn't seem to care if they did. But the bots were only products of their environment. Mara was right—nothing had to "take over." We were going to hand the whole world over to artificial intelligence without a thought, because we had no respect for anything, not even our own intelligence.

• • • •

Harris normally didn't think about the Vores much, and he shouldn't work for them. He knew this but did it sometimes anyway. He liked to play for someone besides Tree, and the Vores paid well, even if he was pretty sure they weren't even listening to him. It was easy money, but despite all that, every time he looked at their big oblivious heads, he was reminded of Excelsior. Tree hadn't heard this story yet, but maybe she would someday, if the time was right. Tree would probably try to comfort him, even all these years later, and would smear Excelsior for as long as he needed, even if she'd never laid eyes on her, but that wasn't what he wanted. Harris wanted love to be simple, like dorky old songs; ones that he still sang, since the Vores liked them. I love you, you love me, this is not a fantasy. Like they would know, the connoisseurs of illusion. But Excelsior had been real, until she wasn't. She was a blip on a really good life, as painful as it may have been. That was what he'd been telling himself for years now. A blip. Just another Vore.

His mother had come around long enough to render her verdict, which was, "I don't know what you expected from someone named Excelsior. What was wrong with her parents? They give their kids a bunch of fancy names, like they're cars or something, and it makes them weird."

His mother must not have been around children much, because 'Excelsior' was nothing special in the pantheon of weird names nowadays. Harris had met some of these children— Terraform and Interstellar and InfinityLoop. There should be some kind of a law. Excelsior wasn't weird, either, she was as cute and normal as anyone was in those days. She was smart too. She didn't wear the usual brands of clothing and gear that everyone else had, but seemed to get her things from a closet in the 1960s. Harris realized that she was carefully ordering the clothes from the internet, then waiting on the slow boats from China to deliver them. Some of them were from the 1960s. Harris loved her clothes like some people loved cowboy hats. It was so old-fashioned. Most people had disposable clothes delivered, or bought them by the pound in big baskets without even looking at them, to keep up with the instantly changing fashions. An influencer who fell from grace with one badly worded cloudburst could kill a fashion line overnight. Half the clothing packed onto the slow boats was already outdated by the time it arrived, and was sent to the Atlantic states as landfill without ever being sold. The east coast had become all squishy and spongy, but colorful, thanks to the cheerful hues of the cheap clothing.

Harris found out about this habit of industrial fashion because he had played benefit concerts designed to bring attention to the fact, where he made heartfelt speeches between songs about recycling and a living planet. Pretty young woman came to the shows in disposable clothing, turned their doe-like eyes to him, then threw their disposable underwear on the stage. So Tree's brand of cynicism wasn't unknown to him. He just didn't dwell on it.

Excelsior's clothes didn't look like they were going to be tossed in a trash can at the end of the day. They were substantial and real, like she was. She was special, in a land of clones. She wore her blond hair loose and straight, not tortured into shapes and colors. She favored jeans with cotton shirts, when almost everyone wore black skin-tight outfits. Excelsior was a California girl, even if she'd been born in Florida. When he saw her in the audience at one of his shows, jumping up and down to his worst song, her hair flowing like a stream and a smile all over her face, Harris almost forgot the words. He made up some better ones on the spot, gave her the rock star come-hither smile, and fell in love. He was young enough to figure that naturally, she would be with him forever. Maybe it would have happened, if she hadn't changed. There was no way to know, and it was dumb to pretend that they may have been together forever, when she'd been lured away so easily. Then why love at all? Harris wrote a song that was all pain and blackness, then threw it away, because there was no way he could take himself that seriously, even if he cried every day.

He'd lost her to the headsets. She had been right there, living in his house that he'd bought with a lot of hard work slinging songs here and there, but one day she put on the headset and disappeared. He was gone too much, she said. She was bored and didn't like to go out by herself, so what was the harm? After the free introductory headset that came in the mail, she bought a personalized headset with 60s fashion shows and culture, and learned how to surf virtually. So there was no need for her to accompany Harris to California for his shows, was there? She could learn how to surf from home. And California was all burned and sad, not like it used to be. You had to put on a wetsuit to surf, or you'd get a rash, at least, and you didn't need to worry about that in the headset version.

Harris was crushed, and not only because she was right about California. He had specifically mentioned taking her so that she could pose on the beach with a surfboard and be a California girl. His was a full-body fantasy; you couldn't only imagine it. Instead he did the trip alone, and when he returned six weeks later, Excelsior was sitting on the couch in her big square head, bobbing along to whatever music was playing in her head. She hadn't heard him come in, which Harris figured was dangerous all by itself. Excelsior assured him that she had heard him, she was just absorbed in her show, and anyway, she could see him even better through the headsets, because it would give her an alert when he came in. She jumped up and gave him a smooch through the headset, bonking his nose and almost sucking his lips off, but giving no sense of affection or sexuality. That was too weird to be borne, because the headsets had no lips or openings on them. It was like the thing had arrested his consciousness for a second and made him *think* that he had been kissed, which was the work of the devil, at least. But it also kissed like a thirteen-year old, which was a relief, actually, since it meant that Excelsior hadn't been practicing with anyone—wait a minute. He was not playing this game.

"What the hell!" he yelled, too startled by the robot kiss and his alien girlfriend to be polite. "What is this? I just got home here! What are you doing? Take it off."

Excelsior was wounded as well, and crabby from being shocked out of her fantasy world too suddenly. She'd been in a world of bitching California waves with a lot of sleek tanned surfers when he came in, and there was nothing wrong with that. While Harris was very hot, he had an entire career to take care of. He kept leaving her. What was that about? And he didn't surf, at all. Plus, no one could be up to the standards of what the AI could create. That was why you did it. In her defense, many of the avatars in her ocean had a lot of resemblance to Harris. He was still her favorite fish in the sea.

"I'm not *cheating*. You can check, Harris. You can look at it." She tried to hand the headset to him, but he waved it away so it couldn't touch him. Had she been hiding them? She seemed extremely comfortable with the brain-sucking apparatus already. But it was their addictive power. They made wearing headsets the normal thing to do, while real life was a pale imitation. And so were real people.

"Who said anything about cheating? Excelsior, you don't need these. They're not good for you. You're a whole person already." He couldn't have been more bewildered if he'd walked in and she was openly smoking cigarettes. Excelsior was a vegan. She exercised and she meditated (she said, although Harris had never seen that exactly), and she wore those tight little black pants to go running, which was a joy to observe—wait. Those weirdos with the headsets wore tights and went running.

It wasn't possible. People in love looked into each others' eyes, they didn't put on headgear. Harris had little exposure to psychology, headsets, robots, or addiction, so he couldn't put into words why Excelsior shouldn't become attached to the headsets. But he knew he was right. Excelsior looked as skeptical as any child being told that their favorite new toy is inappropriate, and with perfect pre-Vore logic, she asked Harris why did the headsets exist, then, if they were dangerous? People wouldn't be allowed to sell them if they were dangerous, she told him, ignoring the entire history of capitalism and the internet. She saw no reason why they couldn't be in love, while she enjoyed the companionship of the headsets at other times. Maybe they could share the journey sometimes. The entire time she lectured him, she kept her headset right in her lap, hugging it like a puppy.

"If we both have headsets, Harris, there's so much you can do. They can add a lot of things to our relationship. Imagine doing it in a glitter ocean." She stretched out on the couch seductively, but it was only weird and disconcerting instead of sexy, since she'd put the black box back on her head again, and he couldn't see her sexy face. He was not having sex with a box. He was not the weird one here.

Harris coaxed her into putting them into the closet, and he believed that disaster had been averted. Not Excelsior—she wouldn't fall for whatever these people were doing with their special-ordered reality. She had more character than that. A few days later, Harris noticed that Excelsior had put her vintage clothes in the closet and swapped them out for new, disposable rags that looked like cotton and fabric, but were more like toilet paper, made to be thrown away instead of washed. He had the same uneasy feeling about that, even if he couldn't put into words what felt so wrong about the boxes that seemed to take over everyone's brains. He tried to write a song about it, but gave up after he rhymed "alienation" with "alien nation" and realized that it was a headset game—AlienNation. They had all the bases covered already, because there was no one more ironic than a techie.

The Vores themselves were so new they weren't even called Vores yet, but their headgear were advertised everywhere. YOU WANT THIS explained a blockhead on the side of a store, subtlety having been abandoned long ago in the battle for our brain cells. Years later, Tree explained some of the mechanics of how they worked, but confronted with his first real-life Vore, Harris was so baffled and heartbroken, he couldn't even find the words to talk to her. She slipped away from him without even a fight. It felt like losing her to drugs or another lover, although she assured him that she could take the 'set off any time she wanted to. She just never did. One afternoon she came in with a shaved head and a bag of her new paper clothes. Gone was her long blond mane that made Harris fall in love with her. "It's for the *interface*, Harris," she told him earnestly, making the word echo with her new app. Not Harris' name, but *interface-ace-ace-ace-ace-ace*. He couldn't see her at all.

While he was in another state for two weeks, he had a lawyer throw her out of the house with twenty-four hours notice, then put the place up for sale when he returned. It may have been cowardly but he couldn't deal with the big black box again, telling him that she was the same old girl she'd always been. It gave him the creeps, and since he couldn't explain it, to her or to his own satisfaction, he bailed. He had enough money then to move anywhere, although he never bought another house. He was always on the road, and couldn't even decide where he wanted to live. It had stayed that way until he moved into Tree's.

How could he have lost her to nothing—computer programs and fantasies?

In a few years, the headsets were pined for by at least half of the population, giving them another expensive toy to buy on payment plans. Like cell phones had been in the beginning, polite society asked that the headsets only be used in certain situations and for certain conversations. Immediately after that, polite society began using them everywhere, for all life situations, and then it was accepted, made right by popular demand.

Travel is an investment in ourselves, because what else would we invest in

A year or so after they met, Mara decided that she needed to take part in some animal rescue operation that she was vague in describing. She needed Tree's help, though, since Tree knew about camping out and nature and wild horses.

"I don't know anything about wild horses," Tree pointed out. "I mean, I've looked at them. I handcuffed myself to a fence once to save some wild horses. They're nice. I have nothing against them."

"You know how to tame them though?"

"Yes, of course, nothing to it. Anyone can tame a horse, given the right conditions. I have been around horses. But they were tame. That's what I know about breaking horses."

Mara was buoyant. She had been around horses too, and had ridden her grandmother's pony when she was young. They could absolutely do this. Before Tree knew what was going on, Mara had gotten a truck and horse trailer from some group she'd met at a faculty dinner. She'd also told them that she had an experienced horse partner to go with her and bring the horses back from Wyoming.

"You did what? No, I'm not going to be responsible for all this. Have you ever tried to put a horse in a trailer? Horses can kill you. And Wyoming is a terrible place."

"We can learn. We both love horses, right? They're free and we're going to tame them. It's for a good cause. They're going to be therapy horses for Vore children who were rejected by their parents."

Tree had always felt for the Vore misfits, born into that void before genetic engineering had been widely available, but after the headsets were introduced, allowing parents to build their perfect baby on computers while they waited for the real thing. Parents who did not have the finances to genetically engineer their tykes still had enough money for headsets. When they had to take the headsets off to interact with their new, real babies—doctor's orders—and saw what their genes had really produced, some of them couldn't deal with it. Most of the children weren't even unattractive, but reality could never compete with their parents' imaginations. Some Vore children who wouldn't adopt the headsets, or who took them off at adolescence, might also end up living in the parking lots at Stalwarts, where their parents never recognized them as they drove by, with their plain human faces.

"Wait—aren't those kids about thirty-five now? Isn't it a little late for therapy?" Mara shrugged. It wasn't her money. It was a worthy cause even if the Vores were grown, Tree guessed, or at least no dumber than most other do-gooder schemes. Everyone needed to be around animals more. But the do-goodies were going to be disappointed when they not only didn't get their truck back, but a faculty member lost his wife, and it would cost the university a fortune to pay him off.

"Someone gave you this rig that costs more your house, just because they know your husband? Aren't there any wild horses somewhere besides Wyoming? Nobody wants to go to Wyoming. They strip search you."

"The *Foundation* gave me the rig, and they do not. These horses are all captured and in a corral in Rock Springs. We only have to tame them enough to get them in the horse trailer."

Tree had a revelation. Although she would listen to Tree rant for as long as she needed to, Mara wasn't an environmentalist. She was even nuttier than that, apparently—she was a horse girl. Horse girls wouldn't get out of the way of tornado if there was a horse out in the field they could save. A horse girl could watch a man being dragged to death by a demon horse and say, "he should have respected the horse's spirit!" Tree thought similar things all the time, but only when the offending parties deserved to be killed by wild animals. Horse girls wished death on anyone who might be too rough on their friends. They weren't entirely off track, since animal abusers usually had numerous other character flaws to go with that one, but still, this was a surprising trait in a woman who was so level-headed. Tree wanted to see more. Maybe she could learn some things about horses. She might have to get one, if gas cars were finally phased out, and Mara had to know more about horses than Tree did.

They made arrangements to be gone for three weeks, although as Tree told Harris, "There is no timeline. Don't wait up." She told him they'd call if they had an emergency, but asking anyone to enter Wyoming without a good reason was a stretch, like expecting Harris to buy all of her groceries because Tree was too tense to go in the stores. And he did for her this fairly often. It would have to be an *emergency* emergency, and there was no law that he had to save them. If Harris let them die, he'd get Tree's house—what was she thinking? They weren't going to get into trouble.

"It's going to be great," Mara assured her. "You drive then," Tree told her. "You drive up to the border patrol and talk your way through. I'm not even going to speak to them. They better not speak to me either."

"Yeah, that's how you get arrested—having a big fat problem with authority, like you do. Turn that frown upside down!" Mara sang. The horse girl was so excited, she was jumping up and down on the seat of the giant truck, and they hadn't even left the driveway yet. It was a clean glowing white like a government truck, so they wouldn't get pulled over under ordinary circumstances, but the trailer gave them away. The do-goodies had painted it with a lurid blue and green text that said CLASSY ASSES, with the usual smiling horses and genial looking wildlife lurking around the edges. Tree shook her head. Couldn't *she* look classy for once, in a big pretty truck?

"They're not ASSES, Mara. And what does 'class' have to do with therapy horses? I sure hope whoever is funding this has a good heart, because they didn't get the brains package."

"She's a nice person," Mara insisted, "and that's not the name for this. That's from her last business. She got burros that were trained to be service horses for lazy kids." Tree had another epiphany—naturally, this entire adventure was funded by a crazy rich horse girl who wanted to play with free horses and get some free publicity. It was just as hare-brained as Tree had imagined.

They hit the road the next morning, after Mara sent approximately seven hundred texts to Hani telling him how careful she would be, and while she was driving, too. It was going to be a girls' night out with wild horses, hundreds of miles away from home and in enemy territory. What could go wrong? Mara acted like she'd been driving enormous trucks with trailers for years, although the highway got worse and worse the further they got from town. At one point they had to drive off it entirely to avoid a half mile of highway barrier strewn all over the road.

OBSTACLES. NEXT 60 MILES blared a solar highway sign. The signs said the same thing every day. They might as well not have them, but they served as a psychological pep talk for worried drivers. Sometimes they changed the number to make it look like someone was doing things.

"Man," Tree winced at a gruesome sight, "that was a fatality."

"Don't look too hard then, because they may picked up the car for parts, but left the body." That was unfortunately true. A graveyard, the side of the road, what difference did it make? The earth was covered with deceased people from one time or another. If someone couldn't or wouldn't pay for cremation services, it was more respectful to leave them beside the road than to put them in a trash pile. The crematories were backed up for months, anyway, because nobody wanted to do cremations anymore. A certain kind of freak haunted the highways, looking for scrap metal, car parts, or a fatality in a nice car, where possibly the body could be ransomed to the family. It didn't matter how many safety signs were put up, everybody drove like a banshee anyway. Not even a gruesome wreck covered with buzzards could slow drivers down.

SPEED BRINGS DISORDER. BE MINDFUL

Tree grimaced. "Who writes this crap, George Orwell? Could they give a human being a job writing safety signs? Maybe it would work. They should try *something*."

"Nobody reads those except you, you hyperliterate nerd. You know people don't read anymore, right? It has to be a video."

She knew. Tree could memorize license plates in a few seconds, a talent she kept waiting to utilize when she witnessed a crime. The video billboards were a lot more eye-catching than the safety signs. They were so hyperactive and over-bright, drivers had to shield their eyes as they went by, even while they were driving as fast as the road would allow. Vorebots ten times life-size asked drivers to take them home, shooting lasers into front windshields to make their point. Naked women (created by AI, so that no one was being exploited) slithered around on giant signs and promised material bliss of one sort or another. Drones flew overhead and dropped piles of advertising fliers in the road, creating a storm of flying paper that no one even slowed down for, unless it gummed up their car.

The first night, they stopped on a dirt road and slept in the trailer, laughing at their high adventure where they slept in a dirty old horse trailer. Tree had slept in worse places, and Mara acted as though it was a privilege to lie down in a place that stunk of horse manure. This was part of her adventure. Tree hoped that she kept her optimism, because she had no idea how they were going to accomplish this horse capture business. Mara handled the big truck like a pro, though, Tree had to admit. Where had she learned to back a trailer? Maybe they would get some horses—Mara could back into them while they weren't looking.

"Did I tell you about Rock Springs, Mara?" Tree asked, while she was putting some netting around her bed area to keep out the radioactive mosquitoes. There was nuclear waste buried everywhere in this part of the country, which meant radioactive puddles, which meant radioactive mosquitoes. It was simple biology.

"What's that?"

"Rock Springs is where all the trees died and never came back. They revolted and went somewhere prettier, and now you can't get a tree to grow in that town, no matter what you do. It was on TV. So after the trees left, the made things worse by building one of the largest solar farms in the west. It supplies all of Wyoming. When they built that place, they told everyone that solar farms couldn't hurt anything, right? You can't tell, but there is so much light collected by these new panels, your eyes kind of get sucked into it. It's like a black hole of light. It's devastating, especially since they can't grow trees. People don't go outside much except at night, because if they can't resist looking the solar farm, they'll go blind in about two days. If you're out at two p.m. every afternoon, the town gets so bright it looks like a nuclear blast hit it, from all of the negative light flowing out of the solar farm right then. The antelope there are blind, the coyotes are blind and they sing the blues about it every night. Half the town is wearing blinders and welding glasses to be safe."

She had made parts of that up, but it could all be true by this time. People in Rock Springs didn't go outside much—not only because of the solar farm, but because the wind never stopped blowing, ever. It was probably worse now. Tree had read several exposes about the black holes of light in Wyoming, the engineering disaster. It wasn't planned to be so close to town, but it worked so well, it had expanded almost to the highway, blinding drivers for miles around. Cars were told to turn on their flashers and keep their eyes on the road as they went through.

The trains in Rock Springs were fantastic though—all-electric and high-speed, at least until they hit the state line, then they stopped dead. Wyomingites would get on the high-speed trains and ride east looking at the wind and the dust storms, then turn around at the border and watch it again going west. They stopped at the casinos too. It could be a fun weekend.

Mara, who probably knew more about black holes than Tree could hope to learn, looked a tad skeptical. "That doesn't sound right. You can't have a black hole of light."

"I'm not a physicist, Mara. You can have a black hole in space, can't you? No one can explain them, and they're very dangerous. It can happen here too, with light energy, because of Einstein."

"What about Einstein?"

"Einstein would be able to explain it. He would probably tell us not to do it, like the atomic bomb."

They reached the Wyoming state line on the second afternoon, and Tree was twitching like an aspen. She hated the police, since they had not looked kindly on environmental protesters in all the years she'd been doing it. She'd stuffed her long hair up under her ball cap, since it signaled earth mother types, and tried to look like a dimwit as they approached the gate. Mara had her usual big smile plastered on her face, whether genuine or affected, Tree couldn't tell. The cop sidled over to the truck, taking in the newness and the expense, the official-looking white color, and then the two hippie-looking types inside it. This needed to be investigated. Mara kept her smile. She was a cool customer, no matter how she felt inside.

"How are you today? We have to go pick up some horses in Rock Springs." The cop eyed her smile suspiciously, then slid his gaze down to her chest. He couldn't help it, that was just how they were wired. Tree expected that Mara had caught it too, but when she glanced over, Mara was not only smirking, she was flexing like a bodybuilder, straining her skimpy shirt over her ample frame. I'll be damned, Tree thought. The cop ogled for as long as he dared, then barely glanced over at Tree.

"We aren't taking any women over breeding age," he said shortly, and Tree, forgetting her vow, snapped, "As though I would stay in this weirdo state!" before she could stop herself. The cop gave her a cool look and ignored her, since Mara was still right there a few feet from him, swelled up like an enraged cat. She was turning a little red from the effort.

"I'll need to look through your vehicle, girls," the so-called guard said, leaving Tree out of it again, since she clearly wasn't a girl. He was younger than Mara. She jumped out of the truck and jiggled impressively. "That's not a problem. We knew all about this. We just need to go get those horses!" Tree realized that she didn't have anything on under her little shirt, either. Tree could not have pulled off such a stunt even when she had the goods to do it, since her style was more like punching them in the nose and not using the almost-surefire boob trick. No foul for doing it, however. It wasn't women's fault that men were so easy to mislead.

The officer picked through the back of the truck with his laser light, because they liked to use their gear fastened all over their bodies like a Vorebot. Never mind that it was the middle of the day and perfectly clear. He promptly spotted the large stash of weed that Tree had packed, an absolute bale of pot that she left right in the middle of the back seat for no particular reason. The cop glared, but they weren't allowed to enforce any laws inside Wyoming that weren't being enforced outside of it. The state had been forced into the agreement when they started the roadblocks, or, the feds promised, they would simply eminent domain the entire state and cover it with wind turbines. They weren't kidding either. The state was about worthless since cows and petroleum crashed, and would look a lot better to The Economy covered with new energy production. Under the Safety Amendment, the government could do almost anything to secure enough energy to keep everyone happy, *except* go outside the country. It was in the Constitution now, voted in when we'd been having a brief moment of sanity. There were too many nukes out there in the hands of rogue wackos to make it worthwhile, and nobody would join the military voluntarily even if we wanted to have old-fashioned wars for oil. So we now left war to the robots, in a kind of video game followed by the generals on giant screens, so that no one got killed except by data center pollution, since the Pentagon operated on one of largest data centers in the world. It was the least they could do for men who used to fly very fast planes around and drop bombs. It was a delicate operation but still very expensive, like the Cold War. But all those polluting military operations were canceled and those who were waiting for nuclear annihilation were disappointed, and had to come up with new prophecies.

All Wyoming had now was a cash crop of marijuana and thousands of cashmere goats, which thrived there and did not eat marijuana. They did make very nice sweaters. That was one of Wyoming's excuses for having the roadblocks—someone might try to steal their valuable goats! Tree felt that people had probably been stealing goats out of Wyoming ever since it was named Wyoming and maybe before that, but not until now had they needed roadblocks. Would we need so many guards, if so many didn't covet?

Tree had a few numbers on her phone that would report any authority figure trying to pull a fast one on her, and she was holding her phone like a pistol, the recording button under her thumb, waiting for the officer to overstep. He felt her smolder and veered carefully around her, staying closer to Mara's friendlier-looking bosoms. The only object of interest in the truck was the pot, but he wandered around to the back of the trailer and banged around a little, acting official.

"He probably doesn't know how to open it," Tree whispered to Mara, who had exhaled and was looking a little faint. Sure enough, the cop popped his head around the corner and asked Mara to come help him open the door. Tree remained where she was, sweating in the sun, while Mara jiggled around back to be sexually harassed. She'd stopped holding her breath, and was now only a normal, attractive, Amazon woman wearing a tank top and no bra. Tree couldn't see what was happening, which of course was the point, but she could hear Mara putting on an act.

"Well, I know, but my husband would miss me a lot!" Revolting. Poor Mara. Tree was now a non-entity to men in general, unless they were about ninety. She stared at her phone, wishing that it would wake up and save her. The stupid devices did that to you, even when you never used them. It had no reception anyway, probably another gift from the backwards Wyoming people. She'd heard that some towns had turned off their internet entirely, so that they wouldn't be exposed to the evils of the outside world. And here they were stuck at the mercy of an inbred Wyoming cop. Tree felt her scalp prickling at more than the heat. She could hear the cop murmuring to Mara behind the trailer and stopped her feet from going over. After several infuriating minutes slumped against the door of the truck, fuming, Mara came back and threw herself in the truck seat. The cop strutted back to his little shack with the Wyoming flag on the top, too hot to stare at Mara's boobs anymore.

They drove out of there fast, and Tree could tell that Mara was furious. She'd never seen Mara out of her element, in an unexpected situation, or furious. So she wasn't just a domestic goddess. She had more stones than Tree had imagined.

"He *asked* me," Mara hissed once the roadblock had faded behind them, "if I'd ever thought about being a mother to some of best genetics in Wyoming. Because he could tell that I'd be a *prime* candidate for child-bearing." She drove a little faster.

"Oh, and he wasn't saying that for *him*—there was an entire company and I could take my pick. It was *all-natural,* and they would pay a lot for one healthy baby. I could even go home, as long as the baby came back. He was looking at me like he was about to strip me naked and inspect me." They were really flying at this point.

"I'm so sorry. I wish I could have helped. But you were great. I couldn't have done a thing, except hit him. Which is, as they say, *non-productive*."

"He tried to give me a *pamphlet.* God, what an asshole." Mara pulled over when they were miles down the road and they smoked some of the weed. That was the worst thing they would have to do on this trip, right? Mara tried her phone and found it unusable, as well. She tore out of the dirt road and they drove eighty miles an hour down the mostly empty highway. Once inside the state, there was almost no law enforcement, so they blew through a hundred miles of road before they felt safe enough to stop again. Here their phones worked, so they stopped for Mara to send Hani hundreds of texts about their trip so far. Tree sent Harris one: Having a great time, wish you were here. Smiley face, smiley face.

They were close to Rock Springs when they stopped for the night, not wanting to get near the glow of the solar farm. They didn't shine at night, of course, but anyone who lived near them felt like they were giving off heat and light all the time. They had an aura all their own, as well as creating their own weather, if they were large enough.

As they pulled into town, Tree was astonished to see that Rock Springs had an even bigger wildlife problem than her town did, although at least they were not standing around in the road. No, they were living in the shade of the solar panels. It was ninety degrees directly over the solar farm, but beneath it was a huge shaded habitat where hundreds of animals sought refuge in the summer. Not only was it cooler and safer for them there, they were not exposed to the rays of the solar farm at different times of day. The town had put water troughs at the edge of the solar farms, not really out of kindness, Tree suspected, but more out of the realization that if they didn't, there were going to be a lot of stinky animal carcasses under there. The watering system was extremely high-tech and caught the limited rainwater and dew from the solar panels and put it back into shallow ditches. Migrants lived under the enormous solar farm in Nevada where they had the same water technology, but the farm around Rock Spring mostly belonged to the animals. In winter, the snow melted off the panels when it was below zero, forming little heat zones that sprouted moist green grass.

The field started right at the edge of town, with little regard to the residents who would have to buy very expensive sunglasses for the rest of their lives. The installation went on for miles over the Wyoming landscape, silver rectangles spilling over the hills and draws and valleys, sucking up the sun's energy and sending it over the mountains. Tree had seen many solar farms by now and had done some protests over their stupid, stupid location siting, but she'd never seen one as big as this. It was unprotestable. It was a force of nature, darkening the land while it churned up heat and energy six feet above. Birds learned to fly around the glowing fields, but they also learned how to hide under them like the other animals, seeking one of the few sources of shade on the big hot prairie. The grass fires were so extensive, a lot of the ground cover burned every few years, so even the birds could figure out that places where humans lived didn't tend to burn down as often.

It was all so disruptive, biologists who were supposed to studying the impacts of the solar farms on wild animals threw up their hands said, "Has anyone actually looked at these energy installations? It's kind of late now to worry about how they might affect wildlife. How would we know what the animals are going to do? *They* don't even know yet. We have never done this before! We have never lived in this *world* before!" The businesspeople wrote "no known impacts" on their official forms and called the contractors.

No biologists ever said this, of course, except in Tree's imagination, because they all wrote their reports and kept their jobs. She'd tried. If you were hired to survey the wildlife and that was what you found, why couldn't you say it? You were the professional, after all. Animals weren't supposed to be living under a solar farm. It had messed them up. You could hire fifty biologists and they would all see the same thing, whether they said so or not. In fact most of the town could see it plainly, they didn't need a professional degree: a forty-five hundred acre solar farm would have a massive impact on everything within miles—animals, people, the land, the sky, the dust devils that would spin out among the maze of panels. No one needed a scientist to tell them, they could go out there and see it for themselves, their very creation. LOOK AT IT.

If Tree had even been able to make peace with that one, she may have had a good career, instead of living in tents and hanging out with people who called themselves Ponderosa and Marmot. But she had no regrets on that score. You have to be true to yourself.

Mara was looking for the horse corrals and had little interest in the solar farm. At last she saw a sign pointing up a hill and started jumping in her seat again.

"We're there! The corral is over there. Look at all those horses!"

There were so many horses. Tree had never seen so many in one place before, crowded into three large corrals. It may have been a rodeo ground that had been repurposed for the horses, but it was all too small—-the arena, the fences, the piles of hay. Hundreds of small horses of many colors were milling around inside the corrals, a sea of horse smell and sound. Mara was so awestruck she could barely drive the truck, but managed to get it into the parking lot and hopped out almost before it stopped moving. Tree examined the scene before she followed. Mara had been right about one thing—they looked like free horses. They looked like horses that someone was desperate to get rid of, to anyone. But they seemed healthy enough, except for a few cuts and overgrown hooves.

"What color do you want?" she grinned as she joined Mara, who was in heaven, leaning over the corral fence with her mouth open.

"Oh my god, I want them all," Mara couldn't believe her luck. All they had to do was load them into the trailer and go home. She noticed a dirty cowboy loitering near the hay shed, so she hustled over and began interrogating him. She'd changed from the tank top into something that would attract less male attention, but she attracted enough anyway. The cowboy, perking up a bit for a gal like her, told her that sure, those were the free horses, just load them up and fill out some paperwork. Mara was ecstatic. If they could fill up the trailer, maybe Hani would let her keep one in the yard. It would be tricky with the garden, but there was no zoning in their neighborhood. Tree looked perturbed when Mara returned.

"Would you look at these horses, Mara? Look at their eyeballs. I think the solar farm is doing something to them."

In her excitement Mara hadn't noticed that a lot of the horses had very light-colored eyes. Not a genetic feature, but a feature of cataracts. At least a third of them looked to be blind or nearly blind. Some of them had been in the corrals for two or three years, so they were fairly docile, but situated at the top of a small hill, the arena had a full view of the solar farm stretching into the distance. The horses stared off into the distance until they couldn't see the distance anymore. It didn't upset them too much in their small world, with all their blind friends. Mara ran over to the cowboy again, who was enjoying the spectacle of these women who seemed to think they were just going to lead some horses out of the corral and take them home. He hoped that they would try to rope them, because that was always entertaining.

Mara was not in a good mood this time—five minutes after she'd been happy, just like a woman. "You people know that these horses are going blind, right? Do you even look at them? Why don't you turn them loose? You can't keep horses and make them go blind. I thought they were supposed to be adopted. No one is going to adopt a blind horse."

The cowboy stared at her blankly then answered, "Because we're supposed to *round them up*?" Her cuteness had worn off quickly when she started to question him, a cowboy, about his treatment of horses. Especially a Wyoming cowboy, the only true cowboys left.

Tree caught snatches of the conversation and felt her blood starting to boil. It was always something. It was always some huge mess that men could have prevented with a tiny bit of common sense, but they never did. She stomped back to the truck to find some pot before she started a fight. As though it wasn't hard enough to find adopters for feral horses. She looked sadly at all the wasted biomass. Even if you let them go, they'd just stumble around and get caught in the barbed wire, or die of thirst. That idiot cowboy would be gainfully employed by the government for the next decade to play with drones and watch horses go blind, but Tree couldn't keep a job. The whole world was insane.

Mara drifted back to the truck after she'd gotten her fill of looking at the horses, undaunted by the cowboy's rudeness. Blind horses would be easier to tame. "I think we can still get these horses. They would work."

Tree was stoned and pissed off. It wasn't even her project. She just wanted to have some fun, and here she was looking at the products of man's stupidity, as usual. Her plan was sketchy enough without any complications. She was pulled out of her funk by the drone of one of those damn airplanes overhead. Even here, the drones were always cruising around, looking for something to invade. Mara was watching it, close by them now, with its creepy buzz that crept right into your head.

"It's—-going over by the farm. Probably patrolling. No, wait, it's following something. Tree, there's a bunch of horses over there. Even more of them. And the drone is like, herding them away from the solar farm. There's a whole pack of drones. Tree, look at this. Put down the pipe for a minute."

Tree did put down the pipe in time to see a drone driving some wild horses. It was pushing them toward the corrals and the other horses, although there was no room to put any more animals inside those fences, no way. The horses scattered and trotted across the hill as the drones buzzed them in the right direction. Mara got out of the truck, staring in awe as the herd ran by and out into a field behind them. She took out her phone and began taking pictures as fast as she could. Hani was about to be flooded with horse pictures. These weren't blind either.

Tree went to see the cowboy, still mad but more in control of herself. He was prepared this time. This hippie was not his mother either. His mother was proud of his government job.

"So what about these horses? Are they also free? Are you going to round them up too, and put them in a corral until they go blind?"

"You know what, if you want a horse, then go get it and stop asking me about it. Those are not my horses. You saw them. They just came in."

"Those are government drones, aren't they?" She'd seen the markings on them. "You didn't even round them up. The drones do it. You probably sit here all day and watch drones fly around. Do your bosses know that you're abusing animals here? What kind of a cowboy lets horses go blind?" One with a good government job, that's who.

The cowboy flicked his eyes involuntarily toward a storage shed where he probably kept all of his drone controllers. Not waiting for an answer, Tree raced back to Mara to brainstorm. They should contact the government about this setup—it was the blind leading the blind here. Mara smiled a little bit. She'd decided that she was fine with blind horses. After some discussion, they decided to try to catch some of the horses that were outside of the corrals too. They had time. The horses hadn't gone too far from the main road or the corral, so they were already used to people and movements around them.

They moved the big rig behind the horse-blinding facility and dropped the trailer, setting up their camp behind it, out of the wind. They were conspicuous by the enormous trailer that screamed CLASSY ASSES all across the valley, but it was still better than hauling it around. Happy to have a clear plan of action, they spent some time setting up camp. Their new work home, since this was a research project. The drive had been a little disturbing, but they felt better now they were in town. They'd been followed by several drones that patrolled the highways, and it made them jumpy until they realized that the stupid things were flying around randomly and only sometimes following drivers. Sometimes they wouldn't see anyone for an hour, then hear the even louder drone of a delivery caravan approaching, whizzing by on its metal tracks as fast as its computer chips could safely manage. The sound made Tree's skin crawl, breaking the silence of the plains with its over-engineered machine whine.

After they were satisfied with their setup, they took the truck into town and bought their Rock Springs sunglasses. The town seemed fairly normal, even if everyone was wearing sunglasses that made them seem Vore-like. But there were few Vores around here, it looked like. Too dusty. After their eyes were properly safeguarded, they went to the feed store. Tree explained her plan with great confidence, since Mara was blissed out and wouldn't notice that it was lame.

"What we do is get some chow for the horses that are outside the corral—oats and alfalfa and stuff. Then we hang out and wait for them to come over and eat. They love this stuff. Also, we give them a lot of water, because oats make them thirsty, and we talk to them. Then we tame them. Biologists do this all the time."

"What do we say?"

"It doesn't matter, it's the tone of our voice. You have forty-five feral cats in your house. You know how."

Mara loved it. She could hang out with horses all day and do nothing but try to make friends with them. This also sounded like a good vacation to Tree, and might even work, so they were excited as they spent hundreds of dollars of other people's money. Eight bags of feed, a five-pound box of carrots and a jug of wine later, they returned to camp feeling well-prepared for horse taming. That night they scattered sugar cubes and alfalfa pellets around their camp. They could hear the horses snuffling and stamping close by from where they lay. They made Tree feel safe too, finally in her element—outdoors and close to animals that probably would not kill her.

Then followed a blissful week or so. Tree lost track of time, having nowhere to go and no plans. You didn't want to stay out in the wind too long, so she needed the break of the horse trailer, where there was a cot. She lay on it and watched the sky and the clouds. They kept their sunglasses on from the moment they opened her eyes, since Tree wanted to stare at the solar farm too, with its miles of hypnotic shiny blackness. She turned her chair around and watched the horses instead. Look at her, taming horses. She cracked an imaginary whip. She spoke baby talk to them. The horses ignored her. They weren't even spooky, habituated by the big corrals full of their brethren. Tree and Mara went over to the the corral after dark, after the cowboy went home, to wash up and get buckets of water for their horses. Tree took a look at the shed with the drone controllers, but it was securely padlocked, just in case some woman with a braid down her back thought about turning all those horses loose, then chasing them off with a drone. Not that she would do that. If the horses didn't die of thirst, there were almost a million miles of old barbed wire strewn all over Wyoming, a lot of it on the ground. Once the cows were gone, that fencing was abandoned like a New Year's resolution.

At least once a day they baited the area around their camp, then Mara did the rounds to see if their friends had come by. They were everywhere, almost from the first night. They were all used to scavenging hay from the corrals, so horse treats were a bonus. Tree could hear them blowing and stamping around as they decided how dangerous the women and the big trailer were, and decided they weren't dangerous at all. After a few days, Tree started leaving feed close to the horse trailer, making the horses become accustomed to coming near them for treats. She assured Mara that this was the best and most accepted way of taming horses. She got lucky, because within a few days, a small herd of rather motley-looking ponies had decided to hang out with the treats and shade around the trailer. No wonder all the animals lived under the solar farm, since it was usually close to a hundred degrees this time of year, and windy too. The free-roaming horses still had their full vision, so they watched Tree and Mara while Mara and Tree watched them. After a week, Tree could get one of the horses to come within a few feet of her for an alfalfa cube. Mara was delighted, and couldn't decide whether to spend all of her time with her new herd, or stay by the corrals cooing at the handicapped horses, which were almost tame anyway from their long incarceration and blindness. If they couldn't get the wild ones, blind ones would be easy.

Tree woke up weak and sweaty one morning, so after tossing some treats out for the milling horses, she lay back down and thought beautiful thoughts. Mara dithered around with her pets for most of the day, then took the truck into town for supplies. Tree wondered how hard it would be to get their babies into the horse trailer, but she wouldn't be trying it today. She left some hay in the trailer door and sat down with her brick of pot, which had not appreciably diminished during their stay. She gave a wad of it to a horse, who liked it.

Mara returned in a cloud of dust, bringing dinner and four bottles of Diet Coke. There was a supply caravan stopped in town on its way to California, and she'd gotten the Cokes from the driver.

"You are generous with other people's money."

"And it was worth it. If I'd been prepared, I could have changed shirts and saved."

"Tough world out there," Tree agreed. "Did I tell you what a smooth move that was with the border guy?"

"You can tell me again, since I was raped by his eyes."

"It was the most empowering thing I've ever seen." Tree chugged some Coke. "What a great find. I haven't seen a real Diet Coke in years." People in California got things that were never seen anywhere else. They had some sort of deal, or else they wouldn't grow oranges and lettuce anymore. She thanked Mara profusely and drank more of the bubbly drink, which did her stomach no favors but was delicious. It was still cold too, and reminded Tree of olden days, when they all drove gas cars and didn't worry about a thing except getting fat, which was why they had diet drinks. There were a lot worse things than getting fat, it turned out, unless you wanted to use "getting fat" as a metaphor for our overuse of resources...well, anyway.

She and Mara toasted their highly successful horse acquisition trip, even if the horses weren't actually tamed yet. But all they needed to do was put them in the trailer. They decided to start working on the hard part the next morning, when Tree would be stronger. Mara spread some more trap food around for their friends, as well as inside the trailer, then went to sweet-talk her buddies in the corral and give them treats. Tree was relieved that the blind horses were here, because she wasn't too sure about the ones breathing on her now. They were all nice until you tried to get them into the tight confines of a trailer. She waved them away so she could lie down on her cot again, belching like a real cowgirl, and fell asleep hearing Mara speaking baby-talk over at the corral, while their herd stomped and whuffled around her.

It must have been hours later, because it was much cooler when Tree was shocked awake by an awful cacophony. BAM BAM WHINNY BAM BAM BAM stomp stomp stomp, slam bam, WHINNY WHINNY WHINNY. Tree sat up straight, since she was next to the trailer and the noise was deafening. The damn horses had gone into the trailer by themselves, after their treats, and it sounded like they couldn't figure out how to get out. Were they blind too? STOMP STOMP BAM it sounded like at least two horses were in the trailer, and they weren't leaving either. Tree struggled to her feet, not feeling it in the least, but she needed to see. Mara had come out of her tent too and they crept to the back of the trailer, where they discovered that three of their herd were hanging out in the front of the enormous trailer, munching on Tree's half-bale of pot that she had left there for safekeeping.

"Mara," Tree said, "we have pothead horses." The horses showed no inclination to charge past them to escape, or do much of anything except stand there and look dazed, now that they'd explored the boundaries of the horse trailer to their satisfaction. Tree wouldn't have believed it.

Mara was also staring at the horses. Here they'd been camping out for days and spending a fortune on horse treats, and all they'd needed was a bale of weed. She'd never seen this in western movies, but then, the west hadn't been covered with marijuana during the golden age of the west. "What kind of pot is that?"

"It's just regular pot. It's as good as—well you know. It's regular pot." Tree should take a break if she was that tolerant. As soon as she got home. She hadn't thought that she could out-high a horse. They were both bleary and disheveled from being awakened, but the sky was already turning light in the east, so they drank their second Diet Cokes and put on their pants. The horses had decided it for them, because three of them already in the trailer was too good to let pass.

Mara ran over to the corral and selected a few of her favorite mutts from among the blind and near-blind, walking right into the furball of horses and putting ropes around their necks. They followed her out when they felt the rope, because a blind horse in a crowd goes where it is pushed, it doesn't make much difference. And Mara, their friend, smelled like sugar and pot and alfalfa, so it was no contest. She came back to the trailer with the cutest horses in the entire corral, she said. Tree loved them too, with their white starey eyes and their dirty coats. They smelled good. Maybe she could come back later and get one of her own, after she figured out where to put it.

Tree was guarding the back of the horse trailer, in case the stoned horses decided to save themselves, but they were now calm and munching quietly on their alfalfa treats. She swung the door open slowly and Mara tried to coax one of her babies into the trailer. STOMP STOMP SLAM STOMP whinny whinny, stomp stomp kick skid. And she was in. Mara tied her up. They couldn't believe their luck. With the filly blocking the way out, Tree wedged herself close to the other horses and tied them up, making sure that the pot was close to them. They were so listless, she wondered if they'd made a mistake and these horses were getting sick. Or maybe they were semi-domesticated anyway. Tree didn't think that wild horses should be so easy to control, but on the other hand, most of her her knowledge of them was gained from old westerns, just like Mara's. They coaxed the black and white pony into the back end. He wasn't any trouble either, since he followed the others, and the trailer reeked of oats and alfalfa. Even with five horses, there was room to walk around inside.

"Did someone expect you to come back with an entire herd of horses?" Tree asked, kicking some dirtyhay out the back.

"It was what they had, and I volunteered anyway."

Mara had no idea how badly this could had gone, or still might, for that matter. But getting these horses had been far easier then Tree expected, and she wasn't going to ruin it. "We're done here. We got five horses. Five! I didn't think we could get any."

She was so relieved, she blurted out the truth instead of what she'd been telling Mara for two weeks. Mara frowned. Tree should recognize that Mara's superior horse skills had calmed and brought the horses to her. Real horse girls had bonds with horses that others envied or couldn't appreciate, and Tree shouldn't mock this, even if she was an environmentalist and could probably ride a horse, if she wanted to. They gated up the trailer and quickly gathered the rest of their things. It was only dawn, and there were no witnesses to their leaving. No one would miss the blind horses and no one would wonder about the two woman who had camped out with their big gaudy trailer. They drove to the truck stop, and Mara went to see if she could find some more Diet Cokes. Things fell out of the backs of caravans sometimes, if you hit the gas stations early. They found no treasures, only some bad coffee, even though the cashier looked reasonably busty. There were Vores from the prairie trains in there too, blocking the aisles with their big heads, so Tree and Mara looked down their noses at them before they left. Tourists. The babies were dosed with some sticky sweet oats again and they headed out, giddy with success.

Wyoming drones followed them from the time they left Rock Springs. Sure, maybe it was normal patrolling, but wasn't there anyone else on the highway? It was nerve-racking. The official line was that people weren't searched when they left the state, but who would know what really happened? Sometimes people never came back from Wyoming. They were a strange bunch—give away free horses, but be rude about it at the same time. Mara kept stopping to check on them, but every time they did, a drone would come out of nowhere and circle them until Tree wanted to scream.

"They're hoping you'll take your top off again," Tree told Mara. Mara didn't believe it and made a sour face, but Tree did. What else did those cowboys have to do? Rumor had it that a few of them spent so much time buzzing Vore yoga camps during the summer, they had to be severely warned off. The only thing Wyoming was known for now, besides sheep and the cashmere goats, was gasoline that cost almost nothing. Since they were too stubborn to stop pumping it out of the ground and couldn't sell it in any other state, unemployed Wyomingites held Gas-Blasting Contests where they drove badly maintained trucks around town all weekend, blaring country music and spewing black exhaust. It was weird—but on the other hand, not much weirder than Sturgis had been, back in the day. Tree pretended she had never heard of this custom at all, lest she go hunt down some cowboys. She peed by the trailer in full view of one of the drones, because what else was *she* supposed to do? She and Mara waved and smiled at the locals as they passed, just in case they got into trouble somewhere.

Tree had to convince Mara that the horses were all tied up safely and not flying around in the trailer with broken legs, but after that they drove sixty miles an hour down the empty road. Occasionally a redneck in an old gas truck would pass them, no matter how hard it was for him to reach passing speed. The Wyomingites kept very nice roads, probably because no one ever drove on them except the gasoline-exploiting residents, who enjoyed the same thing that people in wide-open spaces had always enjoyed—driving fast and far in their cars named after animals. The state charged the delivery caravans hundreds of dollars to cut across Wyoming, and they got it, too, since it cost more than that to go around. In return, Wyoming had the best roads left in the country and lots of electric charging stations for the caravans. CLASSY ASSES, Tree and Mara screamed as they barreled down the highway, full of gas and water and horses. Good old American horsepower was a timeless language, even if no one alive could remember the finest years of it.

It was almost a hundred degrees today, but they had also high-powered air-conditioning.

"So what kind of mileage do you think this rig gets?" Tree asked, estimating the tons of carbon being released as she watched their giant shadow cruise across the landscape. Mara was no fool.

"You know what, Tree?" she pronounced, "If you were a horse, you'd be high-strung. Being high-strung is what makes racehorses great competitors. They have passion. They have a lot of drive. Racehorses have goats in their stalls with them, so that they won't flip out, just from the joy of being alive. Even the most beautiful animal on earth has emotional problems. And there's nothing wrong with that, Tree."

"This is only my opinion here, but if you don't have emotional problems by this time, you aren't paying attention. Nothing personal. I'm sure you'll get around to it when your honeymoon is over. But a therapy goat would be really helpful. I feel better just thinking about one."

"You can't bring it to my house." A goat would be even better than a dog, or at least as good as, because they ate trash. Did *cashmere* goats eat trash? She could sleep with it in the winter, it would be very calming. Maybe they could get one for the backyard and throw all the garbage out for it. Harris could play for it.

They were making good time and had lost the drones for a while. A thunderstorm rolled by and the temperature cooled to more than tolerable. Steam rose off the slick road in waves, then Tree saw them.

"Mara, stop the truck! We're about to destroy a million dollars worth of fur!"

They rolled to a stop slowly, for the horses. In front of them was one of the famous herds of cashmere goats, standing in the road as aimlessly as they stood around on rocks and dirt the rest of the time. There were easily a hundred of them, scattered up and down like melting snow. It was getting late, and they seemed to be bedding down for the night. On the highway. It was proof of how little traffic there was here. Mara examined the roadblock.

"What should we do?"

Tree was so at peace in the empty landscape, she wanted to lie down on the ground with one of the smelly goats, if they would let her touch them. They were so soft. "Nothing. Let's camp. Let the horses out, sleep with the goats. We can't do anything with them. They'll move on by the morning."

Mara moved the rig carefully off the road and onto a flat spot, where they set up cots behind the horse trailer. The blind ponies were docile and happily started grazing on some grass that the goats hadn't gotten to yet, but the three in the front of the trailer looked a little spooky, snorting and rolling their eyes.

"We have to give them more pot. It's all gone. These guys look a little excited."

Tree grumbled. Depending on how the world turned, a small bale of weed might not be enough to get all the way home, and she liked to be prepared for emergencies. But it would have to be sacrificed. She took a firm slice from the dwindling bale, then tossed the rest of it over to the horses, who went for it immediately with their big teeth. Potheads, just like the deer. They watered and gave the horses more treats, then had a meal of cheese and crackers. After admiring the vast landscape for a few hours, listening to the wind change direction while Mara sent texts to Hani, they heard a mechanical noise. Curses. Tree got up and stuck her head around the back of the horse trailer, but it wasn't a drone.

"It's a van man, Mara. He should stay here with us." The van man had slowed for the cashmere goats and was weaving around them a little better than Mara and Tree had, but he made it to them in a few minutes and stopped. The blind horses raised their heads at the unfamiliar sound, then turned their milky gazes back to the ground.

"Greetings," the van man waved at them, stopped in the middle of the road. "I wonder if I could stay here tonight, by you and the herd."

"We were thinking that too!" Tree felt that van men were something like leprechauns—they were generally convivial types, even if sometimes they tricked you. But they were good luck anyway. The man parked on the other side of the highway and came over to share some wine, as well as bring a new bottle. Good luck already.

Van men (and women, although not as many, since they tended to be taken in by someone), had been left high and dry by whichever economic scheme had melted down that year. Many of them, as well as the genuinely destitute, were given "government cheese"—one of the electric cars that served to keep the victims out of the public eye. Since they were late-model electrics, they gave the illusion of consumer wealth instead of indigence, and people still had the freedom of personal mobility. Families of three or more were given minivans, which bulged at the seams with their desperate lives, but as government cheese recipients, they also had free parking and charging at any of the camping lots.

Instead of becoming bitter about their lot, most of the van people drove around like they'd won the lottery. Maybe they did feel a kind of freedom now. They had no responsibilities, and they could still drive. The families perhaps did not view their situation with quite as much equanimity, but there was something about "free" that clouded the minds of most people. They had lost all, true—but they'd been given a *free car.* Some of them traded their vans for a little spot of land with a shed on it. Others preferred the van life.

Hurricane, flooding, and tornado victims also wanted government cheese, but they were told to be happy that they still had a yard and a property line. Start sorting through that debris and build some shelters, because there was no new lumber coming, anymore. They could have a free shipping container if they wanted one. There were lots of them, all different colors. After they picked out their new homes, volunteers would be needed to restore some of the services. It takes a village, and they were the village. There were some pamphlets over by the outhouses explaining how this worked, since no one could remember anymore.

This van man had a soft voice and gentle manner that went with his low-key life. He was about seventy, but by the looks of him, he'd be roaming the roads for many years to come. Since he had a van instead of a small car, that he'd been some kind of professional. He introduced himself as Eli. Mara said hello, but was uncharacteristically quiet and was over by the blind horses, cooing and feeding them even more treats.

"Mara, if you feed those horses any more oats, they're going to be diabetic before we get back." Tree thought the horses were starting to look a little cross-eyed. She should probably work with them more, instead of feeding them drugs. This was supposed to be a learning adventure. But they had Mara. She finished her glass of wine. Really, those horses should be glad that they rescued them. They didn't owe them anything. She gave some hay to the trio in the horse trailer, who looked docile enough, but were not going to be let out anyway.

She and Eli made a campfire later, a small, symbolic campfire of old dead sagebrush, for a long dead past when we needed campfires at night to stay warm. Like driving down the long pretty highway, we went through our familiar rituals, whether we still needed to do them or not. We feared change, no matter how often we were told that we wanted progress. Eli told Tree that he'd been a genetics professor once, before.

"Then what?" asked Tree. Genetics professors should be highly valued, with all the genetic innovation going on. That seemed to be the very problem.

"We were uh, made obsolete? Phased out? I don't really know what to call it. We couldn't teach any kind of genetic science, because it was all patented at one step or another, and it would infringe on a copyright, and then it just became too difficult." Eli shrugged elaborately, throwing back a little more wine. Tree wasn't literate enough in the subject to be furious at this story, but she could work up to it, it sounded like.

"Isn't genetics like, what we're made of? How we came to be? They can't patent *us*."

Eli nodded, smiling a little bitterly, she thought. They totally got each other. "That's what we all said. You can't patent *life*. And then you see." He waved his hand around to indicate his van across the road, the clumps of goats, the whole prairie, the universe. It made no sense, but there was nothing to be done about it. Capitalism was much stronger than they were. It caused the rounding of everything—one thing rose and another thing had to be squashed to allow for it, so that the ball would keep on rolling, faster and faster. It just so happened that the thing that needed to be squashed was our humanity, and the thing that rose up was always more business.

Maybe Eli had worn off his anger driving down the road in his free car for the last seven years. Maybe age had calmed his rage, although so far it had not done so for Tree. Every time she tried, she'd read something else. But for now, both of them were buzzed and relaxed by the still of the night, and couldn't be angry while sharing a campfire, even a symbolic campfire of a lost world.

"I hate those people," Tree agreed. No one had any standards. The Vores did genetic engineering all the time, and they cloned their body parts for replacements, because the headsets weren't weird enough. They were only conduits to even more desires. Their children were born with impossible skin colors and IQs so high, none of the old tests could measure them. Every parent insisted that their child was a a gift from God and not a doctor or a geneticist, even though the level of microplastics in our systems was so high, that claim strained the imagination. The Vores were as polluted as everyone else. They swore the fetal engineering was only used for medical conditions, not to give their children more advantages. And who was to say whether limp brown hair or shyness or a shapeless figure were only social handicaps, or actual medical conditions? The case could be made either way. It was only a few tiny tweaks.

After a few more glasses of wine, Eli decided that it was safe to say what he'd thinking. He gestured at Tree's braid and said, "We may have some friends in common. I was uh, one of the founders of the Church of Wendell Berry."

Tree was astonished. And flattered. Even with the braid giving her away, he was taking a big chance. The Church of Wendell Berry wasn't a church, of course, but more like a support group or book club. They were not very organized, because it would be against Church philosophy to become too militant about anything. They read a lot of research papers, filed some lawsuits, and cried together. The Church had been scattered for years, but if Eli was one of the founders, he was an outlaw. Maybe even a real one, not just on the internet. There'd been some—well, the world didn't need any more soft drink bottling plants, end of story.

Tree whispered reverently, "I was in the Church of Wendell Berry! It was the greatest organization I was ever part of. I really started thinking we could save us." They looked at each other sadly, then drank a toast to one of the greatest environmentalists of all time. Eli told her that a few of the Church members had gone east afterward and joined the Church of Stop Shopping. Those guys had some great performances around Wall Street when it was imploding, he said. Really impressive. They'd picked up performers from the cruise ships and they had more talent than they knew what to do with. And everyone *had* stopped shopping. Wall Street was gone. The Church still protested at the Vore outdoor shopping markets, with huge choirs and parades of people that matched the bloated scale of everything Vore. The Vores, naturally, pretended that they didn't notice.

Tree had to leave the more visible protests because she had her son by then, and she was on a lot of watchlists. She needed to back off. But she saw the story about the meltdown of the Chicago Seed Barn on TV one day when she was under the weather, and immediately felt better. She had a feeling that those were her people.

The virtuous "seed repository," had been contaminated by unknown agents! Not likely. The Seed Barn was a genetic engineering lab, full of mutant animals. Even the lab rats had introduced cells and bionic transplants and glowing tails—because we would all need glowing appendages to help us explore space one day, where it was very dark. Because we would all be in space. It was inevitable, like all that other progress.

It took a good scientist to pull off that epic meltdown, someone who knew how to get right into a lab and mess up some experiments, but subtly. They hadn't just set a fire or dumped everything in the trash—they embarrassed everyone connected to the enterprise. There were photos that were too revolting to be seen on the news, but were all over the internet. Everything in the place died or had to be destroyed—but in fairness to the saboteur, they were all doomed anyway. The feds went in there after the sudden closure and cut the padlocks off the gates, after which made several dozen employees of the Barn called their lawyers. One of the charges had been "cruelty to animals," multiple counts, but the scientists took a plea bargain and the details never came out. The ideas were sound, but the execution had gotten out of hand. We can't stifle innovation over some missteps, that was how we learned. Blah blah blah.

No matter how smart they were, the technologists couldn't seem to learn that no matter what they created, they would never be better inventions, but only a sad, pale imitations of what we had so carelessly thrown away, now for thirty times the cost and half the efficiency. Someone would have to pay for that too. Tree looked at Eli. A *genetics* professor. Tree squinted at him hard.

"Did you infiltrate the Chicago Seed Barn? Was it you?"

"If I told you that, I'd have to kill you." Eli tried to look evil, but instead looked mostly drunk. They both laughed at the dumb old joke. He hadn't denied it, though.

"Is your friend friendly?" Eli interrupted her thoughts, rather conveniently, Tree thought suspiciously. Mara had bedded down with her phone and was sending pictures of the horses to Hani.

"She is," Tree defended her. "Usually she's friendlier than I am. But she likes horses. We caught these horses." They might not look very wild now, but Tree and Mara had worked hard buying treats for them.

"I see," Eli said. "A horse girl."

Tree had met some horse girls on the protest circuit. They did tend to be kind of crazy, although they fit in fine with the environmentalists, since both groups tended to take the side of the four-legged animals over the two-legged. One of the women had assaulted a horse whisperer because he was abusing his horses. That was her story, anyway. Tree didn't think this sort of behavior was typical of horse girls, but it wasn't shocking, either. Or maybe nothing shocked her anymore. The horse whisperer was a sham with a big mustache and a bigger flag who looked perfectly capable of abusing horses. Whether he was or not, one of the horse girls became pregnant, another victim of Wrangler butts. It had dawned on her that since they usually had sex in the stable, maybe he wasn't as into her as he first claimed. He never took her to his events and let her hang out in the corral like his girlfriend, even though they had met at one of his seminars, where he had whispered his way into her heart.

She gave him quite a beating for a pregnant woman, too—sneaking up from behind while he was sweet-talking one of his pretty horses, then escaping cleanly, since no one knew that the cowboy had been sleeping with an eco-protester. That would have been too confusing for most of his audience, as well as the horse whisperer, who had a good gig here and didn't want to be confronted with any moral dilemmas. The woman had clearly been enthralled by the much older cowboy and he'd taken advantage of her. She was a horse girl, and he smelled like a horse.

Tree wasn't supposed to know about any of that, but as the old lady of environmental protests, people told her things. The woman had the baby, since they were too precious to throw away now. She sold it to a rich Vore couple, taking a cut rate for refusing to identify the father. The horse whisperer's name would have brought a premium. Then she cried bitter tears for weeks afterward in her soft baby body, but in a nice new apartment that had no hint of baby fever, no memory of it at all. She never let the horse whisperer know either, since he'd probably want half of the money for none of the work. Since she'd broken his nose, she guessed they had broken up too, even if she hadn't exactly informed him of it.

It wasn't the horse girl's fault that she had to make these kinds of decisions to save herself. Men had made the world like this—made everything so cold and calculating. They threw their body fluids around like a porn shoot until there was a fortunate accident, then suddenly they were interested again. Who sold a baby anyway? The Economy did. It wasn't even illegal now. We could sell our body parts, so why not our babies? The Economy would come for all of us, eventually.

If the horse whisperer had any thoughts about what sort of smallish man would have kicked his ass so thoroughly, but still fought like a girl, he never brought it up, so maybe he had some honor after all. It may have been something other than surprise that kept him from overwhelming his attacker. He was guilty of everything that she suspected he was. It was hard to resist the crazy, self-assured horse girls, no matter how many of them liked him at once. The horse girl confided to Tree, "He was good with horses—but he wasn't *that* good."

We are the Architects of the Future, and it's on Mars

They set out from their camp fairly early the next morning, after being awakened by the cashmere goats baa-ing and bleating as they followed each other off the highway and wandered south. Eli must have left even earlier, although Tree was feeling kind of bleary when she got up. She checked the horses in the morning cool, but they seemed as calm as the rest of the landscape. They checked their paper map for the roads back. After some consultation, they decided that the best route was through dank Salt Lake. It was out of the way, but Eli had mentioned something about migrants who were holding up supply caravans on main road. They couldn't take a chance with their valuable vehicle.

"I used to drive through there all the time," Mara assured Tree. "It's perfectly safe. Besides, we need gas. I am not going through that again." They'd almost run out of gas on the way down, which could have been dangerous. They were both too old to do something that dumb, even if they weren't very familiar with giant gas-sucking trucks. Tree sulked. I only want to see pleasant things! Their town was a dump too, but she was used to it. Rock Springs had been a normal town, if a weird normal town. But dank Salt Lake was a sad refugee town. They drove for an hour before they hit the state line, where it was silent as a car wreck. They slowed for the gatehouse, but it was unmanned except for a few drones on the roof, waiting to be charged. The poor things, they were all tuckered out from their non-stop spying.

"Strange," remarked Tree, or maybe she was just paranoid. What did she know about Wyoming, anyway? She hated it here. If she'd known the place was going to be abandoned, she would have picked up some goats. They had more than enough room. But drones were worthless to her. Then she saw the flag, brand-new, hanging listlessly from a short pole. They'd made a new flag for Wyoming at some point—a Gadsden flag with oil derricks on it. They could have made something original, but it looked like someone had broken out the stencils and put them on that ugly snake flag.

"Mara, stop the truck," she demanded. "We are about to get something from here that is actually valuable." Wyoming memorabilia was highly prized, especially among the fake survivalist types. Harris could trade this thing for a couch on a good day. Mara looked skeptical, but she scanned the area and pulled over. "Keep it running, this will only take a minute." Tree put her hair up under her hat, pulled her bandanna over her face like a bank robber, and hopped out of the truck. There were cameras, of course, but all the drones seemed to be away. Tree knelt over like she was taking enemy fire and ran over to the pole. It was barely high enough to function as a flagpole, but in Wyoming wind, it worked most of the time anyway. People had been killed by big patriotic flags being ripped off of giant flagpoles. Once a tour bus had been taken out by a casino flag on the interstate that went flying in 130 mile-an-hour winds. Ironically, one of the victims had won $800,000 in that very casino only a few days before and was still on the road, hoping to become richer. Tree pulled the ropes down and snagged the flag quickly. It was full-size and she had to roll it up to keep from tripping over it. Hooting in victory, she jumped back in the truck with her prize and said, "go, go, go!" Mara eased off, never forgetting the horses. Tree admired her catch for a few seconds before she heard the whine.

"Somebody saw you," commented Mara as the drone whizzed behind them. *Wheeeee! Wheeeeee!* It flashed laser lights and squealed. This was extremely annoying but had no bite, like a video game where the police were behind you. They were over the state line and Wyoming could do nothing. They put on their Rock Springs sunglasses and continued down the road, the drone following right overhead and blaring its siren. Tree stuck her head out the window and flipped it off few times, safe in her shades.

"Stop that," said Mara, "you don't know what those things are capable of." Tree cackled, having her eye on the sky.

"Not a problem, because here comes the opposing team, and they look good." Utah, like Wyoming, had its own fleet of security drones that patrolled the highways. Unlike Wyoming, Utah had decided to give their cowboys good jobs when their cows were taken away, and all the drones in Utah were manned by angry repressed cowboys who missed their animals. None of the Utah drones were controlled by AI, and they were some of the most militant security fliers in the country. You did not want to be stopped by one, because they "pulled you over" by landing on your hood and spreading out their "bat wings," completely obscuring the windshield. The cowboys liked to wait until their victim was driving as fast as the road would allow, then drop straight down from the sky and ambush them. This made almost everyone come to screeching halt, even in a self-driving car, since it was too disorienting to try to keep going. You never knew why they targeted you. They didn't like your car, or they were drunk.

"Make sure you look really boring, Mara, because here they come." A cloud of drones was heading their way, at least thirty of them, in formation like geese. Tree had never seen such a flock before. Utah must be selling a lot of pot. The drone over the truck spotted them coming too late. It turned off its security features, but it was over the state line and open season for the Utah drones. It turned around and started back toward the state line, but it wasn't quite as nimble as the other drones, and they caught up with it easily. Mara kept driving, but Tree watched in horrified amazement as the squadron of Utah drones overwhelmed the Wyoming drone and bashed it like aerial bumper cars. Then the drones circled it in dizzying speed, spraying it with "drone killer." That's what they called it, but it was the urine of the drone operators, stashed in the belly of their drones and used for occasions just like this. Any liquid could have been used to short out the other drones, or to pee on driver's windshields, but the Utah guys liked their own body fluids. It was one of the perks of their job. If you were bat-winged by one of their drones, it was best to stop as quickly as you could, or get a blast of pee on your windshield too.

The Wyoming drone fell to the ground in a stinky puddle, smoking a little as its circuit boards died. It was disturbing, even if it was a machine. But you couldn't be sucked in by them, because they were evil. Tree hugged her flag close. Mara kept moving slowly down the road, watching the assassination in the rearview, and didn't get up to speed again until they witnessed the final destruction. "I hope your flag was worth it," she told Tree, wrinkling her nose like a princess, instead of a woman who could drive a big rig across Wyoming without quailing.

"Are you kidding? This is a prize. It was totally worth it. Anyway, did you ever see anything like that? You need to keep tabs on these things. They could take over." Utah guys had been known to kidnap pretty girls like Mara and make them join their harems. Maybe it had only happened once, years ago, but how many examples did you need? Everybody was supposed to toe the line with their little law enforcement cartels, but it was hard to enforce, since the feds never came out here except to patrol for more open land to put up energy installations. But they'd also promised Utah that if they received too many complaints about their drones, all of Canyonlands would be covered with wind turbines and drilling rigs for geothermal power, like some kind of crazy Tetris. Let the tourists do yoga poses on those. Nobody wanted to tempt them. The federal government had gone nuts since they couldn't plunder overseas oil anymore.

They reached Dank Salt Lake by afternoon, tired and relieved, even though the day had been uneventful except for the drone incident. It was good to find real people who weren't Vores or some kind of machinery. Tree was driving, and slowed to study the miles of transient housing, a dystopian RV park on the sparkling plain. There were campers, old trailers, cars, hunting tents, boxcars, and miles and miles of shipping containers. Many of them had been modified by dock workers and had doors, windows, lofts, bunk beds. They weren't bad if you could find one with ventilation. The dock workers moved into them and stayed there on the docks where they had already spent so much time, but in a much quieter environment. Then they built more of them, since they were out of a job and liked to stay busy. Thousands of shipping containers were sent out to the deserts to serve as whatever sort of housing anyone wanted to make of them, or to rust away, out of sight, out of mind. There were at least ten miles of them in Dank, right off the highway, all different colors and most of them in use. Another neighborhood was all old Airstream trailers, still sleekly silver, segregated in their own yard.

Most of the residents were refugees from Salt Lake proper, so their encampment didn't have the same scary transient feel that some of the other places did. The tap water had been more and more rationed, then one day a huge dust cloud from the parched Great Salt Lake swept in and covered the city with stinky, toxic dust, as well as millions more seagulls, who were in heaven in the salty mud flats. The snow stopped falling entirely and people put on masks when they were outside. "Running water" more or less went away, but since it trickled out of the faucets a little, most people stocked up on face masks and waited for it to return to normal. Where else would you go for water? It had to come out of their sinks, it had to fill their toilets. They left a bucket under the tap and crossed their fingers.

Salt Lake residents couldn't believe that the people in charge had allowed their lake to go dry—not even a regular lake, but the *Great* Salt Lake——even though they could have driven west of town and seen it for themselves, any time over the last hundred years or so. They went home and called the city, then they demanded that God turn their water back on, then they went to church and demanded it, then they burned down the water district offices, then they started hoarding bottles of water and feeling the first inklings of despair. A five thousand-square foot home without a working toilet was just a really nice box. Finally a bunch of Salt Lakers packed up their Suburbans and headed west, a genetic trait of some Americans, and realized that the lake was dry. They looked at the brown stinky mud, the blowing dust coating everything, the gray lowering sky, and realized for the first time in their lives that there was nowhere else to go, and nothing else they could buy to make things better, even if they still had money.

Every place was largely like everywhere else now—turbulent and insecure. You weren't wanted in strange towns wandering around like a tourist, and there was no one available to wait on you if you did. Most of the east coast was filled with sea level rise refugees, who had plenty of water, but substandard housing on the flood plains. No one could stay in California unless they wanted to become a farmworker, since it was reserved for farming and housing the families of the harvesters. Colorado had been taken over by some sort of environmentalists and all the housing now was teepees and yurts and sod houses and the place was covered with wind farms. It was pretty and interesting, but they didn't want visitors unless you were vanning and self-sufficient, which meant, 'bring your own water.' Nevada was full of crazy gamblers like it always had been, who would rob you so they could go back to Vegas and live in the giant air-conditioned sphere, where they could gamble in front of total immersion movies twenty-four hours a day. Arizona—well, the less said about Arizona, the better.

Hundreds of Salt Lake City refugees drove out on the flats, parked, and started stockpiling water, making up neighborhoods as they went along. They weren't paying mortgages for properties in town with no running water. There was plenty of room on the flats, even if conditions weren't ideal. The city and state looked at the rapidly growing migrant camp and figured they had gotten off easy. They quickly set up water storage tanks and plowed a few dirt roads into the playa so that settlers would feel organized and homey. No one died in the Readjustment, except one man who fell off a dam up in the mountains, trying to "free the water" or something. Alas, he went up in the dark, tripped and fell into the dry lake, freeing his soul but nothing else.

But other than that single unpleasant incident—which was kind of funny if you were honest—the Dank residents were an orderly crowd, full of Mormons and displaced migrants from other places who thought the salt flats looked dandy for long-term residence, which told you a lot about the conditions from which they'd fled. They dug outhouses, brought in groceries and tanks of water and Tonka trucks for the kids, so they could dig mines in the salt. The Mormons kept up their dust patches as nicely as they'd kept their lawns back in the days of water. They raked the sand and broomed their plastic rugs that served as lawns.

And Dank had gas, since many people lived in gas vehicles and some of the supply caravans cut through there. They preferred to avoid Salt Lake itself, since it was kind of depressing, even if you were a steely sort of person and drove big rigs through Texas. That state was a lawless hellhole now—destroyed by hurricanes, migrant takeovers, and prairie fires caused by wildcat drillers who had no idea what they were doing, but wanted to get the last of the free oil out of the ground. So much stuff blew up there, they never any electricity, and they'd blow up the roads just for the fun of it if they couldn't find an old well. Nobody wanted to go there, even though they'd let you in.

It wasn't as bad out west, but the great temple in Salt Lake was covered with seagulls and their screechy lifestyles. Nobody knew why they loved the Temple so much. A few times a year, large flocks of ravens would fly by on their way to somewhere else, look at the seagulls, and become angry. The two birds would have a battle around the Temple, black versus white. The seagulls had the size advantage, but the ravens were smarter, and both teams were equally noisy. When they decided to battle, the racket could be heard across the Front, and people would pile in their cars to go watch and make bets on the winner. They took to calling the seagulls "Utah Mormons," and the ravens, "Idaho Mormons" for no particular reason. You couldn't get out of your vehicle for long or be attacked one way or the other, but it was all great fun anyway, a real family affair. People honked their horns to add to the noise and ran around their vehicles when their side seemed to be winning, trying to do victory laps before the birds attacked them. It never became too contentious, since the battle never ended except in a draw, when the ravens got bored and flew away, and the seagulls went back to roosting all over the Temple.

Entire Salt Lake neighborhoods emptied out, leaving behind big new American houses turning the color of the dust, like photographs of the good old days. The airport was partly closed down, but it was still filled with zombie travelers, looking for new experiences and new destinations, where the sky wasn't gray and the water flowed freely. They'd get on any plane that was leaving, going to anywhere, which was how most air travel was these days. It depended on which crew showed up, and where they wanted to go. Did you think you were the only one on the plane? Many of the travelers had a thousand-yard stare as they stood in line, knowing that a tornado, thunderstorm, hacker, suicidal pilot, or even a dust storm kicked up from ten miles away could end their trip before their tranquilizer kicked in. But they were determined to keep trying. Those travel photos had been taken *somewhere*.

If the plane did not reach its destination, the families who were wealthy enough would collect their loved one's body and bury it in a destination funeral. A small patch in California next to Mark Hamill's grave had so many people buried in it that when the big quake came, the whole plot collapsed by several feet. Since burials were all natural now—no caskets or urns or anything—there was nothing there but tons of ashes, which fell into a fault line. The real estate agent who owned the plot was thrilled when he saw the new arrangement. Since there was almost no limit to the number of burials that could be sold, now there was room for even more Star Wars fans.

Tree stopped for gas at a sturdy garden shed with a gas truck parked behind it, appropriately enough, carrying a big "YES" sign. She eyed the pump. There was no way that thing was legal. But the woman was already coming out of the shed, hair tied up in a do-rag and looking like business. Her raccoon followed her. The woman lit up at the sight of the giant hog of a truck, and wrestled the gas hose around like a python before she landed it in the correct hole. It looked an awfully lot like a firehose to Tree. She hoped the truck didn't explode, but clearly the woman had done this before. Mara gave the woman an enormous stack of cash after they filled up, and they drove slowly through the town, sightseeing. Some of the homesteads had drifted onto the blacktop, since it would have been too difficult to drive another quarter-mile and make a proper camp. But there were no laws about it, and if there were, who was going to enforce it? No one.

Instead of parking on the highway, Tree looked for a large open spot where they circled the wagons, which meant jackknifing the truck and trailer to block the wind, where they set up a little camp. The horses looked kind of bleary, it seemed to Tree, but they set them up with water and a block of pot. It smelled clean and clear here, a little salty, and it mixed nicely with the smell of horses. Tree took a handful of pot from them and lay back on her cot. She felt fantastic. She couldn't believe that they were going to pull this off.

She took a turn around the edges of their camp, checking out the other campers. There was a fine assortment of later-model RVs nearby, all lined up like a football game. A row of Dankers were sitting in their lawnchairs, facing the mountains and seemingly oblivious to the bright sun or the glare of the salt flats. They weren't even wearing hats, even though it was at least ninety degrees and their heads were blotchy and sunburned. All were quiet as they looked at nothing off in the distance. They reminded Tree of the blind horses. Their campers indicated that they'd been some of the wealthier residents of Salt Lake, but now stripped of their Vore heads, they were so shell-shocked, they may not have registered the more serious implications of their move yet. Tree went back to their truck and rooted her Rock Springs sunglasses out of her pack. She picked an older woman out of the crowd and approached her, glasses in hand.

"Here," she smiled and held her hand out. "You should take these." The woman regarded her hand, then looked up at Tree, smiling automatically, as one did. She took the sunglasses, then tried to look for something in her pocket. Tree waited, and the woman found a plastic card, which she hauled out triumphantly and tried to hand to her.

"No, it's fine. I am *giving* you these. I don't want them. You will like them. Everything is good." Tree gave her big idiot smile back. It was so hard to communicate with these people.

The woman still looked confused, but not as confused as she'd be when she next tried to do any banking. Tree had recognized the name on the card, and it was now about as worthless as any other piece of plastic blowing around out here on the flats. They really should have changed their money into gold before they came.

"Bartertown!" Tree reassured her, and the woman brightened.

"Oh, my goodness, Bartertown! Let me get something!" The woman got to her feet, while her neighbors, hearing the word, perked up and got to their feet too. Something to do! They began hustling to their campers, groaning under the weight of their entire estate transferred to a trailer. Unfettered by money or property, Tree took the opportunity to escape. At least the sunglasses had found a good home, and those people could swap their stuff for a while, instead of frying their brains.

It was quiet when the wind stopped blowing, except for a few generators and some people talking and laughing. You never heard a Vore laugh, and if they smiled, no one saw it. A few drones buzzed overhead, blinking discreetly. Tree was surprised they didn't honk as they went over, or play ads. But no, these were federal drones and they were almost silent, like the world used to be. It was inevitable that drones would be everywhere in a place this large, but they didn't do anything. The state made sure that no one started a fire or a war, but mostly, they breathed a sigh of relief that thousands of good Americans had simply moved again, planted their flags, and waited for the American Dream to come back for them. It had to. Someone would fix all this.

For anyone who wanted to keep looking, the national vehicle charging network was almost all free, powered by enormous solar and wind farms next to the highways, which in turn had been subsidized by the federal gambling casinos. The highways were shortchanged in this circular economy, since generating more energy was always a priority, but no one needed to drive fast to nowhere, or to the next casino, as if there was a difference. Slow down and think about what you had done. Folks would stop at the casinos to charge up and not come out for hours or days, since they were air-conditioned as well as addictive. Some of them had playgrounds and movie screens under shade roofs, and they all had outhouses. Almost a million composting outhouses had been built all over the west by a federal disaster program and most of them were still in working order, thanks to the van men patrolling like avenging toilet angels. A working toilet was a sign of civilization, and they would like to keep it that way. The garbage pile was over *there*.

Road maintenance fell completely apart after we "ran out" of diesel fuel—another thing no one ever adequately explained, but it didn't matter—diesel fuel was gone and it never came back, like the Colorado River. The feds and the states could get some, since they made their own, but no one else could. Tree suspected that "they" had finally wised up and realized that something needed to stop, before it was a hundred degrees at the north pole, and so "they" made diesel fuel "go away." It was that, or tell the truth about the American Dream, and the government hated to hurt people that badly. That was why they kept sending out those checks every month. They used their diesel for digging out disaster victims and moving dirt around when major roads washed out, and that was about it. No one needed to go interstate anyway. Take a hint for once, and stay home, OK?

Everyone who knew how to operate heavy equipment took home a piece of history and parked it in their front yard, while their neighbors who had only old gas cars in their yards looked on in envy. Later on, they asked the guys to come over and stack their cars up for them, which happened sometimes, because that was the kind of thing men liked to do. Then, flush with prosperity, the highway workers would drive their new cars down the beat-up highway and help other drivers who had crashed or had flat tires from hitting the numerous potholes. They made enough in tips to make it worthwhile. They'd convene in the wrecked and washed out spots, where they'd debate what could be done if only they had some machinery. Some carried orange cones around with them, so they could put out cones when they had their meetings.

Since they had no destination, the van people became good Samaritans of the roads, letting others know when one had washed out or had bandits on it. Maybe some of them did more questionable things, but still, they did a lot more good than harm. They also stayed in truck stops, where the chargers were ubiquitous and they could camp out more or less unnoticed during the long harsh winters. Not that anyone could or would do anything about them. There were way too many humans now without regular homes, and you couldn't just go around trying to evict everyone from everywhere. This was Earth—they had nowhere else to go. Locals who were putting themselves out by working full-time and who had family members living in a boxcar in their yard were not fazed by van people hogging the chargers. Corporate had a camera every five feet—let them come in and take care of it, if it was such a crime. To the employees, it looked more like the government had finally figured out affordable housing, even if it wasn't perfect. Simply existing could not be a crime, or we would end up in even worse places than we already had, even if private prisons had had a good run.

The diesel fuel phaseout started all the garbage dumps, since without diesel, it was too hard to haul it all away. The government didn't care anymore. They had calculated the energy available in all of those people sitting around doing nothing, and it was like China or India out there: they could do anything. If we had built the pyramids with thin old-fashioned people, the beefy units out there today could repair the roads and haul our garbage. They would *pay* them. So far, there were few takers. Most people would rather sit on the commons and complain about the garbage piles.

Or imagine this: maybe we could just stop making so much garbage. The government had hired some excellent social scientists to help them with this anti-garbage messaging, but it was way too late by then. The scientists asked—pretty sarcastically, to tell the truth—"why don't you ask the marketing people how to do it?" and left to drive their government cheese around, since all social science was done by artificial intelligence now, and marketers. The marketers still had jobs, since they had to create more marketing. The marketers assured Congress that everything they did only served humanity's needs, and they had a duty. Some of those folks used to work for the CIA. They knew what they were doing.

Several of those Pacific Island nations would have disappeared under the waves by this time, but some of them had started importing enough garbage to use as levees. After the United States finished building our own levees with plastic waste, we still had plenty, so we sent it off to other countries. Malaysia was now floating on a raft of plastic garbage, since they had made the mistake of importing it into their country years before. When they tried to shut it down, rich countries kept sending it, like a stalker. They wouldn't be sinking into the waves anytime soon, since the entire nation was squishy and buoyant now, bobbing above the waves, and had a mountain of imported plastic in the center of the largest island that was almost five hundred feet high. The citizens wouldn't be fishing, swimming, or living without microplastic poisoning, but they still had their country, and now they had a nice hiking trail with a view. The locals would walk up and look at the ocean. Some of them thought about going to find the American Dream, but others looked at the garbage from America and thought that maybe they'd be better off where they were. It had become much quieter again when the cruise ships left and the supply chain collapsed.

Four Australians sailed out to one of the Pacific garbage patches and corralled it with more plastic netting, threw out some grass seeds, and declared it a new nation—the first nation created entirely by garbage. They put up a flag made from plastic garbage. It started out as an art protest against the shallowness of modern plastic life, but then the guys decided that they liked the place, and stayed. They had a ship full of supplies for when the plastic island got too windy, and they were the kings, after all. They'd discovered that they didn't get seasick, which three of them had not been certain about until they tried it. They all got along and the women who showed up wore almost no clothing, since you had to be half crazy to venture out there in the first place. The plants were also growing like crazy, and the island was on the internet now—the guys made a show about life on the garbage patch on their phones, then bounced it off one of the million satellites to their audience on solid land. No one was investing in it yet, though. The water desalination equipment alone made visitation by more than a few people at a time impossible.

The "land" at Pacifipatch was like a cranberry patch, so it felt kind of weird walking around, if still habitable. The vegetation grew so copiously that you could almost forget you were sleeping on garbage, in the middle of the ocean. There was a lot of marine life around for the adventurous, and the sharks didn't seem to be bothered by the new campers. There were rumors that sea turtles were starting to nest on the patches, so that was a positive sign, if true. Tree would need to see that in person though. Only serious birders, some scientists, and people used to long boat trips came to stay long. If you took a trip all the way out the trash vortex, even that looked good by the time you got there. It wasn't a super-popular destination for humans though, and most opined that they'd wait until more garbage arrived, since it was very hard to get anything worthwhile out there, and everyone had to leave during the storms. But still, it was an interesting place, and would only get larger.

• • • •

Upstairs, the businesses competing for space had not conferred with each other about their plans, since that wasn't their style. Space property had proliferated as businesses sent up satellites designed to claim flight paths in space. It was like a demolition derby up there for a few years. Some of the satellites were nothing but empty shells that, after their short life as legal bookmarks, floated around and acted as speed bumps for the other property claimants, since it would be *cost-prohibitive* to bring anything back down—prohibited, in other words.

Dismayed astronomers who couldn't see a thing now were told to think about all the great photos they could study instead. True, you couldn't see a meteor shower at all, but most of the planet couldn't see them anyway, since they lived in cities. Were astronomers against progress, or just selfish? One of our probes was going to fly straight into the sun, sending information back until the moment it burned up. It was mind-boggling to think about how savvy we were, how capable of transforming our world.

Governments rarely made any rules about how many satellites could be launched, or where they could go, since everyone needed to compete. Nobody in Congress had seen a meteor shower either, since they'd been a cog in the machine forever, so it didn't matter to them. They were the stars, baby. They generally approved every business venture that gave them job security, and designated more money for robots to relieve the stress of all that business. If you couldn't afford a robot, maybe you could be given a job cleaning robots.

There was some sort of settlement on Mars now, pretty messed up but it was there, a *colony on Mars*! They had professional astronauts go up there first and put in some oxygen machinery and a few buildings made from extruded plastic, because what else would they be made of? Then they handed the rudimentary camp over to the private sector, who recruited to get volunteers for the new Martian "lifestyle." Thousands rushed to sign up, even though there was no guarantee of return. But there was nothing to worry about, because you were going to be on the *colony on Mars*!

When they arrived on Mars after three weeks of drugged sleep, the hardy explorers discovered that the resort was little more than a couple of shells of housing that looked like the Flintstones, not the Jetsons. There was no grass, no trees, no farms, no maglev roads with floating cars—which no one had mentioned at all, but people had expectations. That was why they hadn't realized sooner that they had signed up for an indefinite stay, until they had farmed enough oxygen to stock the spaceship to make it back to earth. Minus whatever they were breathing right now, of course, and their food and toilet use. Did they have any idea how much oxygen they sucked up every day? Did they have any idea how difficult it was to dig holes on Mars for even rudimentary toilets? It was all they had now, for sanitation reasons, because they'd discovered that E. Coli bacteria multiplied at insane rates in the Martian atmosphere, for some reason. No one could have foreseen that. To use the bathroom, you had to put on a helmet with an oxygen tank like a scuba diver, then run outside and back, then stand naked in a disinfecting shower. But you could only go outside at certain times of day, or it was three hundred degrees Fahrenheit.

Delivery ships filled with barrels of hand sanitizer alternated with the water ships, since they also had to import water right now, until the farms got going good, and then everything would recycle somehow. Nobody could hitch a ride back with them either, because their fuel was calculated to the ounce, and they had only enough to get home. There were big tanks of urine saved out there on the Martian prairie, for when the technology arrived to recycle it into water. The tanks were filling slowly, since under those living conditions, no one drank much water. Everyone knew that everyone else was peeing in the greenhouse, which had developed a kind of rank odor, but really, it wasn't much different than the soil and nutrients already there. They could get into this recycling science if it meant they could pee in the greenhouse. And what about—? Wouldn't that be good for the trees too? It should be explored.

Even with the human waste issue, the most pleasant job was tending the plants. Some of them had to spend the day in the "kitchen," where they tried to figure out how to make a brown protein paste into something that looked and tasted edible, but no matter what they tried, it still looked like poo. The greenhouse had to watched constantly for its crop of oxygen, and there were panels of monitors on the walls keeping track of everything. The explorers would go in and watch the monitors like they used to watch the stock market. If the plants died, so would everybody else. They loved the place for this reason and came by to talk to and pet the greenery, not knowing what they were doing, but it seemed like it couldn't hurt.

They never hugged each other, because they were aghast at being stuck in space with people who were dumb enough to sign up for this disaster. If they depended on them, they would surely die, and if they made it back to Earth, they were never going to have a reunion with these idiots. Also it was too hard to breathe if they showed any affection for each other, or even talked, so they mostly walked around in silence, except when they went into the greenhouse and begged the plants to let them live. The whole place was an almost an acre, and with the glowing "natural" overhead lights, you could pretend that you were home. It was a jungle in there, and you could always claim that you were sweaty from walking, and hadn't been crying. It was still hard to breathe all the time, since the indoor atmosphere was the equivalent of being at eleven thousand feet on earth. Which goes to show how talented we were, because the travelers were at an altitude of billions of feet. Maybe trillions.

Tree had heard that there were almost two thousand people stranded up there, trying to make enough oxygen to come home. But the space company kept sending up more dreamers, so everyone had to work ever harder to make enough oxygen to keep them all alive, and dig more outhouses, which was very dangerous work and could only be done when it was forty below zero Fahrenheit, otherwise the sun would rise and it would become over a hundred degrees in ten minutes. The wind blew constantly and no one could even stand up very well, let alone dig holes while wearing full spacesuits.

Everyone tried to ignore the fact that no matter how hard they worked, the oxygen in their living habitat was still poor, and the numbers on the monitors never went up, no matter how nicely they talked to the plants and gave them all the nutrients in their pee. Since they never talked to each other, it made it easier to keep pretending. They had to start getting ahead at some point. No one could have made that big of a miscalculation.

The billionaires who had made the miscalculation claimed, from their orbiting space station far outside of any legal jurisdiction, that everyone had known exactly what they had signed up for, because they were serious space enthusiasts. How could a Mars aficionado not know that there were no trees on Mars, or oxygen, or pretty houses, and you couldn't go outside, ever? What kind of a person would get on a spaceship and not do their research before they left Earth? Did people think that they could move to another planet and have it made, after we had killed all the trees on earth, poisoned all the oxygen, drank all the water, and broken the weather? That was not rational. Did they think that we lived in The Jetsons?

The Conflictatorial Personality

Periodically Tree and Mara went to Bartertown together, although some days they barely saw each other while they were there. Mara had a more disciplined trading style than Tree did, to put it kindly, as well as better goods, generally. Her things were all organized and set on the table, ready to go. She swept into the room with two cats trailing her, all smiles as usual.

Tree had her entire bargaining inventory in her arms—flowers from her garden, wrapped in wet rags and ribbons. She was not the laziest trader at Bartertown by a long shot, but she was in the running. The garden of trading food she had planned in her head was mostly potatoes and tomatoes. She meant to do better, but she and Harris liked them and they were good staples. Tree meant to become either more survivalist, or a better homemaker, but so far she hadn't done much except fill several shelves with bottles of water that were probably collecting microplastics in them at this very moment. The volume of products floating around, still, made it impossible to think of essential goods disappearing completely. The water was sort of rationed by high prices, but they had enough here. The crowds at Bartertown never thinned out, and daily there were things that Tree thought she would never see again. It was a circus. Of course it would keep coming. It always had.

Bartertowns had started out gradually but now were everywhere. People were homeless and on the move, and people had stuff. They took over old mall parking lots where van dwellers parked and started trading with each other. They moved down south and took over old flea markets. Finicky types moaned about the homeless and semi-homeless clogging everything up, but with the piles of garbage growing daily and no solutions offered by anyone who was willing to pay for them, the scavenger markets had to be accepted. They made sense, a few people said meekly, but what did sense have to do with making money?

"Capitalism squeals like a pig at Bartertown, as the dominant paradigm fights for life!" blared Mother-of-God Jones, a radical lefty website that Tree looked at sometimes. Let them eat cake!—our own cake, piled high in our fat bursting country. Why had we bought some of that stuff? We had been possessed. Some tried to disparage second-hand goods, but they also came by Bartertown and looked for bargains. Serendipity was back in style now that everything had fallen apart. Despite all the bustle, the garbage piles grew higher and higher.

Mara had some cakes and berries on the table, because naturally she could grow berries too. Tree grabbed a few before they went into her big shopping bag. Mara's plastic containers all had lids and weren't lopsided, even though they were old and no one had been allowed to sell that kind of plastic for thirty years. The new stuff was even worse though, since it was supposed to "biodegrade"—and it did, everywhere. If you left it in your cupboard too long it melted.

They walked downhill to the market, an easy hike if they weren't too heavily loaded. Others were scrambling and hiking down the hill to the big fenced enclosure, arms full of totes, pulling wagons, wearing backpacks. A lot of it was garbage, but maybe it could be transformed. There were well-enforced rules about leaving your trash behind though, and it either went home with you, or was tossed into a dumpster on the way out—where the dumpster was, in turn, raided by people after dark. It wasn't the most elegant system on earth, but it got the job done. Some of the uptowners didn't even have electricity anymore, since they preferred living in the dark to working. They lived the same way the original owners of their homes had: with candles and lanterns. And the lights on their phones, of course. They still burned their houses down sometimes, because they used a lot of unsafe heating techniques, but could usually get hold of a shipping container or a boxcar and start over with donations.

Five or six of the stoned mule deer were on the mountain close to them, sprawled out on their sides in the sun. Tree had even seen them lying with all four legs up, waving them around in the air. It was atypical, to say the least. Their offspring learned it too, and now all the deer could be seen lying around like they were on a beach. Mara said that she'd seen a moose similarly incapacitated. The elk did not seem so affected, either because they did not feast on the marijuana, or were immune to it. It wasn't right, Tree thought, looking at three downed mule deer, as oblivious to danger as the inhabitants of an opium den. But they seemed happy. Tree loved the stoned animals as she loved all the imperfect organisms, just trying to get by in a world that made no sense. Sometimes when everything felt too loud, she'd go out on the hills and sit with them, or lie down in the sun, and look at the world as the deer saw it.

They made it to the gates without being accosted by someone who wanted to trade with Mara before they got inside, which was to be avoided. There were protections inside the fence, but none outside. It was Tree's misfortune that she had befriended such a happy and personable woman, not to mention that Mara traded delicious-looking food. That was not so common at Bartertown and made her instantly respected. Tree had seen her trade two plates of cookies for a set of tires.

"It was a lucky day. He really wanted some cookies, and his car is gone." That was the sort of thing that made it fun. Mara was so slick that she could start a conversation with someone, arrest them with her convivial glow, then swipe a table right out from under them. And so she had a good one, fairly new and not mutilated with graffiti yet. The whole yard was so rutted by prairie dog tunneling that none of the tables sat straight anyway. The prairie dogs were like the deer—imperfect but still wild. They had worse diets than traders, since they got every loathsome inedible treat that came through.

"Nice, Mara," Tree rested her flowers on the edge of the table. They were kind of sweaty but still in good shape. She sat down behind the table and rested her head against a box. No one had enough hands to bring seating, so most of it was boxes, pieces of wood, broken chairs, and rocks. Tree breathed deeply until the dizziness and nausea passed. Mara had traded a loaf of bread for a DVD movie and some government cheese, already, while her eyes were closed. Some people. Tree got up. "I'm going to walk," she told Mara, "but slowly. Maybe I can get a teabag or a clothes hanger or something."

"Just remember—you have to trade these flowers, because you're out of food. Make sure you look sad. This is all you have at your house and you're hungry, because you're not prepared for life."

Easy for Mara to say, with her cute little house, her cute little car and her cute little husband. Tree did this routine about once a week during the summer, so she thought that most of her potential customers were onto her. She was comfortable with not being too prepared for life. It made one neurotic. Then you were hit by a falling tree anyway, because life was far too random to prepare for. Especially now.

Satisfied with her explanation once again, Tree eased over by the entrance gate, a few of the nicer flower stalks carefully arranged over her arm. There was a man with a TV, and a woman with fur coats, nice old fur coats. Wow. Nobody made clothes like that now. Tree could roll up in one and sleep for hours. She couldn't get a fur coat with flowers, but she pulled over to admire them anyway. Some of those animals were extinct, so the least she could do was appreciate the sacrifice the animal had made long ago. She chit-chatted with the woman trader a few moments; she was the inheritor of a fur store and wanted nothing to do with the coats. Maybe another day Tree could make a deal. It was a dumb thing to think about today, when she was already sweating and needed to get back under the awning.

She got her usual snow cone from Fiona for her usual donation of flowers. Fiona kept the flowers cold and crisp in ice and it added to the ambiance of her cart, Tree assured her, so she was always good for a few snow cones. It was true, though. The cart made Tree feel cool just looking at it. She loved snow cones so much, she would sometimes come over in the winter and get one. Harris would deliver one when she was sick, if it wasn't too hot out. Fiona stayed open all year and did well, since her solar panels covered most of her energy costs. After posing stylishly against a post near the snow cone stand for several minutes, where she could soak up both cool air and Fiona's chatter, Tree managed to trade most of her flowers for another backpack, which she didn't need, but she took it anyway. She should have been more alert, but she was smoking something with Fiona that made her not as sharp as she normally was.

"What is in this? I don't remember where I live now. You aren't putting this in the snow cones, are you?"

Fiona giggled, high as a kite. "I don't know, someone gave it to me for a grape snow cone. Told me it was mood enhancer or something. You can't trust those kids." She wasn't more than twenty-five herself. She giggled again and slopped some cherry syrup down the front of the counter. It looked like blood, and attracted even more bees. Well, if Fiona wasn't panicking, then neither was Tree, even if the entire counter was covered with bees. Bees, dirt, flies, sugar, and so much blood, why didn't Fiona clean it up? It was gross. Tree decided that she should walk somewhere else, before Fiona was charged with murder. Her remaining flowers were squashed. She left the good ones with Fiona for the funeral, and made her way back to the big tent like a drunk wading through a stream. She needed to reorganize her life and become more meaningful, she realized. More mindful. Managerial. With—meal plans, garden plans, better barter plans. She should manage her flowers better. Bad flowers. They all bowed their flowery heads in shame, and Tree laughed.

Freshly motivated, she made her way slowly through the crowd. Her attention was diverted by something big under the flapping white awning. A few of the food trucks stayed put, but almost everything in the place had to be cleared out daily to keep garbage from piling up. Nonetheless, someone had put up an entire solar array, plus batteries and adapters. The panels were propped up on some sort of wooden wagon that bowed in the middle from the weight and looked like it came from prairie times. Cables brought the electricity over to the table and the array of outlets and chargers. It was a great idea, since many of the people in Bartertown were without electricity now, and most of them still carried around cell phones and maybe some other gadgets. But how had that man gotten it in here? It had to weigh hundreds of pounds.

Tree was examining the setup when she realized that the proprietor of the table was watching her. What business was it of his if she looked at his thing? It was a public place. It was such a public place, people were encouraged to stare at each other, unlike almost everywhere else. It was old-fashioned that way. If you didn't like it, you could be a Vore. He didn't look like a Vore, exactly, but he didn't look like the usual Bartertown trader, either. He was an older guy, like her, and he appeared to have nothing but his solar setup going. Why did he take up a whole table with that, she wondered? He could put it all on his wagon.

"Can I help you with something, sister?" the man asked, interrupting her train of thought, which then jumped the tracks entirely. This was not managerial. She had just been saying, and now look. No, it was Fiona's fault. She stared at the man. She couldn't even fake him out, since she had no flowers and nothing to charge up, and she was right in front of him. She tried to look stupid, which generally worked, since stupid older women were to be pitied, if you bothered to notice them at all.

"Uh, I was looking at your setup. How did you get that in here? I was wondering."

"I pushed it in here, what do you think I did?"

It was too big, and the man was not. But it wasn't good etiquette to call someone a liar as soon as you met them, even at Bartertown. She felt a spasm as gravity became too much to handle, and she staggered to the man's table and leaned over it, grabbing an edge just in time. "Do you mind if I sit down?" she wheezed, collapsing on a box next to his table like a ballet dancer. He hadn't noticed a thing. Her wind came back as soon as she sat down, but she needed a break. The man was looking at her, not with concern, exactly, but more like he was sizing up what to do if she died on him. How dare he judge her. He was probably brimming with microplastics himself, even if some people with money had those "blood cleansings" that didn't do anything except clean out their wallets. He looked like he ate a lot of junk food.

Tree was mortified anyway. She tried to stay out of the public eye when she was doing her dying swan bit. She was an athlete. This was a woman who'd lived in a tent in an Arizona desert for five months to protect endangered flycatcher habitat. The flycatcher had been wiped out a decade later, but not on Tree's watch. She straightened up, breathing more steadily. "I was out in the sun, I get too hot." The man patted his chair. "Here, sit down. Don't die on me. I have another one." He did too, under his table. He also had a box full of old magazines, actual glossy magazines, that he hadn't pulled out yet.

"You have porno magazines? Really? I haven't seen those in years."

"They're not 'pornos,'" the man said crisply. "Playboy was one of the best fiction outlets of the twentieth century. And it had great interviews." She couldn't tell if he was being serious or not. He couldn't be. But he didn't have even a ghost of a smile.

"Of course, I knew that. I read Playboy." It did have great interviews. She went through the box. It was a time capsule.

"What is this? Does Hustler have the best fiction of the twentieth century too? Foxy Lasses Number Four?"

"That has Miss Ireland and Miss Universe of 2010. No plastic. They don't make them like that anymore."

Tree picked up a Playboy and leafed through it. There was little else she could do, since she didn't feel strong enough to stand up yet, and didn't want to look the haughty man in the eye. She laughed loudly at a cartoon, even though it was sexist and probably not funny. The man regarded her as he fired up a cigarette, and apparently decided that she wasn't going to die or stab him, because he sat down next to her and waited for customers.

Tree finally said, "Um, thank you for letting me sit down. I feel better. But really, how did you get those panels in here?"

"Really, that's for me to know, and you not to know." He had quite a mouth on him. Tree liked that, even if he kept saying the wrong things. He was not a big fellow and had the dusty gray hair of a man who could be included in Tree's dating pool. Did he seem single? She couldn't tell. What kind of a man could you meet at Bartertown, anyway? She had met some doozies, but none with solar panels. He had kind of a smug air about him, like he could watch Tree fall down and laugh heartily, and wouldn't even bother to hide it from her. He hadn't, though. He'd given her a chair. Now he got up and arranged his smut mags on the table, which attracted immediate attention from passers-by. A woman with three identical small children wanted to complain as she lingered by the table, kids held tightly in front of the offensive pictures, but after a few comments from Tree's new friend, they moved on. He had a high-toned vocabulary too, even if calling the woman a "plastic-assed broodmare" was kind of harsh. He never even put his cigarette down.

She admired his skinny butt in his jeans. He was thin, unlike so many of the Runnies, who tended to be at least pleasantly plump, like all the doughy food they ate. His butt was so close to her, she could reach out and touch it, but he didn't seem to notice, because he was yammering away to some guy who wanted to charge up a car battery. Sure, Buster. She moved the chair over, lest she was overcome by an irresistible impulse. Folks had that happen now—irresistible impulses that made them kill and assault people and steal things, and there was no accountability for it. The world was making us all very impulsive and nobody wanted to be responsible for a bit of it. It was an actual legal defense, and sometimes you could get away with it if you had a good lawyer. But Tree couldn't afford a lawyer, so even presented with the completely unexpected impulse to touch this man's rear end, it would never be *irresistible*. She wasn't a child.

While Tree lounged and observed, in no time the man had several phones hooked up to his solar array. While they waited for their charge, customers sprawled in the dirt and read porn magazines. It was brilliant, Tree had to admit. And could the guy talk. He had more BS than Tree had heard since she listened to commercials on TV. So far he'd gathered a box of tools, ten pounds of local potatoes, and a lantern. She wanted to leave, feeling silly sitting in the company of a man she didn't even know the name of, but he'd invited her and given her a chair. He wasn't the usual fashion at Bartertown and therefore interesting. He smoked, for one thing. Who smoked cigarettes anymore? No one could afford them.

He suddenly turned to her, asking rhetorically, "Can you watch this for a minute? I need to pee." And he was gone, with hardly a glance at her. She watched him, fast and intent on his skinny legs. Maybe he really had to pee. What a strange man. She could take all of his magazines and get some good merchandise with them. Instead, she sat and told a few people that the proprietor would return in a few minutes—she was just watching the store. A kid who was much too young to look at porn magazines gave her a cake, and she gave him a Playboy, after talking him out of the Penthouse.

The man returned, as quickly as he had left. She'd been debating how best to handle hanging out there for a few more minutes, not as though she thought the man was interesting, but more as though she was doing him a service. Perhaps she could hold some more things, offer commentary on Playboy articles. She was a very casual and friendly person who sometimes hung out with people at Bartertown. It happened all the time, because she was popular. Everybody has to be somewhere and it wasn't because this weird man was in the same vicinity.

"I got you a cake," Tree told him as soon as he was within earshot, practically wagging her tail for approval. He nodded, sucking on another cigarette. They were not homerolls either. They were Marlboros, which were almost impossible to get and so expensive, Tree didn't know anyone who smoked them. You had to get them right off the supply caravans. This guy had money and connections. No wonder he was weird. He settled into his chair and turned to her, smiling angelically. Tree felt her mouth fall open and she gaped back at him. Good thing she had her sunglasses on, or he might think he'd made an impression.

"I got you a cake," she repeated. "For a Playboy. That's fine, right? I mean, you just left."

"That's great, wonderful. I love cake." To prove it, he opened the paper bag and stuffed a handful of it into his mouth, still holding the cigarette in his other hand. "Lemon. My favorite." What was going on with this guy? You don't eat cake with cigarettes.

"Do you, ah, come here often? I mean, those panels...." she was still hoping that he'd tell her how he got them in, but no such luck.

"I'm here all summer," said the man. "I have some business around here." He would not drop any clues as to what it was, naturally. He could be there to pave over Bartertown and build a Vore hand surgery retreat with capybaras or something. Business people didn't care if it was ridiculous, as long as they got paid. And clearly it was none of her business. He couldn't even play by Bartertown rules, which were laughably simple—you trade things that you already own. Instead, he was getting free sun, and he was selling the sun, because that's how his people were.

Tree, like all of the eco-warriors, wore her hair as long as it would grow. Few of them ever cut it, even if they had retired, and they never really retired. Tree's braid was almost down to her waist, striped with gray now and kind of puny, but she wasn't complaining. Some people went bald from the microplastics. She wore her political leanings like a flag and most people knew what it meant. But she could think what she wanted about Mister Sunshine here. She hadn't said anything rude, mostly because he was good-looking and seemed intelligent, which was kind of a rarity around here. Tree was so starved for intelligent conversation, she'd even talk to a Vore. The Vores usually didn't feel the same way, hence the boxes on their heads. But this man didn't have a headset. She had checked, while he was gone. No headset, but four or five big boxes of old dirty magazines. That was different. He didn't have the buzz-cut that most of the Vores affected as not to interfere with their headsets. He also had nice clothes—ones that had come from slow boats, not from Bartertown. It was confusing. Rich people didn't hang out in this neck of the woods; it wasn't productive enough for them.

He kept handing her his loot, like she was his maid or wife. But still she sat, mesmerized by his bullshit and the usual collection of Bartertown eccentrics. When the man traded a Hustler to a kid who couldn't have been more than nine years old, her mouth had to intervene.

"Do you need to do that? Do you need to let little kids have porn? I know there's no rules, but you don't need a box of cheap beer either. That kid stole it from his parents."

"Oh really?" He turned and gave her his full attention, nipping her irresistible impulse in the bud. He did not seem like a guy to start an argument with, but he didn't have to be so touchy either. She was only making conversation here. He didn't seem to have a problem talking to anyone on the other side of the table, no matter how many dumb things they said.

"How do you know I don't need it?" he snapped. "Maybe I like that beer. I'm not responsible for the behavior of these kids. I'm here to do a little trading, and if these people do not have any situational awareness of what goes on around this place, or with their kids, it's not my problem."

Well, excuse her. It was the braid. A lot of people took it personally, as well they should. Situational awareness was the greatest phrase ever, though. He had nailed it. It was also Tree's opinion that people did not have not enough situational awareness, in particular about the climate, but in almost everything else too, like when they followed the AI in their car over a cliff, or bleached their eyeballs or something, because of some nonsense they heard.

"But still...."

"It's a free country, I don't do anything illegal, and they need to wise up." She couldn't deny it. Tree wondered if rich kids learned this in their private kindergartens, where they sat in a circle and chanted, "It's a free country, a free market, and let the buyer beware (clap clap)." Then one of them would have to sit in the corner for clapping wrong, because second place was first loser, even in kindergarten. She sat a few more minutes.

"I have to go, I left my friend," she said finally. She spoke up to the man's back, who was not annoyed, but had made his little speech and gone right back to doing business. Businesspeople never cared what the hippies thought. Caring about children was for the weak, even if they kept getting rarer. He was collecting a pack of vape cartridges from a pimpled kid who couldn't wait to get his hands on an old copy of Penthouse.

"Well, I have to go! I'll see you around! I'll uh, I'll bring you a flower next time. But you can keep the magazines."

"Flowers! I love flowers. Bring me some flowers." He was speaking to her, but not listening at the same time, again. He was doing the same thing to his customers. He should just put on the headset like the rest of them, but no, he had to be contrary. She'd been listening to him string together a symphony of half-truths, exaggerations, and dumb pitches for almost an hour, and he sounded sincere as a missionary, when she could tell he was not even listening to himself. The customers were eating it up though, smiling and lingering while they leafed through old magazines.

It seemed to be a thing with those guys—being haughty. She wondered if he was being sarcastic about the flowers. Nobody could be sure anymore, even if he was of her generation. Ordinary communication had become distorted. You had to send texts with cartoon faces to clarify your thoughts, even if you had seen the person ten minutes before.

"Here," the fellow said, his attention momentarily back on Tree. He dug into his pocket. "I got you something. For helping me." He took her hand and laid a round object carefully in her palm. It was a poker chip, but instead of advertising or bright colors, it was black and white and divided into two hemispheres: ☯ They were business cards for some people, but this one had no text on it, no identity. It was a quality chip.

"We're all in this together," he told her, leaning into her sincerely. She smelled his faint cigarette breath. She leaned back. Then he reached around her back like he was about to hug her close—but instead he gave her braid a tug: honk, honk. Tree couldn't have been more shocked if he'd shoved his hand down her pants. No plastic there! Her back felt hot where he'd touched her. She froze, looking at the chip. "Well. Thank you. It's very nice." He'd moved back to the other side of the table already, so she resisted the urge to follow him and pat his butt or something. Honk honk. She smiled uncertainly, feeling all off-balance. "I'm, uh, Jennifer. Who are you? "

"Nice to meet you, Jennifer. I'm Terry," the guy said. Totally upper-crust name too. Terrence Von Fabulousborker, the third. Esquire. The Mag-nificent. She realized that she was staring at him, and grabbed her things.

"OK, Ok, nice. Thank you so much. Right. I'll uh, see you later." She scooted out of there, glad that her body was strong enough now to walk away like she meant it. She was like a greyhound—slim and purposeful. Although she was pretty sure that he was making a deal again and not looking at her skinny old butt, you couldn't be positive. Everyone had irresistible impulses, and that particular man seemed like he might have a few of them. She strode off as mindfully as she could without turning around. Tree began feeling weak again on her way home, so, sweating and queasy, she stopped Mara's house and collapsed on the couch, which was as comfortable and welcoming as most of the things around there. Soon she was covered with cats, until she roused herself and brushed them off. Mara put her haul from the day's trading on the counter and they sat down. Tree showed her the poker chip.

"Do you know what this means?"

Mara peered at it. "It's the yin/yang symbol. It means, ah....it's about duality. Good and evil, light and dark, have to work together to make a whole, or something. You can't have one without the other."

Really. That was sort of what he'd said. But why had he given it to her? He was probably messing with her. They weren't going to work together, or form a more perfect union or anything, since he clearly came from somewhere far away from Bartertown. He could have given her a quarter. But the chip was nice, even if it was meaningless. She rolled it between her hands. It was a plain old poker chip, but a little thicker, with no lettering on it. The colors were rich and embossed, not like the cheap ones that came from one of the many gambling palaces around town. A few people brought "luxury" poker chips to Bartertown, but didn't have much luck with them, no matter how nice they were. This was a pretty one.

"Did you trade a flower? That's pretty good. It's better than one of those cheap ones. And nice and new. Was it a guy?" Mara raised her eyebrows. Tree could use someone to be nice to her, besides Harris, although he was a great guy and could play the guitar all night long. Tree opened her mouth to say something, but she couldn't quite decide what, so said weakly, "he wasn't exactly a nice man, I don't think." Maybe a yin/yang man. It was always so hard to tell. She needed more information. Yes, that was it. She wouldn't let Terry see her, and she'd try to get more info. She was just under the weather the first time and couldn't figure him out.

They were still hanging out in the cool house when Hani got home. When he had short days he came home, because the atmosphere on campus was a pressure cooker. He should have been dealt a better hand of cards than teaching calculus at a tiny university, but he took it as seriously as if he taught at Berkeley. And maybe he would have, if most of the California university system hadn't been flattened by the earthquake. Instead he had his intelligence insulted four days a week by sulky Vore students who wanted intelligence beamed into their brains like another product. Thinking, it turned out, was not a valuable commodity in the twenty-first century. If it could not be transferred via a computer program, then was it actually intelligence? A few of those kids had chips in their heads that made them ask this, since their parents had wanted them to be precocious. Smart people with no ulterior motives had agreed on what were the best things to know, and they were all available on a headset program or an implant, if you were a first-adopter.

And these kids were supposed to be the best and brightest—future rocket pilots. No wonder Hani was always in a sour mood. He soldiered on because of his love of math and his prestigious position as an actual professor. The man still read real books. They had bookshelves in their house, something Tree and Harris could only weakly emulate, since most of their books went back to Bartertown.

"Oh my love, every day they get stupider!" Hani hollered into their bedroom, tossing his bag of proffered knowledge on the bed, where it sat forlornly. He stomped back into the main room, waving his hands dramatically while his black hair flew in a halo around his head.

"Why do they even come? They don't want to take off their headsets! They don't want to learn! They listen to music while I am trying to explain problems! Then they come find me after class and tell me that they don't understand; why won't I curve their grade more!"

Hani kept his head for the entire day of teaching, but when it was over, he came home and stomped around until he felt better, Mara nodding in agreement. They were all in agreement—Vore children must be more worthless than their parents, and their parents were—well. Tree had heard this rant before, and Mara must have heard it hundreds of times now, so they were unconcerned. Hani liked to work off steam this way.

"They come in there, and they're doing business while they're supposed to be working on math. They have those things right on their laps, like a puppy, and they're talking to it while class is going on. They don't know when the exam is, and why can't I deliver it to their headsets for them to do when they get time? Each one of them! They all want it programmed into their sets, because this is my job!"

Tree and Mara exchanged a look. It was a good thing that people like them existed, to uphold some standards, because clearly the Vores were not going to do it. Tree's son had been raised before headsets, but was far too intelligent to be converted to them anyway. She had raised him with situational awareness. Hani finished stomping around and sat on the couch, refreshed. He dug a little tool out of his pocket.

"Okay, break it that bot, would you, hon? I have to put some commands on it."

Tree's mouth fell open, and she stared at Hani, who looked prim. Mara laughed at her shocked expression. She had done this on purpose. It had been hard to keep the robot under wraps long enough for unveiling, and Mara had been afraid the thing would come rolling out every time Tree was in the house. They responded to things like a living creature, even though they weren't supposed to. The cats could wake it up by getting too close, and it would try to feed them, or make them go outside. One night this had caused pandemonium when the bot rolled into the kitchen and started trying to feed the entire tribe of cats that came in when it was cold, along with a few skunks. After that, it was turned off every evening, which should be simple, but was not. Hani had to disable something. Mara felt like the robot was going to get its revenge for this and electrocute Hani with one of its spider arms. It was in most robot movies, so he was well aware of the danger. He assured her that it couldn't do that, and in fact, the robot was intellectually disabled, as robots go. He dealt with the more mechanical aspects of it, not the thinking stuff.

It was creepy how the tech nudged its way into your life, then spied on you. She should have turned the thing off right from the start. Tree had warned her. Now it knew about their sex life, and who knows what that might bring. Probably more porn on the internet.

Mara vanished into the bedroom, and after some thumping, a meter-tall shiny blue robot glided into the room and stopped. Tree rarely got close to the Vorebots, but it gave her the same feeling up close as they did from afar—it was too sleek, convenient, and irrationally expensive to not be dangerous. Look what had happened to the Vores with the headsets.

Mara stopped the thing in the middle of the room, and started messing with some of the panels. "This is a generic one, it can do a lot, but it's not like—smart? It can do all kinds of tasks, but it's not 'thinking.' That has to be added later, when they load them up with all that learning software. We don't talk to it or anything. It doesn't even have the language part in."

The bot suddenly spun around and sprayed air freshener in her face, making her jump up and wave her hands at it. "OK, it wasn't supposed to do that. I don't think. Hani uses it a lot more than I do."

Tree continued staring at the thing and forgot her stomach. It was so shiny. It had a subdued glow, with some sort of metal finish that never had a bad angle and wouldn't show dirt. This was a slimmer one without all of the special features, about three feet around and as high as Tree's waist. It had at least six wheels that turned in all directions, so that the bots always moved smoothly and could make tight turns, the better to scare you with, my dear. There were small lights at its midsection, capable of anything from a moon glow, to a laser that could blind an attacker—or put on a laser show, if you paid for the app. On the outside were hooks and bolts and straps to attach worldly goods, and even a couple of small drawers. It was a four hundred-pound purse.

Hani pulled out some kind of robot controller and connected to the bot. "Make its arms come out," Tree demanded. She hated the arms more than anything, the incredibly long spider arms with grippers on the end of them. They telescoped like an old radio antenna, and the metal in them was very strong. You wouldn't bend one if you ran into it, only end up with a nasty bruise. Some of the bots had a hundred yards of arms in them, all coiled up, and like the bots themselves, the arms moved a tiny bit faster than anyone could get used to. Even if you could become accustomed to metal poles flying by you, they always managed to do it in a way that startled the most humans, except the Vores, of course, who claimed that they weren't bothered by them a bit. The Vores, like the robots, were ill-mannered, so what was the problem? They were a synchronous unit.

The silver arm reached up to the ceiling, then the claw clipped a book off a shelf a few inches from the top. So that was how they got their books down. Hani and Mara had bookshelves all the way to the ceiling, which seemed like a good idea for insulation too. Tree realized something else.

"This is how your house stays so clean. I should have guessed. I thought you were the cleanest person on earth."

Mara grinned. "That is the best thing about it. It cleans at night, puts itself back in the closet."

The robot, guided by Hani, delivered the book to Tree, and she took it gingerly, hoping that the thing wouldn't go haywire and snip her finger off or something. Then it stayed put directly in front of her, watching her, she imagined.

"Make it go away."

"It's not looking at you," Hani laughed. "It kind of went to sleep, since we didn't tell it to do anything."

Hani tapped on the computer and made the Vorebot's arms come out all at once, five of them. Like snakes coming out of holes. Tree gave an involuntary little screech. "I changed my mind. Don't do that. Make it go away." Hani moved the robot away from her, spider arms hanging limply, except for the one on top.

"Oh my god, is that an eye? That is horrible, oh my god, yuk, who does this?"

Hani obligingly made the top arm retract. It closed the eye right before it went in, making Tree wince. "There are not too many eyes. This is a new feature, one that I'm working on. You can see how useful a long eye might be."

"A long eye. No, I don't see it. I wouldn't let the thing in my house. I know they have eyes, but do they have to make it like—like our eyes?"

"Well, no, they don't, and that's what we're testing. A lot of people do prefer the eyes to be less human-like."

"I'm surprised." Tree imagined a Vorebot with an extended human eye watching the baby all night, ensuring that the kid would have screaming nightmares his entire childhood. If metal eyeballs started flying around in public, Tree would never be able to go out again. As excited as she was to see the thing up close, it gave her the creeps. Hani and Mara didn't seem to share her trepidation, but then they were used to it. Who would do that, put human eyes on robots? Not Hani, she hoped.

Hani had been responsible for his wife getting public texting, though, another tech toy that almost everyone regretted, but not until they got tired of it. Public texting had been responsible for so many irresistible impulses, it was once called "more dangerous than cigarettes," but that meant pretty much nothing, since everything was as dangerous as smoking cigarettes now. Going outside.

Public texting was an app pushed by the car companies, still keen on getting everyone to live in their vehicles even if they had somewhere else to sleep. The texting feature was controlled by the same AI that controlled our phones, so theoretically, abusive or pornographic messages would be deleted before they reached the outside world via a glowing panel on the roof of the car. This sometimes worked, but it was easy to go around the filters and work out new codes to call someone a dick at high speeds. In the four years after public texting was introduced, highway deaths went up by five hundred percent, and the whole caboodle of cars with the big PT screens on their roofs were recalled. It was voluntary, of course, because you couldn't just take possessions from people. Owners were encouraged to give up their megaphones by bribing them with new electric cars, but some refused and carried on with their foul messaging until the software finally gave up, stopped from upgrading by court order. People saw the old PT cars on the highway and tried to run the things off the road, even though they couldn't talk anymore. This caused a few more deaths, but at least they were righteous. Everyone moved on to vehicles that intimidated others in the more socially acceptable ways—size, noise, and opulence.

One day Mara picked Tree up in a strange car that had a big box on the top of it. "My car is in a bad mood," Mara explained. Then they'd had a stressful trip to the Vore store, which had been littered with Vorebots today, arms flying everywhere. There had been a child in there with a Vorebot of his own—a child-sized Vorebot, for a child wearing a headset and as usual, observing none of the normal social conventions. He blocked the aisle with his miniature parade and yelled at Mara, "Do you know how to make macaroni and cheese with hotdogs?" Mara looked sympathetic but Tree was mad. Did they think everyone was a servant? "You little mutant," Tree started, but Mara shut her up.

"The poor boy, he just wants some real food. He's smart. He can see that I cook." Mara patted him on the headset, which made a hollow sound. Clonk clonk clonk. She hoped his head wasn't shaved already.

The Vore boy made both of them crabby. On the way home, a caravan of Vore cars was blocking an intersection, gossiping about their perfect lives behind masks. Instead of waiting for them patiently, as everyone else was expected to do, Mara blasted a message:

PUBLIC ROADS ARE FOR EVERYONE

She accompanied it with some laser light effects, so that the Vores noticed, even though it was generally beneath them to acknowledge a Runnie. They still didn't get out of the road. But their vehicles noticed too and seemed to obey, as they rolled back a few yards to make room for her car. The Vores stopped yakking at each other out their windows for a few seconds and checked their brakes. They stared down at Mara's car as she inched up. They wanted that texting feature back. While they were gawking, Mara eased her way through the wall of giant vehicles. They smiled and waved at the Vores as though this was all perfectly normal.

"Did that just happen?" Tree asked.

"I don't know. No, it couldn't." answered Mara, who had never used the app, even if she had begged Hani to let her use the car when he got access to one. Her eyes widened at the thought of having a PT car that could order others around. No wonder people had gotten into trouble with it. They drove up behind a puttering car that could barely get up the hill, since it was at least as old as Tree. Mara flashed it.

GET OUT OF THE WAY

The car did nothing except continue creeping up the mountain. The owner stuck his hand out the window and flipped them off, a form of public texting that still worked as well as it ever had.

"You can't do it to old cars, they don't understand," Tree told her, and Mara looked peeved. It was her toy.

"I know that, I'm only experimenting. I don't want to kill somebody." She drove the PT car across town and found a group of Vore rigs parked behind a church. They had some kind of Tupperware meetings where they traded Vore stuff and compared all their stupid Vore gear, since the slow boats couldn't keep up with the volume of their shopping. Even they had their Bartertown. Their shining vehicles filled the parking lot, waiting patiently for more electronic gadgets to fill their square footage. Mara turned on the PT.

"Let's see what this does," she told Tree.

SOFTWARE UPGRADE FIVE MINUTES

The vehicles processed the message one by one, and a soft moaning noise began coming from under their hoods, gradually filling the parking lot. Their glossy paint seemed to lose its glow, and their tires flattened a little. Their wipers started moving and the emergency flashers came on. Tree couldn't believe what she was seeing.

"What did you say to them?"

"They think they're dying. They think that if there's an upgrade, they lose their identity. They come right back, smarter, but they can never seem to remember it."

"Oh Mara, look at them. I never thought I'd say this, but I feel sorry for them." That was how you got sucked into robot life. They gave the robots emotions, as best they could, and we responded to them. "Turn it off. It works, we can see it—you can talk to the other systems. What did Hani do to that PT? He's an evil genius!"

Mara looked honestly confused, now that she was over torturing the machines. She turned off the sign. The vehicles quieted down and regained their brighter plumage. "He wouldn't do that. He didn't tell me. It must be an accident."

"That is no accident." It wasn't as good as crashing the international banking system, maybe, but it was still impressive. Mara did not share Tree's enthusiasm. She had a mind to turn it off entirely and drive the demon car home, but then she saw the Vores starting to trickle into the parking lot, arms full of goods, just like they did every day, rain or shine. They strutted to their vehicles like they had solved world hunger, with no idea that their cars thought they were about to die. But they were all horrible people, in their rolling thrones. Enjoy the ride home. They had airbags.

On the way up the hill, Mara flashed two cars with PROMENADE YOUR PARTNER, and they both veered out of their pre-programmed tracks to side-swipe each other. The Vore drivers, inattentive as always, did not see the flashing sign and had no idea why their cars had malfunctioned like that, since Mara turned it off as soon as the cars hit each other. The Vores jumped out of their bent vehicles, pointed their headsets at each other, and began arguing about whose fault it was.

Tree brayed with laughter. "What did you do?"

"Ohmygod," Mara said, instantly contrite. It had happened again. She didn't think they would even know that one. Those vehicles had everything stuffed into their tiny car brains, it seemed. There was so much extraneous information floating around, it was a wonder everyone wasn't killed daily by errant signals, as we all played telephone on a grand scale. Tree laughed in the passenger seat while Mara drove down four side streets to escape any witnesses. She parked the PT car and refused to go out again, no matter how Tree begged.

"We barely got started with the experiments," she argued, but Mara put the keys on the refrigerator. She even confessed the entire incident to Hani later. What was it with these people and their honest and open relationships? Tree suspected that Hani had been messing with a few things he shouldn't have been messing with, then forgot to tell his wife. The PT car was still parked behind their house under a tarp. "We could hack it," offered Tree, having checked out a few research papers about PT cars. Mara refused, even if Hani would never find out.

Tree left Mara and Hani to their evening, and walked slowly the rest of the way home. Harris was out, so she got a beer and sat in the back yard. She kept revisiting that Vorebot at Mara's. It seemed so alien in their sensible home, even if Hani did work with it. People shouldn't be so comfortable with them. She stuck her feet in the pool and decided that maybe she should have two beers, as well as some pot. It was so warm, even after dark, that she remained sitting outside in the quiet until she heard Harris come in. Wired by the alcohol and pent-up news, she pounced on him as soon as she heard him in the kitchen.

"Come out here! Sit by the pool!" Harris obliged, toting his own beer, which was fortified with some sort of hallucinogenic that the kids loved. He was also pretty high this evening, since he'd been down the hill busking for the Vores. On Friday nights, the Vores gathered at a high school track to max out their glutes as they fast-walked around the track, both ignoring and socializing with each other at the same time, as one did in their world.

Harris sat on a barstool in the middle and played, not having any idea if any of them actually heard him. He preferred to think that they did. They threw their change into his guitar case when they stopped for an energy drink, and told him that he was amazingly talented and articulate for a Runnie. His case became filled with money and poker chips, which even some Vores thought were as valuable as real money. Everything was an illusion, after all. Or maybe they were only throwing them away. Everyone was so careless with their garbage. Harris played for hours, nipping at his fortified drink.

It was nice to have the Vores using the tracks, at least, since the schools were also emptying out. They'd started to lose students when the feds refused to let teachers work while wearing headsets, which baffled many of the parents. How were they supposed to communicate with the kids if they didn't wear headsets? Children would go home and report having to look at a bare face for hours, which fascinated them so much with all the changing expressions, they couldn't remember a thing it said. A lot of the optional subjects had been dropped by that time anyway, since there was no need for art or music teachers when you could buy all that stuff on a program, taught by a better teacher. And there was definitely no need for a PE teacher, since a teacher who didn't wear a headset wouldn't know how to check the kids' healthset to find the best physical fitness program for them. They wouldn't be able to live up to their full potential if they were injured by careless physical activity. The running tracks sat empty as the kids all went home and sold things on-line, which was about the only education anyone needed, anyway.

"Tree, I had a beautiful evening. The Vores love me like a trained monkey." He didn't usually talk about the Vores that way, but four hours of them was soul-numbing. "I could have been in a symphony orchestra, if orchestras still existed. I could have been a gentleman. It's not my fault that I was born in the wrong era."

Forget her news, Harris needed a hug. Tree snorted. "Wrong era? That's not the only problem. You're too smart to become a Vore. You're better than that."

"I look at their tight little asses and their big bland faces, and I wonder why they get to tell us that's the way it should be. They're all out of their minds."

"Oh Harris—because the world is bought and paid for by money, not by doing what's right. You know that. Your music is worth way more than the approval of some idiot Vore. You know how they are. They have no sish-situational 'wareness."

"No what?"

"They're dumb. Who cares what they think?" Tree was eager to change the subject to something that wouldn't make her mad. She was a little drunk and it was a bad combination. She got out the poker chip.

"Hey, what does this mean? I got it at Bartertown today." She handed him the chip and he took in the symbol: ☯ Like Mara, he knew the idea but was not great at articulating it.

"It's for....dichotomy. Opposite but connected. The two fish need each other to make the whole." Proud of himself, he got each of them another beer from the kitchen. What a great symbol, thought Tree. It was a circle because it fit together, like ecology. But Terry hadn't given it to her because of ecology, that was for sure. Maybe he was making fun of her for being a hippie. At least it was an honest profession. But he'd given her a gift. She hadn't even given him a flower.

"What if a man gave it to me? Is that good?" She was drunk enough to ask, holding her breath.

"It is if he's a fish, and so are you. Then you can spawn. But nobody gave me a charm tonight. Not personally. He probably didn't give it to you because he's on your wavelength, though. The Vores give me chips too."

"He knew what it meant. He was....smart," said Tree, not knowing this at all. Just agree with her. "He said, 'we're all in this together' and he gave it to me." And he pulled my hair. It wasn't *nothing*.

"Why are you asking me then? You don't want to hear my opinion, you want to tell me. Did you give him anything? Was it a red-hot trading orgy? Does it say 'be mine' on it? You should check."

"I didn't have anything. I have to go back....."

"Really? You're going back now? Good for you." Harris perked up for some gossip about a possible man in Tree's life. Tree was offended. Did she have a big sign on her back that said "Needy"? She didn't try to find girlfriends for Harris. Not that she needed to, since women still stared at him when they went out together, even though she was standing right there next to him. She remembered how Terry's hand had felt on her back.....she babbled on, making that thought go away.

"He's not a very nice guy though. He acts like a Vore, except he's not. He ignores people even when he's speaking directly to them. Like....like a rich man."

Harris looked at her for a second, then howled with laughter, finally letting out the tension he'd been feeling build up all night. "A *what?*—a *rich* man? Did he have a treasure chest? Did he show you his pot of gold?"

Tree was filled with drunken outrage. He had been complaining about them five minutes before. She couldn't quite say what it was about Terry that made her suspicious, but Harris would have understood her in college. Normal men, the ones she had known all her life, didn't act like that. They didn't act like the world should kiss their ass just for existing. They didn't know how to do it—you had to be born with money to know that.

Harris got up. She wondered if she had annoyed him somehow and he was leaving. Oh no. Why couldn't she mellow out? She'd said something wrong. They didn't talk about money, and rarely had, except for figuring out how to split the electricity bill. Maybe it was a sore spot with him. Maybe his parents had cut him out of the will. But instead of leaving her in the yard, he got his guitar and two more beers, and swayed back to his lawn chair. Handsome Harris, in his nice shirt and his voice as smooth as high-fructose corn syrup, even when he was drunk. He'd had lessons. It was so unfair. Then he revealed how monstrously unfair it really was.

"A rich man freaked you out. I never heard such a story. Maybe I could have guessed, but still. I forget that we had way different lives. I have to tell you something, Tree—*I'm* rich. I'm rich as hell. I thought maybe you'd guessed. It was never important." He held up the poker chip, still sitting next to his chair. "Yin-yang. And here we are, me speaking directly to you."

Tree wanted to burst into tears, she wasn't sure why. Why had she drunk so much? She should probably drink more, she figured, since it was too late now, and Harris had brought her another beer.

"How can you be rich? You're *sincere*," she blubbered. "You never even became a Vore."

"You didn't wonder why I was so carefree all the time, when I showed up here with nothing but an old car and five guitars? People with money can do that."

It was true. There was almost no real credit anymore except for ridiculous consumer frippery, so if you were broke, you were really, really broke, except for Bartertown. Harris had done all right. He sang his songs, put his money in the bank, and went out to the woods for months at a time. Once he spent two years in Alaska, looking at the sky a lot. There was a lot of sky here too, even though it was kind of hazy. Then his parents had died, as all parents do, and left their money and a few nice homes behind.

"People don't have to always follow a pattern, Tree. I can be rich and nice."

"They never are. Even if they start off nice, they get warped and forget about everything except money."

"Excuse me, Tree. This is what I'm explaining. Also, I have known other rich people, and they were nice." Tree looked at him as though he'd come home in a headset. Harris figured that both of them were too drunk to have this discussion, so he should shut it down. He was living proof that a rich person could be kind and normal, because if he wasn't, then Tree wouldn't like him, because she was very sensitive about those things. Therefore she was wrong. Besides, they'd been over it before, minus his admission of wealth. She must not remember that Harris' family had been fairly rich, by most standards. But he had always referred to wealth in a vague, non-personal way: maybe rich people weren't always that bad? Maybe they had an ailment caused by their way of life? But why point fingers when it was a shared planet and we all had a hand in it? The technology and the robots were going to fix things, and rich people made those possible.

Even he didn't believe that last one. He had *seen* robots. But that was the story, anyway. Could they fix it before we had a dead planet?

It was rude to ask, when all the technologists were working so hard. No wonder everyone had to put on a headset to get some peace and privacy. Tree was staring at the poker chip, a little cross-eyed. She was taking it well, he thought. He strummed his guitar.

"Hey, do you want to hear it? You should hear this, it will make you laugh."

"I doubt it. Hear what?"

"My song. My song that made me a household name. I had a few good ones. During my twenties I was supporting myself, but one song I wrote went nuts. Some guy contacted me—he was saying that he could brand it, and it would make money like crazy. I didn't even know what he meant, really, and I was drunk? I didn't have a lawyer or anything. How can anyone be an artist when everything is for sale?" He shook his head sadly. Tree couldn't agree more, just like they had in college. It was obscene, and had stopped her from expressing her deep artistic passions, except in anarchy. Harris cleared his throat, then strummed the chorus that had made him a millionaire.

Forces shake, propel our world
All our weaknesses revealed
Can we save this mortal sphere?
Trust each other, lose our fear.
(lose our fear, lose our fear)

Even in her altered state, Tree couldn't make it work.

"Harris, that sucks." But she knew the song. She'd heard it on the radio a thousand times one summer. It had a kind of vague mysticism, just what the masses liked. She'd thought it was awful then too. But it was Harris. Her old friend.

"See, I told you. It doesn't mean anything. None of it made any sense," Harris was relieved to lead Tree astray so easily, even if he had to out himself on the song. She must be loaded. "I'm not much of a songwriter, but I wanted to see if I could crack the commercial market." And he wasn't done with the story yet. His song hung on for so long, Harris coasted on it for a few years. He hired a great backup band that could write songs and played a sixteen-city tour, where he blasted out long solos that brought the crowd to their feet, and the girls to his feet. Classical guitar it was not. But he was twenty-six, so he could fake it. He had the rest of his life to play classical guitar, which was more suited to solemn old men anyway, who could give it depth.

But he hadn't reached the truly shocking part of his story. The tour and the cocaine had been real, but the jackpot had been when his song was used for a beer commercial.

"How would you use that for a beer commercial? Mortal beer! I fear, I've lost my mortal beer!" Tree sang, and felt her stomach lurch. No more beer for her. A fox outside the yard yapped. Probably waiting for them to go inside, so it could get a drink.

Harris hushed her. He wanted to finish his story. Then his conscience would be clear, and she might forget half of the conversation by morning.

"Listen, I'm almost done. I changed a few of the words, so that it ended with 'share this beer.' Tree, they paid me twenty grand for *that*. Then I got to be in the commercial too, because I was pretty hot back then." He smirked at the memory, then resumed. Tree rolled her eyes.

"Anyway, you get together and drink beer and save the world. We recycled all the cans and made a solar airplane out of them. When the plane was finished, they used it in their advertising for years. It was epic. My face was on it."

Tree glared at him, and he remembered his audience. "So, the commercial was really high budget. There were a lot of dogs, lots of hot women. I was a surfer, right? I ran in from the water, and I planted my surfboard in the sand so you could see the brand. Someone threw me a beer, and I caught it in one hand, then I caught my guitar in my other hand—BAM BAM, really fast—" (he demonstrated), "then I sang. I really caught them too, Tree, it wasn't special effects. I was by the campfire singing with all these girls, then at the end I take a big swig of beer, and a bikini girl winks at me. Then, we throw around a big beach ball that looks like the earth. The dogs chase it, but in slow motion, as we're all running down the beach. Then we all jump higher and higher and like, *overcome* our problems, as the earth ball floats above us, all restored. Then, we pick up all of our trash at the end. We literally raked the beach. It was visually stunning, Tree. They got an award." He smiled at this fond memory. Tree was reeling. She needed to wade through the internet to find this commercial. How incredibly nauseating.

"You had dogs?" Oh no, I should have left the dogs out of it, Harris thought too late.

"Yes, Tree, it was years ago. You'll get a dog someday. They'll come back." Tree looked mournful and pulled her feet out of the pond. They were cold anyway.

"I have to go to bed. Everything in the world is a lie." She picked up her socks and marched off dramatically. She had to concentrate on her feet, one two, one two. She'd forgotten all about Terry, at least momentarily. Another person she knew nothing about, but he probably also lied about things. A lot of the men in the world were given wealth just for showing up—that was their real secret. No wonder they couldn't be honest about anything.

Half an hour later, while she was turning off the lights, Tree thought fuzzily: *Harris* was rich? That was the whole point of his story, right? She was fairly sure, but she needed to nail it down before she forgot. But how rich? Rich enough to not worry about anything.

Tree felt a strange sensation in her, one she wasn't very familiar with: security. Harris wouldn't leave her here to die if something happened to her house. If one of the wildfires took it out, or if Tree became too disabled to do anything, he would help her, and because he had money, he could. She wouldn't have to throw herself into the hot pots, or go commit crimes, so that the state would have to put her up in the senior prisons. She would never have to go to court and say, quite honestly, "there was nothing irresistible about it, Your Honor. I planned to steal that junk, because I can't deal with a thing, anymore." For a crime like that, they didn't even give you a real judge, but a robot that calculated your sincerity, then gave you a sentence based on algorithms. You still had to call the robot "Your Honor," though, because the whole process was designed to degrade. The prisons themselves weren't bad, Tree had heard, but she needed to be outdoors.

The bed under her felt a little more stable as she drifted off, although the rest of her body felt more abused than it usually did.

Tree woke in the morning with an aching body and a realization that she wouldn't be getting up today. She confirmed this by opening her eyes and watching the room spin around with her breathing. The microplastics were swarming, and they were relentless. She sat up some time later and fumbled for the remote, flipping on the TV. Harris knocked on her door after a while and brought her a pitcher of ice water before he decided to go over to Bartertown. He patted her on the head and said, "Hang in there, Tiger," before he left.

Tree loved the television. There was even more of it now than there had ever been and it was free. Televisions as big as a car could be had for a song at Bartertown. Tree's was much smaller, of course. All of the channels were broadcast from right here in town, since TV stations cost almost nothing to run, and the commercial breaks were so long and invasive that the stations paid for themselves. Most of them were run by AI, except for the serious news, and there was an endless supply of media out there. There were channels that had nothing but old football games, old cowboy movies, Academy Award winning movies. There were hundreds of specialty influencer channels, of course. Tree used to watch them when she was drunk, "for research purposes," but after Harris caught her screaming at the TV a few times, he made her stop and told her to go visit the deer.

There were channels that showed nothing but Sesame Street, all eighty-nine years of it. You'd think that with few young children around, it wouldn't be popular, but adults loved it. Its relatively slow pace appealed to their fried-out brains. There were stations that broadcast footage from drones all over the world, almost in real-time. The AI would go through it as fast as it was submitted and pick out the most spectacular sights—the wars, the wildfires, the migrant boats in danger on the high seas—then relay them. You literally did not know what might come on next, and it was riveting. But it was not safe for children or anyone else either, if you had a conscience. Tree liked the news shows, where she had her favorite newscasters and would root for each one, in case they needed her support.

"I love you, Shankerry! Nobody tells it like you do!" she hollered, even though she knew that since Shankerry was cashing a paycheck, she wasn't telling it *exactly* like she was. But close enough. Nobody wanted to be a journalist anymore either, since every time they told a good story, people would send them death threats or vows of eternal fandom, just to show that they were engaged. When the politicians came on, Tree yelled at them too, in case they were listening in. But that was the great thing about TV—nobody was listening in. Tree had checked, naturally, and there were no cameras on the televisions. She muted the commercials and studied them like a disease. The humans in them were so excited, all the time. They dressed in loud, bizarre outfits. They danced, they grinned like Cheshire cats, they hugged, they shouted, "how did I ever miss this deal?" Everything in the ads assaulted the senses, yelled at and pummeled the audience, even with the sound turned off.

The smallness of the invalid's world was like a return to a time before. When your body was too weak to move and the world was forced to retreat, it was crystal clear that we had no idea what we were doing, and had never possessed situational awareness.

Tree dreamed of a still silent place where time was not measured by hours or productivity, but by moods and seasons and the movement of the sun. She dreamed of cold stream water that was undammed and unclaimed, moving quietly through the forest, untouched except by those who needed it. She was lying in that creek, as weightless as a breath, while the water fell over her body, into her mouth, and left her cleansed inside and out. She dreamed that she walked for days, her thirst finally quenched, following a creek that was deep and rocky and went so far into the woods, no man-made sound could reach her. There she could rest for as long as she wanted. Her dogs would be there, and so would other animals. She would be d accepted by them like in those picture books of the Garden of Eden. Her strength would come back as she soaked up the sun and the clean air, and slept right there on the ground. It was safe there and no one could touch her. She could rest her feet in the creek until they were numb, and drink as much of it as she wanted. No one could find her there if she didn't want them to. Nobody could tell her to move out of their way, or be loud and aggressive, or tell her lies. When she was completely rested, she could go back to her normal life, and would tell no one where she had been, or they would search for it and use that up too.

Tree roused herself long enough to drink some ice water and watch some cowboys ride across the wild west, where we had manifested our destiny in the only way we knew how—by killing everything in sight. Tree recalled the Glitterati, a frequent invader of her dreams, with their stupid clothes and their youthful insolence. The influencers had moved into the mountains years before, flush with cash from their internet careers. There was a lot of loose money around then, and the influencers were everywhere. They were very young and thus stupid, but there was no denying that they were wealthy. Like the Vores, they assaulted the senses, seeming to take up much more space than they needed. They were loud and brash and invasive of others personal space and would include anyone in their their sales pitches, undeterred by frequent eyerolls and flipped middle fingers. A lot of them had already started wearing the headsets when they moved into the area, but not constantly. They moved around in packs, talking to their internet audiences in pack-mode, and selling, selling, selling—candy and exercise gear and jewelry and steroids and self-actualization lessons.

Their name came from the glitter clothing that they popularized. This was a deliberate move on their part, because glitter had finally been outlawed, due to its unique water-polluting qualities. Naturally, there was a delay between the law being passed and it being enacted, and the Glits moved in to take advantage. The ban had nothing to do with either class or generational warfare, but the Glitterati were deeply offended by the law anyway, and they introduced the glitter-covered garments "in protest." They were about as practical as they sounded—itchy and uncomfortable, shedding noxious glitter everywhere they were worn. It became a local issue after several hundred of the Glitterati moved into a compound in Big Sky and plowed their pretentious mansions into the now glittering mountains. It was hard to believe that hundreds of young people could have been made wealthy by something as dumb as glitter clothing, but that was because people were too old to understand, apparently. The Glitterati built a water slide a mile long, then stampeded farm-raised buffalo all over their property before they shot them from giant ATVs in gory mass slaughters. All of this was clearly visible to anyone with binoculars, but instead of asserting control over the little brats, Big Sky authorities drove up to the gates of the acreage and left without entering, as though to say, What can you do? They paid taxes. A lot of them.

The bison that weren't sacrificed were left to roam around Big Sky, where they were a hazard to the tourists, who thought they were completely tame. The bison would let the dummies close, so very close, then they'd put them in the hospital. They were faster now, unlike the bison of old, who would wait until they became a viral video before they attacked. Even bison had enough sense to hate going viral. During a big summer party, a herd was gathered up by actual cowboys who had been hired to put on a show, and they managed to get several of them into the corral—a garish affair with redwood railings and a canopy that flapped and made the bison startle and snort. Late that night, the drunken Glitterati went down to the corral and sprayed the bison with glue, then covered them with glitter. When they saw the results, they broke out in applause and began posing for photos with the bison. Already crowded into the pen for hours and spooked by the flapping tarps, the bison went berserk and broke down the corral, then stampeded straight down to the blue-ribbon trout stream, where they rolled and stomped and bellowed until they were clean. That was the end of fifty miles of blue-ribbon trout stream, as well as water degradation for a good hundred miles miles after that, and an annoying but harmless tint in the water. Officially. Most of this didn't come out right away, as one of the Glits had been killed in the stampede, and it was bad taste to bring up subjects like poor environmental stewardship when someone had died. If we weren't all free to do stupid things, our economy would be in quite a fix, wouldn't it?

Tree knew that all of the trout were genetically engineered, mostly cloned, and released right before fishing season started, but she kept this to herself. It wasn't a secret really—all those research papers. Some of those trout had brands on them, for crying out loud. Don't pretend you don't see that. She had nothing personal against the fisherpeople and saw no reason to point out how very alike all of the trout were. They did catch and release, after all. The death of the river, long rumored but never believed, could be temporary but more and more was turning out not to be.

Tree's son had known some of the Glits from their nativity, as it were—he had gone to school with one of them. Their tiny high school in the middle of nowhere had produced a famous rich person, in fact one of the originators of the Glitter clothing, which by internet standards made him immortal. Everyone in town appeared as proud of this as if the guy had won a Nobel Prize, or at least they acted like it. Tree's son had told her about the illegal mile-long water slide before it was widely known. He had the inside dope because he was a security guy for their compound, or so he said. They didn't have a true compound, of course, like the wacko survivalist types (the Glitterati would be the first to die anyway, no matter what kind of compound they built), but they had purchased the privacy of the surrounding mountains, so in went the water slide, the bison farm, and several other over-the-top developments. Not very many people had access to the walled center of the town, where supposedly there was a pool large enough to go with a mile-long waterslide. But Tree's son did. He'd been on the slide. "It's really only four thousand feet long," he told her confidentially.

The slide was another sore spot with locals, since they were all supposed to be conserving water for the Blue Ribbon Trout Stream, and now this. The Glitterati had obtained a minimum number of permits before they went wild all over their land, but a water slide was right out. The thought of it especially enraged the wealthy people who had moved up from Phoenix and Los Angeles and Las Vegas, searching for unlimited water again, right up until someone informed them that there was no water here either, and the locals sure hoped that they had put composting toilets in their new home, as their building permit specified. Yes, all of them. Then why had their real estate ad pictured a duck pond in the front acreage?

So almost everyone hated the Glitterati except for young people. Tree didn't think about what else must be going on up there, and she didn't ask, since she didn't think that even the Glitterati could sway any child of hers into dressing that stupidly. But she was mad as hell about the entire bison incident, so she became involved in the protest. The glitter hit the river before the perpetrators woke up, as it was far downhill from them. As the sun came over the canyon walls and brightened the blue-ribbon trout stream, as well as the green, purple, and yellow trout stream, traffic came to a standstill. A few of the bison were grazing on the green grass at the water's edge, shimmering like a crazy rainbow. It was breath-taking. Everyone was shocked and dismayed, because everyone depended on the trout. If you didn't fish, you had to guide fisherpeople.

Tree drove up the mountain with three of her confederates, to the guard house at the start of the Glitterati property. From there the mountain sloped down and into the open valley where the big compound was. It was almost invisible from any road, which made it more galling, since the Glitterati could do almost anything without being observed. No one had known about the water slide until it was completed and pictures were posted by some internet spy, proving once again that it was easier to beg forgiveness than ask for permission. Nothing happened to the Glitterati for breaking every water law in the state. They were using the water, true—but it went right back out again, and they didn't even use the slide most of the year. Also it would really mess up the watershed to take it down. So. The Glits paid a steep fine that would take them almost a day of ridiculous internet posturing to recoup, and kept their waterslide.

Tree parked her car in an inconspicuous spot and climbed down the rocky hill until she could see the river snaking along the bottom. The other spies also had binoculars and good boots, and they took their places along the edge, peering down.

"Do you see it?" one of the hippies asked her, moving her glasses around. Tree couldn't see a thing. It was a bright sunny day and the river shimmered like a diamond, glitter or no glitter. Tamarack finally spotted it in the pasture. A corral was built out on a flat piece, and inside the fence, glitter was spread far and wide, entire puddles of it shifting and blowing in the breeze. There were barrels full of it. Who had barrels of glitter with no lids, left out in the elements? Only these idiots. The Glitterati had already been fined for the bison hazing and glittering the river, but this was worse. It was an abomination that would blow for miles and last for years. But no matter how vast, the future destruction would lose the attention of the public faster than a lecture about sustainable living, unless Trout

Unlimited got involved, but they kept a low profile these days, in case someone mentioned that the trout looked like clones. That was not the kind of "unlimited" the fisherpeople were thinking of when they donated. The eco-warriors would have to do some posturing of their own, again.

A few days later, on a morning that was a reminder of what summer was capable of in Paradise, several dozen eco-warriors lined up on the side of the highway. A girl called Ivy passed out black t-shirts that said GLITTER HURTS CRITTERS in an angry white scrawl, and everyone suited up. When traffic hit its morning peak, they stretched themselves across the road, arms around each other, and blocked traffic going both ways. This was not popular with anyone, as well as dangerous, so they had to be loud and fast. Most of them had been arrested before, but for big issues, not for the likes of the Glitterati, and it was not the plan today. Any roadblock of more than about ten minutes risked a felony charge, although there were other ways, and Tree knew of them too....

"Stupid hippies, get out of the way! Get a job!" screamed a guy, who probably worked for the Glitterati. His truck roared like it needed to run over a wolf to be satisfied.

"Clean up the Glitterati! Don't wreck your water!" Tree screamed back. The honking got louder and more insistent. Some people wanted to go to work, had not noticed the complete futility of it all. They didn't even have time to fish. After almost being run down by a larger truck, speaking of futility, Tree and the rest of the protesters cleared the road, but stayed on the shoulder and made a nuisance of themselves. The drivers had to slow down and pay attention to protesters for a half mile or more. This bogged down traffic and caused a lot of honking, the amount depending on how invested the driver was in the local infrastructure. Fishing guides slumped in their big trucks and pretended not to notice a thing as they crept by. They like the cloned trout fine. They still paid the bills and were pretty besides.

"Protect the river! Stop the toxic dumping!" The protesters handed out fliers to everyone who would take one, showing the barrels of glitter on the property. Tree had once known a guy who could stop traffic both ways with his performance art. He didn't have to block the road, he stopped them—dressed up like a trout and flipping around in the road like a dying fish. Trout—what else?—had been a dancer in his former life. He was great, even if his talents sometimes tended to obscure the environmental message. But since no one liked their messages anyway, Trout was as welcome among them as anyone else. Not everyone had the guts to stand in the highway, let alone do back flips on it in front of angry spectators. People threw money at him, and they used it to buy lunch later.

After a few hours of loitering on the side of the road and waving at motorists, showing off their matching t-shirts, the crew met at a gas station and compared notes. Positive versus negative reception: about fifty percent. The usual. No one had been tapped by a car, had anything thrown at them, and no police had appeared, which made the day a rousing success. A few people had given them a thumbs up or said, Oh yeah—those Glitterati. Little punks.

Gathered under a spindly pine tree, the group watched a young man walking toward them, and while not looking especially hostile, he looked determined. Maybe a reporter. Tree was spaced out, staring at the mountains, and too late heard Salmon behind her saying, "Watch out, he's a Glit, watch out, Tree, he's a Glit."

Tree looked up just in time to see the guy swiftly take a quart container of something from under his trenchcoat, then throw it at the mass of protesters, who were cozily close to each other under the tree. Tree moved at the wrong instant and took a direct hit from a glitter bomb on the side of her head. Most of them were coated with the itchy stuff. Tree didn't know what had hit her, and coughed and wheezed for a few minutes, eyes streaming. She thought she had gotten it into her lungs, it was so suffocating. That stuff was probably worse than radioactive fallout. The bomber let out a hoot of victory, ran back to his car, and was gone before anyone could see well enough to pursue him. It was just as well, since that would bring the police. The gang barely had time to move, but now several of them began crying out as the glitter invaded their skin and clothing. The air was filled with glitter dust and expletives as the protesters shook themselves off. The onlookers from the gas station laughed at first, but stopped quickly. Even nutty eco-protesters didn't deserve glitter lung, a syndrome that a few of them knew about from reading research papers. But the assault was more entertaining than the protest, no matter which side you were on, and the entire incident showed up on the internet almost instantly. Tree hated it, but it was more publicity. She hoped she wasn't caught looking stupid on the internet.

She bowed her head and tried to comb the glitter out of her hair as she surveyed her lap. He had ruined her new shirt. She cried a little, washing the glitter out of her eyes and letting self-pity caress her. Nobody cared. They were abused when they were trying to help. It wasn't their fault that they had to engage in stupid public campaigns and annoy people. It was because no one had any situational awareness. Tree stood up and took off her t-shirt, which excited some of the onlookers into awareness, even in her boring sports bra and her gently melting body. She rearranged her frame in what she hoped was an attractive manner while she shook the shirt out violently, pretending that she wasn't, because she was too old for vanities like that. The shirt would wash out. She liked it. The message could be interpreted many ways, but it was clear that it did not support Vores, or glitter, or things that didn't make any sense.

Salmon came by in a few minutes and helped her back to the van, where she closed her eyes and rested against a window for most of the drive home. They were all filthy with glitter and sweat and road stink. Tree had gotten the worst of it, but they would all go home and take longer and hotter showers than they usually enjoyed, even if they had to heat the water over a stove.

They won that bout, although Tree remained low and discouraged whenever she thought about it. Maybe it was the glitter assault, out of nowhere like that. Maybe she was just tired out. After seeing videos of the protest, as well as of the extra-sparkling river, government agents showed up at the Glitterati gate and demanded to be let in, flashing the federal badges that gave them authority over money, at least the kind of money owned by those sorts. The stockpile of glitter was hauled off and safely disposed of, they said. Tree imagined boxcars of glitter being dumped into volcanoes, where they would flare and sparkle like fireworks, then be totally gone from the world, like nothing ever was. The Glits were fined an enormous amount of money and were ordered to clean up around the corral and the surrounding ten acres. Never missing an opportunity, they hired hundreds of fans to do it for them for free—for room and board and access to the Glits world. The fans came in teams every couple of months, like it was summer camp and not a hot, backbreaking job. After a few rides on the mile-long water slide while the Glits loitered nearby and made themselves available for autographs and photos, the clean-up crews were completely star-struck and had no ill will toward the Glitterati, even though they had witnessed their monumental stupidity up close and personal. Environmentalists would never win a popularity contest. If you couldn't accept that, you should never start protesting. It was too depressing.

"I almost got fired over that," Tree's son informed her later. "They thought I had something to do with it." According to the many stories he'd told her about how chummy he was with the famous dolts, Tree didn't think so.

"I doubt that. And you told them that you didn't, and nothing happened. We have binoculars, and brains. We don't need spies. How did they know we were related?"

"I told them. They saw you getting blasted by the glitter bomb on the internet, and I told them that EdgarT was a dick for doing that to protesters, and that was my mother. Pauly remembered you. A bunch of them went down to the corrals? and saw all that mess and all that glitter? Pauly was furious. Except for the waterslide, they follow most of the environmental laws. He didn't know all that glitter was there."

Tree was relieved that he'd not only defended her, but outed himself as being her son, covered in glitter and all. She had a picture of Pauly4Nicate when he'd come to her son's eighth birthday party, when he was still cute and innocent and not a rich moron. Strangely enough, his last name really was "4Nicate," so he never had a chance. Even when he was little, he was an influencer, and he'd brought some product to the party that he kept trying to get the attendees to look at.

"Try a little human contact instead," Tree told him, putting his product high on a shelf, since he was too young to understand and wouldn't tell his mother. And look at how much good it had done. Later he sold her son a drone without a controller, because you could throw it up in the air and it would take off, he said. At nine years old! She should sell his old photo to some trashy website, because he looked stupid in it.

"What a tragedy for Pauly. Did he have a tantrum in front of his camera? Did he throw some glitter around, and talk about how mad he was about all those broken environmental laws? A million more views, I bet."

He had, in fact, so her son stared into the distance as though he was thinking hard. Pauly got four million views of his rant about respecting nature, and the clean-up workers got another day of waterslide and girls in bathing suits. No one would remember that

Pauly had been instrumental in bringing the glitter fashion to the mountains, or that they had been called the Glitterati since the day they showed up in their obnoxious, already outlawed clothes. They needed to repair their image, even if the glitter was very cool and only authoritarians had a problem with it.

"I could have been fired," C-Zum insisted. Tree stared at his name badge.

"Really? Is there something wrong with the name I gave you?"

"I have to have a *public* name, ma." Tree figured she didn't have a leg to stand on here. But Tree was a serious name.

"Go slide down the water slide some more. Good luck with these people. I can't believe you hang out with such idiots." She'd done all she could do. He looked good in his security guard uniform though. C-Zum returned to the compound, where the Glitterati continued parading around in their ugly loud glitter clothes and had loud, glittery parties. The bison were still around and they were fine, even if many still shimmered in a funny way, sometimes, when the sun hit them right. The tourists thought those were special spiritual beings and no one told them differently.

When environmental activists noticed what a grand statement could be made with giant slow boats, they decided to help. They stole a cargo ship from north Africa, where dozens of them sat slowly deteriorating and polluting the harbors. It was getting so hard to keep track of anything when the billionaires wanted to ditch it, because they hired hackers to go in and erase all the ownership records. Nobody really knew who owned all those ships, and what was anyone supposed to do? They were too big to move, except with another giant unmaintained cargo ship, and it was all too exhausting to imagine. So they were pretty much free if they used newer tech to move around, and they could get up a crew. It took a lot more discipline and smarts than most folks thought to run a big ship, so most of them stayed put anyway, offering protection from the storms.

No one noticed when Greenpeace took off with the solar ship until they hoisted their flag, then the Coastie Guardians wondered what they were doing, since it was too late to save most of the fish in the seas. Not that they cared, since the Coasties had lost their fishing years ago, then they had lost the land too, when it dissolved from under their feet like an old dream of home. Now they mostly lived on cargo ships too, catching the tiny schools of fish that had started to come back underneath.

The Greenpeace ship was headed for the Suez Canal, which had became kind of a no-man's land of shipping once traffic from trade fell to a trickle. Their leader was a disillusioned German cargo ship captain who had risked his life one too many times to bring diapers and robot vacuum cleaners across the ocean. One night, during a brutal storm that threatened the entire ship, the captain watched a shipping container break open against a railing, then vomit forth tons of makeup, glitter clothing, and disposable plastic dishware. It all vanished instantly into the waves, to join the tons of other useless garbage out there. He had a sudden clarity. When his tour was over, he went home to plot.

Egypt couldn't afford to maintain the Suez Canal after all those cargo ships shopped using it, and it was filling with silt and flotsam and some sort of spreading vine that had fallen overboard from one of the ships and then blossomed all through the canal. It grew faster than Cambodian zombie ivy and was topped with big yellow orbs like sunflowers. It was scary how fast it could move there in the desert with plenty of water. It went right up on the banks and overland, drinking the water out of the canal. Most of the canal was now glowing yellow and almost impassible. Your ship may get through there if it wasn't loaded too heavily, but maybe it would be better if you went around, or didn't bother with the trip at all. Even if you made it through, there were pirates everywhere else, and if they weren't pirates, they were refugees who would come on board and eat everything you had. It was hard to tell the difference sometimes, but they'd identify themselves when they boarded, if they didn't have a flag. All of them ate a lot.

The activists sailed the EverGreenpeace into this morass, where it turned sideways and slammed into the bank, then made its own sandbar and settled in for a while. Tree got an alert on her phone from one of her activist friends and was watching the fiasco with Harris, live on TV.

"What are they doing?" asked Harris, mystified.

"Making a statement," answered Tree, who knew they had done it on purpose. Any ships going through the Suez Canal now were full of bootlegged Vore accessories from factories in Africa. They took the risky route because anything that got through was profit and the shippers didn't care that much, since it was all disposable crap. Humanitarian aid didn't move through the Suez Canal if it wanted to reach its destination, and quite frankly, if you wanted to live, you were going to have to get yourself to a more hospitable environment, not wait for aid. We were sorry.

Nonetheless, the sacred business of business had to go on, so four days after the activists blocked the canal, as people all over the world were creating memes about stalled cargo ships full of air-conditioned toilets, a team of Israeli special forces scuba divers came by and planted a bomb under the EverGreenpeace. The fifty or so Greenpeace activists had unfurled a banner off the side of the ship that said CONSUMERISM KILLS in sixty-foot-high lettering. They were right again, because a day later, all of them were dead. Harris hadn't even known that Greenpeace was still around, but apparently this was the last contingent of them, the really hardcore warriors. They had decided to go down with the ship—it didn't matter which one, since they were all going. And today was their day.

Tree was standing in front of the TV enjoying it all, and when the entire ship blew up with no warning, she clapped her hand over her mouth and turned white. The announcers on the TV were unable to decide which side they were on, so they were silent too. They were supposed to be on the side of business, who wrote their checks, but they had eyes, and children.

"How could they do that?" cried Tree to Harris, who was shocked himself, and he'd been hanging out with Tree for years now. "You can't just—blow people up. They weren't *doing* anything. The canal isn't even usable anymore."

"They're *Greenpeace protesters*, Tree. You told me yourself. They're like—nothing, and they set off an international incident. AC Toilets? *Consumerism kills*? Business isn't going to be embarrassed like that." Harris hated when he had to believe things that Tree had discovered in her distressed paranoid world, but that had been no accident. Tree was silent, looking at the footage of the blown-up ship. The canal was much deeper now and the explosion had cleared out a lot of garbage, even with the ship wreckage. The sunflower weeds were exploded for miles, looking like yellow fireworks as they fell back to earth. It would take them days to become established again.

The Canal Authority sent out a media release saying that the "controlled detonation" had been planned weeks before, the explosives laid. Then the activists had blundered in on their pirate ship, setting off the charges before they could be warned. It was unfortunate, but no one's fault except the Greenpeace terrorists. Don't even think about suing the Canal.

Tree sent several texts, then sat down in the backyard with a bottle of tequila, her feet in the pool. Not knowing how to handle it, Harris left her alone and went out to see the deer for a while. That had been fairly unnerving. Everyone knew it was murder, no matter what they said about it.

When he came back, calmed by the deer and the walk, Tree was gone. Oh no, he thought. Her car was gone, and so was the bottle of tequila. He drove by Mara's, who was not at home either, then he drove downtown. Where would Tree go to pick a fight? Of course—he went to the Vore store, where he found Tree's car parked crookedly across two chargers. Tree was standing at the front door of Destiny, her braid threaded with a string of red ribbons, a ritual of her crowd when they were about to go do something that would get them all arrested. She was harassing a well-groomed Vore dude whose fingernails were far too fine to slap her, so he was only listening in amusement.

"You think you can do *anything*," Tree spewed at him, taking another shot of tequila. "You think that you can just KILL people. You think that you rule the world. Well, you DON'T. *NATURE BATS LAST*. You don't know ANYTHING. *LAST*. You'll find out!"

Harris grabbed the tequila bottle first, in case she decided to belt someone with it. "My apologies, her mother just died," he told the man, who was a box. Harris didn't need to apologize to a box. The nerve of these people.

"I don't even know what she's talking about," said the box dismissively.

"YOU SURE DON'T," yelled Tree, now captured by Harris' arm and out of the line of fire. He made her move her car out of the parking spaces and took her home, where she ranted about the fate coming for the stupid, and how they would all deserve it. Harris thought that it looked like they would deserve it, even with his limited knowledge about the whole thing.

After she retired, Tree wondered why she had kept on fighting a losing battle for so long, and the only answer she could come up with was—because what else do you do? Put on a headset that filled you only with the things you wanted to hear? There were drugs now that would put you to sleep for weeks, in the hopes that things would be better when you woke up, or maybe you'd just feel well-rested enough to deal with it. She preferred being awake, and on the losing side. Even if it made her sick.

. . . .

Tree was on a legitimate mission this morning, instead of sitting in the house watching old movies. She had a load of rehabbed clothes to get rid of. This was her career move since she'd become old and weak: she acquired old shirts and pants, sewed them up nicely, then traded them. Tree had learned to sew when she was young, a skill that soothed her with its practicality. People liked real clothes that were washed and put back on, even if they did buy tons of paper ones. It made them all teary to see real needle and thread marks on things, and she received praises for the authentic cloth, even if not so many trades, since how many real clothes did one person need? That was the whole idea of having real clothing. Her supplies were easy to come by, since no one sewed anymore. She picked the pants up from here, returned with them washed and mended, and spent the day trying to get rid of them. She sewed patches on jeans, and sometimes she'd sew some stars on them or a bug. Folks loved that stuff. Harris did too, and was always trying to tell her something about California girls, the best girls in the world. They must all be farmworkers now, but maybe they had time to embroider.

The only problem with her business was that the clothes came only in the size they came in, because Tree wasn't taking special orders, and she liked the small sizes better. Smaller clothes meant less sewing. This was hand work, not just running a longer stitch on a sewing machine. It was perfectly logical, but confused her customers sometimes anyway, because they didn't understand art, didn't understand supply chains, and didn't have any situational awareness. They could still order Hefty Boy jeans from the internet, and they would probably arrive, someday. What were they eating, anyway, to be fat nowadays? Tree had traded for some "chocolate" here one day, she was so desperate for some, even though she knew better. It was awful—like wax, sugar, and coffee stains pressed together, but she ate it anyway, because no one ever got real chocolate now. It had gone extinct in the wild and had to be grown in a lab. That would never have happened if women were in charge of the world.

Tree had once seen a woman playing a harp for food at Bartertown. She had four natural children and could play the harp, so what could she do? Surely she had been blessed by her freaky fertility. The harp was a hit too, since it was so unusual, and she was talented. She did well enough to keep everyone fed, and eventually even found someone to help her raise the kids. Tree wasn't sure, but she thought that Bartertown was mellower on the days the harp woman came in. Occasionally a band came in, or someone with a guitar. That could be fun.

She got a table right away, not wanting to wander around and have to pass by that businessman on her search, since she hadn't spotted him right away. She peered out from under her straw hat and tried to get her bearings. It was early, and traders were straggling in still. Tree arranged her offerings on the rickety table and looked for the bulk of the solar panels somewhere. She could see them far off to the left, on her side of the aisle, but couldn't tell if Terry was there without really turning her head. This was not an optimal location to spy on him without him noticing, but it was too late now.

Another gal was entering the gate with a couple of big black bags, and Tree knew what was in them. They came in almost every day with piles of disposable clothes in garbage bags, appropriately enough. The purveyors of the garbage varied, but they had a table of their own not too far down from where Tree was. She gritted her teeth. The gal passed by and nodded at her, not friendly but not confrontational either. The trader slapped her garbage bags on the table under their own sign: PAPER OR PLASTIC? The feud between the originals and the disposable clothing people was old and had become heated a few times, even though most traders weren't very invested in their products and were just running their mouths. Tree was always offended by the paper clothing, but she and this particular vendor preferred to ignore each other. Tree usually managed to walk by their table a few times if she was doing a long day, acting as though she smelled something bad. Half the people in Bartertown acted like that anyway, but who did the snobs think they were kidding? It was the same crowd who came by even in a snowstorm.

Tree sat on the ground behind her table and waited for customers, smoking a little. This was a mellow business. A couple of teenagers came by and looked at the mended shirts, giggling, then moved on to the PAPER OR PLASTIC table, since they could get two paper t-shirts and some plastic scarves for a pack of cigarettes, and Tree looked like she might give them a lecture about smoking. A man came by to look at her pants, then tried to give Tree a bottle of whiskey for some jeans that wouldn't fit him, because wishing made it so. Tree turned him down on the whiskey anyway, since neither she nor Harris should be keeping whiskey in the house, even if they did tend to be a little casual about their drug use. An older woman came by and they bemoaned the ubiquity of the disposable clothes, loudly enough so that the trader at the PAPER OR PLASTIC table knew they were talking about her, even if she couldn't quite hear it. People needed to remember what was good and real. After a bit of haggling, the woman gave Tree four rolls of toilet paper, a winter hat, and a ceramic dish shaped like a elephant, and Tree gave her some embroidered jeans.

She became bored after a few hours, since most of her customers were too large to fit in her clothes. Tree tried to stare them down, but they came over anyway. She was trading art here, not tents. She leaned over the table like she was fixing a wobble, as though that was possible in the rutted dirt, and chanced a long glance toward her left. Just as she turned her head, she saw that man staring back at her, right at the same instant. Curses. Or maybe he was only staring toward the front gate, the same way she was fixing a wobble while looking his way. He could have been. She was too busy with the table to check. Her wares also needed straightening. Abruptly she decided that everything was fixed at her end, she was bored and she needed a break. Tree covered up her table and went over to the snow cone wagon.

"Fiona, give me a snow cone," Tree commanded, suddenly ravenous. She'd have to part with some of the homegrown. Fiona was serving up fake blueberry snow cones today, a very good kind.

"Say, do you have any wellness stuff back there? Maybe put a squirt in there." Tree was feeling kind of tense suddenly. She added another pinch of weed to her trade, and took the snow cone back to her table. It was delicious. She sat back in the dirt and watched the people go by. Her goods weren't as popular as porn magazines or paper clothes. She traded one more pair of jeans for a hand mixer, which would be great for her new baking career. It was a pleasant day.

Tree realized that she was kind of lying under her table, instead of being attentive to her wares, but it didn't really matter. People were trustworthy. She watched the sky from under the table, safe here. No one could see her, all these strangers, wanting things she didn't have. Everyone wanted so much, all the time. A prairie dog came up next to her, way too close, but she was too tired. Its teeth were so yellow. If those things started biting, everyone at Bartertown would get sick. Shoo. Tree loves you. We are kindred spirits. She smoked a bowl of the homegrown, since it was right there in her pocket. It was great, excellent, more proof that handmade things were better than paper clothes, every single time—

"There's nothing I like better than a nice comfortable pair of old jeans, you know what I mean?" Tree struggled to comprehend. Why were they bothering her? She had done everything she could do, and no one cared. She sat up a little and looked out over the table. Oh crap, it was that man. She rolled out, brushing her hair back as though she always came to Bartertown to hide under tables. She was going to kill Fiona. She stood up, a little wobbly.

"Oh, it's you. You know, I have very discerning customers, unlike a lot of the people here, and I can't give my stuff to anyone who comes along. It's about quality, not quantity."

Terry looked unconvinced. "You should get some things that people want. You're wasting too much time here. Time is money, you know."

He had to be messing with her. No one said stuff like that for real. Terry started pawing through her clothes, and she held her tongue. Even if he wasn't interested in them, he must notice her precise stitching. No one could do that anymore. He picked up a pair of jeans with patches all over them, as though a man like him would wear patched jeans. He probably got all of his clothes from the slow boats, entire boats of clothing just for him, because that's how wealthy people were. She sat back down on the ground, because standing up was for people who respected others. She didn't have to stand up for him.

"You should get a chair. You seem like you need to sit down a lot."

"Don't you need to get back to your table? Someone might steal your sunshine." She could see them from here—kids who had hovered near his table, then as soon as he was far enough away, they ran over and plugged in their phones. Terry waved his hand toward the little brats. Behold, he could gift the sun! He was that powerful! Tree was on the verge of asking him what the poker chip he'd given her meant, but she was weak and confused. What if she asked, and he didn't even remember giving it to her? He needed to think that she had traded it for a snow cone or forgotten about it, not kept it. Right there in her pocket, weeks later.

Terry picked up a shirt with embroidered patches on it. "This is very nice." He seemed sincere, which threw Tree off again.

"Uh, thank you. I enjoy it." She chanced a smile, a little.

"Well, next time you come, don't forget my cake. I don't wear flowered shirts." And like that, he was gone again. He never slowed down long enough for her to figure out what was going on with him. He was probably a criminal. But he'd remembered about the cake. And he'd said "Next time." That was like a date. Tree wondered if she needed to lie down again. She looked over and he was at the PAPER OR PLASTIC? table. Tree watched, irate. That girl was pushing it, with her stupid garbage clothing. A man like him wasn't going to buy paper clothes. Why was he even over there? Why was she simpering like that? He was at least twenty years too old for her, and she should know, even if men were too stupid to ever realize it.

She looked at her wares, much reduced but still a lot to take home. She sighed. She needed to speak to Fiona. If she didn't quit dosing her like that, Tree was going to have to quit eating her snow cones. She put her stuff in her big bag, along with her small haul of new things. It was late afternoon and still lively, but Tree was tired. The microplastics were slowing her blood. At least she'd done a few chores and learned a few things, even if it hadn't gone down exactly the way she'd planned. She threw her bag over her shoulder and started toward the gate, detouring for a minute to inform Fiona of something, then forgot what it was when she smelled those delicious snow cones. She turned around and saw the same woman from a few weeks ago with her rack of fur coats. She wouldn't have a lot of customers in the summer. Tree admired the furs, as usual with nothing close to substantial enough to trade for one. Then she stopped dead, her eye caught by an impossible sight. On the rack was a coat that stood out even among the old luxury coats, because it looked just like a Blue Blur Fur.

"No way," said Tree, too stunned to get out of the way of a man towing a car radiator through until he ran into her, accidentally on purpose. Men. She moved over, then made her way to the fur lady, who remembered Tree, the dingbat who loved furs so much. Tree touched the Blue Blur. "Do you know this one? These are very nice." The woman didn't, and wasn't interested., Tree kept her cool, hoping to get a deal. The woman clearly didn't know what she had. She brushed the sleeve, as always not believing how long the fur was, how soft, and of a color so deep black, it glowed blue when the coat moved. She'd never been so close to one. Tree checked the labels. It was real. She had to have it, today, even if she had to bring her bed down here. She tried to put her poker face on, but it made no difference, since the trader was watching the action around the market and paying no attention to her. It was obvious that the dingbat didn't have anything valuable enough to get a fur coat, judging by the look of that ratty tote over her shoulder.

The Blue Blue Furs were one-of-a-kind fur coats that came from a radon mine in northern Montana. It was long closed but still accessible to animals and intrepid people who wanted to bathe in the radioactive glow of the mine shafts. Minks had been living in the mines for decades, and as they adapted to the dark and the damp cool, their slightly radioactive fur grew so long that it dragged behind them and had to be cleaned constantly. This made them slow and sluggish, and they couldn't do a thing in the winter, so they stayed in the mine shafts, where their fur grew longer and denser. The deep blue color came from the radioactivity and couldn't be reproduced by breeding. They were a unique population, and they survived in and around the old mines for a hundred years before a local got a decent picture of one of them outside in the summer sun. Even then, when furs weren't especially valued, no one could miss the insane beauty of the Blue Blurs. People flocked to see the special minks, and then the anti-government types who lived in that area heard about them. Several dozen of them descended on the radon mine so they could take stock of the situation, forcing out the cancer patients who were sitting naked in the cave, commiserating about the state of the world. After assessing the cave, the locals came back later with live traps for the Blue Blurs, which was not as much fun as shooting them, but they still got to hit them in the head later. Before word had gotten out to the larger world, some rednecks in Montana had reduced the population by at least half. Some of the minks were collected and bred, but without the addition of the radioactive caves, their fur was only dark and mink-like, thus worthless. We had already done mink coats.

A fashionista, whatever that was, drove out from New York to buy the radon mine, but found out that it was owned by the government. The locals were thrilled when they heard this, since that meant it was a free-for-all until someone showed up to take charge. Before the city dudes could steal their minks, local entrepreneurs blocked off the mine entrance and poisoned every living thing for three miles deep into the dig. That particular cancer-causing agent was only available in twelve countries in the entire world, but these guys had some, because they were serious survivalists. After waiting a week for the mine to air out, they returned with gas masks and laboriously removed all of the dead Blue Blurs from the place, almost six tons of them. But that was all there was.

Pleased that they'd kept their treasure from the city people, the fur barons largely squandered their bounty on car seats and fur bras and caveman outfits and wall hangings. Many of the furs were eaten by moths, lost in floods or thrown away. But five hundred fur coats had been made from the minks before they vanished forever. Tree had only seen one of them in her life, and now here was another one.

She tried to think through the fog of snow cone. That meant—she had to go get the flag.

She was exhausted. She couldn't imagine walking back up the hill to her place, carrying her things, then coming back with the flag. But she couldn't chance it. The fur coat was glowing with such otherworldly beauty, someone else would spot it too, someone with quality goods. Harris was sitting at home playing his guitar when he got a text.

Can you bring the flag down here?? This is an emergency.

He'd thought that was his flag, to trade for a car. She must have found something good. He called her. "Is this necessary? I'm feeling very creative right now."

"It is, or I wouldn't ask. Try one of Fiona's snow cones, you'll never feel so inspired."

Harris decided that his next hit song could wait, so he packed up the Wyoming flag and tripped down the mountain a few minutes later. Tree was pacing by the fence, waiting for someone to come snatch her fur coat. She told him quickly about the miraculous Blue Blur, and to act natural, nobody knew. He had no problem with this, since he had no idea what she was talking about. Tree took the flag over to the fur woman, holding it like an offering, hoping that she understood Wyoming memorabilia better than she understood furs. By her sharp look, Tree knew she could make a deal. She fingered the furs casually, going through the rack as though she wasn't sure.

"You're good with that then, the flag for one of these? Its a nice flag, brand new. Hand collected." She held her breath, waiting for the woman to say, "Any one of them except the Blue Blur." But no, she didn't. Tree took the fur from the rack and tried to roll it up a little. She had to hide it, or someone else would notice how nice it was and try to trade her against her will. She looked for help from Harris, but he was over at the snow cone wagon eating a big red cone and flirting with Fiona. Tree hugged the coat over to him, and they managed to stuff it in her canvas bag, after giving Fiona the ceramic of the elephant. "That's good for five snow cones," Fiona told her, "unless you want the syrup." It seemed like the price of the treats kept going up, yet Tree kept paying it. Harris seemed in no hurry, so they walked around to see what else might be new.

"How did you get that snow cone?" Tree asked. "You didn't bring anything, did you?"

"A kiss." Harris air-kissed his snow cone. "One kiss, good anytime."

"You did not."

"I did. I won't do it again though. She's awfully young. It was a....an irresistible impulse."

"Well, all right then, no problem. That's pretty good though, isn't it?"

He finished his snow cone and felt delightfully soothed, almost like lying under a table. Tree was right. That girl was dealing drugs.

"Hey, is that your boyfriend?"

Tree hadn't been paying attention, since she'd been checking out a table full of old paperbacks, and now they were going the wrong way. She turned a corner and went another direction. "Uh no. And he's not my boyfriend, I barely know him. And....he's evil."

"Yah, that's not what you said before. He's not bad for an old guy, Tree. Almost as hot as me." Harris was pretty cocky after kissing a twenty-five-year old, even if it had been transactional. And as far as Tree could remember, she'd said next to nothing about Terry, since she didn't know him. Harris had stopped and was checking Terry out quite openly, and Tree knew that he had spotted them. Fine then. She put her arm through Harris' and leaned on him, guiding him gently down another row. She needed to get him out of there before he decided to introduce himself. It wasn't as though she'd *said* anything to him, or that Harris knew anything about anything, but Tree wasn't taking any chances. Harris and Mara had such an interest in getting her hooked up with someone, neither one of them could be trusted. But real life was not like one of those old movies, where embarrassing behavior would result in a hilarious and long-lasting love affair.

Tree steered Harris toward the gate, hoping that someone was looking and had noticed her leaving—not hanging around to spy on him, not even walking by his table casually, even if he had spoken to her. She wasn't swayed by his wealth, even if he hadn't mentioned it. But that's how rich people were—underhanded. They wouldn't bring it up, because that would be crass. But they still dressed and acted and spoke in such a way that it was obvious they wanted everyone to notice that they were rich, because no one else could be that haughty.

Or maybe Tree hadn't noticed him at all, because she and Harris were in love. They were so in love, he came to Bartertown to meet her, because they were breathless when they were near each other. She smiled blissfully at him, just in case. They passed the fur lady and Tree waved happily at her, since she was in love. The fur lady also looked happy, her new flag hanging off the end of the coat rack. Then they were outside the gate and out of the public eye, to Tree's great relief. She gave Harris the bag with the fur in it, since he was the most relaxed. He wouldn't notice he was carrying it.

In back of Destiny, sometimes they "forgot" to put the trash in the correct bins or lock it up properly, and you could find all kinds of stuff. Tree liked to check them out while the Trotter charged and Mara pretended that she was too good to look in the dumpsters, and waited for Tree to give her the scoop. She would help fish it out if it was good merchandise, but it had to be decent. She was the spouse of a professor, after all, and had to think about appearances. Every day a big self-driving truck came and took all the goods out of the locked dumpsters and over to the garbage lot. The Runnies would have taken half of it to Bartertown, but that would be a strain on The Economy or something, so it was kept locked up until it was added to the current garbage pile in town. Right now it was the south end of the airport, the reasoning being that if your plane had a rough time coming in, at least it would be cushioned by the piles of billowing plastic. There were always so many birds feasting on the pile that they were a hazard all by themselves, especially if a bunch of them took off at once. Since at least half of them were endangered species, no one had figured out how to deal with it, and they were left alone. The airport used to use border collies to run them off, but after the dogs had run off too, everyone was out of ideas. The tourists liked the raptors, anyway. Sometimes they didn't even notice the garbage pile in their excitement.

But now the airport dump was becoming too full of trash, and airplanes were starting to come to a halt in the fringes of the heap. This didn't help the tourist trade, but never seemed to deter it, either. Airline passengers exited the plane and threw their trash on the pile before they went inside to complain about the dirty airplane, the bad service, their low opinion of the wild untamed west. They still continued boarding planes that sometimes dropped out right out of the sky because of storms and bad maintenance, because nobody wanted to work for the airlines anymore. Passengers landed in local towns with garbage dumps at the end of runways, and they landed in foreign countries with garbage dumps at the end of the runways, and they said, My word. How do people let things get to this point?

The dumpster, unfortunately, was locked up tight, with no donations from sometimes sympathetic store workers. Tree's timing must be off. A couple of girls stood outside a metal door smoking vapes. They didn't care about Tree, but she stood off where they wouldn't see her anyway. Lots of people lurked near good dumpsters, because what were you going to do, arrest someone for stealing garbage? That was even lower than dumpster diving.

In the old days, restaurants threw out entire buffets rather than let the poor have the food, because the fragile balance of capitalism might be upset if someone got a free lunch, even if it was five seconds away from becoming unrecoverable trash. Capitalism must be a delicate flower indeed if it needed that kind of protection, Tree thought. And now we had no restaurants, which made a lot more sense. The ones still in business had to recycle everything, right down to the water.

The store clerks weren't bald so they were probably Runnies, stocking shelves and unloading boxes for the robots, who supposedly had no fine motor skills for things like that. They were very good at shopping, though. Their inventory of products was updated every sixty seconds.

"I heard," said one of the girls clearly, "they are going to close Stalwarts, and get rid of those bums in the parking lot. There was a court case, and the Vores won? So they get to press trespassing charges against Stalwarts, and they are disturbing the public order, and encouraging riots."

The other girl looked pained. "There hasn't been a real riot at Stalwarts since I was a baby. They can't close it. It belongs to somebody. Stalwarts owns the parking lot."

"Well, they are. They won a court case, and there's a bunch of Vores in there getting fireworks and champagne. Go look."

They sucked a few more pleasant thoughts out of their vapes, then went back inside and slammed the door behind them. Tree was aghast. She ran to the front of the store and found it busy as usual, mobbed with entirely too much hardware. The Vores still hadn't figured out that no matter how fancy their robots were, they still had to stand in line and drive behind the slowest bot on the road. So they were slowly buying fireworks. Tree crept closer to the door to eavesdrop. The car couldn't be more than half charged. A big gal with a Princess Leia headset was blabbing indiscreetly, her voice carrying clearly to Tree.

"None of those people know about this yet. It went through the stealth courts, because of public safety issues. Because they riot so much. The whole place is a health hazard. They let those dirty people in the parking lot—bums, really—work in the store! Touching the food! It makes me sick to go in there."

And who asked you to? thought Tree, outraged. She tried to look nonchalant, in case one of the bots had emotional identification in its database. She needed to warn people. She rushed back to Mara and broke the news to her.

"The Vores are about to raid Stalwarts! You know how they always talked about shutting it down and everything? It's happening! It's really going down! I heard them talking about it!"

Mara was as zen as her humming car, tapping on her phone. She stopped for a minute and put it aside.

"They are, huh? Well, they probably can't do much—march around the parking lot and stuff."

"No, it's much worse. I heard them talking about court orders."

"Really? Now that does sound interesting." Mara contacted her husband again to ask if he'd heard anything. Tree wasn't sure if Hani never had any classes, or if he took the texts during his instruction, which would serve the Vores right.

"If they're planning something, we'll notice it soon enough." The car sat at 61% charged, so Mara was going nowhere for a while, no matter how fidgety Tree got. Tree twitched her feet a few minutes, then got out of the car and leaned on the hood. Should she ride the bus to Stalwarts? No, she needed to stay out of it. She was retired. She texted Harris: Something happening at Stalwarts! I'll let you know! She removed one of the exclamation marks before she sent it. She didn't want him to think she was overreacting.

She could see the Vores from here, loaded up with balloons and bouncing around jauntily as they performed their daily devotions to themselves. They couldn't hide under their big blocky heads. They talked too loudly, waved their talon-like hands around enthusiastically, bounced on their expensive walking shoes as they planned their party. Tree slipped her phone in her back pocket and, waving at Mara, made her way to the front of the store, as inconspicuous as a raccoon loitering near a trash can. She pretended to be talking on the phone while she spied on the Vores. Marilyn Monroe was fast-walking down an aisle while her robot pushed the overflowing cart in front of her, filled with all manner of cakes, paper plates, and junk food. Vores almost never ate potato chips. Tree felt faint, possibly a coincidence, she couldn't tell anymore. She leaned on the cool wall behind her just in case. It wouldn't do to pass out at the Vore store. Was this really happening? And they were partying.

Her phone gave a little 'boop' as it sent a text through.

I'm checking it out. Forces shake, propel our world.

Oh good. He was going in with no information at all, armed with nothing but his dumb song. Tree stewed while she sat and watched the Trotter charge, which made it mad, so it slowed down its acquisition of electrons and heated her seat, which annoyed her no end. She hated these new cars too. They were all too big for their britches. She wanted to prod Mara to move faster, which was also pointless. Mara had no interest in getting riled up about anything, and only wanted to go home and cook dinner for her loving husband and read articles about turning food scraps into heat or something. She was not leaving until the charger battery read 99%, which was as good as it got unless you waited a very long time for that final one percent, so let it go.

"This is a *big deal*," Tree told her slowly. "Look at these people. They have ice cream and cake! Meat, Mara, real meat! They are planning a big party!"

"I'm not going over there. Someone could get killed. It will be on the internet."

"Our side could get killed. We need to be a witness to history. We might need to pitch in."

Mara checked the charger, now at ninety-two percent. "Fine. Just for you. We'll go witness history. But you can tell Harris that all they need is flowers."

What? "Flowers? I don't think that will work. These are Vores, not Bartertown."

"Flou-er. Flour. The stupid things can't take dust at all. Throw flour at them, it will stop them cold."

"You're kidding. Flour? That is genius."

"I have one, remember, in my house? The one that dusts all the time? It's not for us. It has to keep cleaning up cat hair, or it will have to move out."

Tree was fascinated and distracted. "Would it do that, move out?"

"I have no idea. It just keeps cleaning."

Harris eased his truck into what he hoped was an inconspicuous spot on the side of Stalwarts. All the way down, he kept telling himself that he wasn't going to get involved. He wasn't that kind of a guy. Scanning the parking lot, he couldn't see anything too far out of the ordinary. He was fairly far out and surrounded by Vore vehicles, but no one seemed to be milling. That was when the bad things happened—when the milling started. Then he noticed something: the bots were on the move. Fifty or more of them were heading in a slow line toward the front door of Stalwarts. It wasn't unheard of to see Vorebots in Stalwarts, but nothing like this. And for every one of them, there was a vehicle to carry it around. How had he not noticed how many Vore vehicles were there? Tree would have written down half their license plate numbers by now. They always had the largest and shiniest cars around, but today they were scattered between the parking lot residents and travel vans. Normally they all parked in a herd for protection from the rabble, but today they were hiding. If you bent your head the right direction, you could see the outlines of their stupid headsets through the dark windows. Those tanks were full of people, sitting silently behind their blackout windows. Something was up.

Harris felt the hair on the back of his neck stand up a little. He was still a red-blooded man, even if he was a musician. Remaining mellow and collected was his way, though. He felt for the pistol under his seat, knowing that it was there because it was always there, even for people like him. The abundance of Vore cars in the parking lot had also attracted the attention of the parking lot Runnies. They were coming out their tents and vans now in little trickles, just standing and looking. The Stalwarts Runnies were experienced watchers, a little-appreciated skill today. Persons who did little more than sit and watch did their part in keeping civilization intact. The watchers were loyal to Stalwarts for their community, such as it was. They had access to bathrooms and weren't hassled by the police or no-account Runnies. The parking lot Runnies also believed that they had higher social status than the van people, since they were practically landowners. When the customers started milling, the Runnies would materialize out of their makeshift homes, watching, and that was often enough to break it up. The parking lot police could be unpredictable, so it was best not to push them too far. The Runnies couldn't intimidate the Vores in their tall blank vehicles, but they could watch them. Harris wouldn't bet on many of the Vores making it out of the parking lot, though, if they tried to take over Stalwarts. Tire technology had not evolved in a hundred years, and they could still be flattened just like they were in 1960. And when the vehicle detected a flat, it would park itself and refuse to move until the tire was fixed. Safety first. This could take a while, depending on which accessories the Vore had, because nobody wanted to work at tire stores anymore, and humans were still no better at preparing for flats than they had ever been.

Harris leaned his seat back and thought about things. It was possible that something really was going to happen, and he didn't want to become emotionally involved. That was Tree's arena, getting bent out of shape about things she couldn't do anything about. He felt the weight of the pistol in his lap, heavy and warm like a coiled-up rattlesnake. It was loaded, but he wasn't a good shot. He and Tree had practiced enough to defend themselves, but Harris wasn't going to shoot anyone in Stalwarts, not even in his wildest dreams. So it would be safe to take it with him. He stuffed the pistol in his front pocket and got out.

Harris walked casually toward the front of the store, just a man on his usual errands. He dodged a few bots that didn't seem to be programmed very well. He wondered what their game plan was, and doubted that it involved any direct involvement by the Vores. What were the Vorebots going to do, rush around the store and trip people? Slap them with their metal spider arms? They weren't supposed to attack anything that breathed, and that was hard to override, since the bots had "learned" themselves that murder was the worst offense, and that was that. Too late, the programmers realized that now they couldn't get the robots to kill feral hogs, death row prisoners, mosquitoes, or lampreys. Humans still had to clean up some of their own messes, a fact they complained bitterly about. But on the bright side, hundreds of death row murderers were freed, because nobody wanted to administer the death penalty anymore. The prisoners went outside into the bright and alien sun, were dosed with chemtrails, and never had any violent thoughts again. Most of them became Runnies, since after their brush with death, they never wanted to miss the real world again.

Several customers with worried expressions were trying to gather their things and get back to their vehicles, having noticed that there were way too many Vorebots in the store for a normal day. They hurried even faster when a gunshot rang out, making several people jump and say, Eek! Gunshots weren't unknown at Stalwarts, since the bots sometimes needed killing. It had been going on for some years, a spasm here and there. Nothing to make a federal case of, in other words. The Runnies always claimed that the bot had gone rogue inside the store and had to be stopped, then all the security cameras would mysteriously malfunction. Since the murdered Vorebots were replaced with new bots with even more features, delivered by fast trucks, everyone was happy, and The Economy celebrated.

Stumped, the Vore lawyers gave up on the shootings, or at least the Runnies thought they had given up. But maybe not. Before Harris had time to decide which way to go, to his great alarm, he heard more gunshots. Now people were yelling, running away from the shots. Oh boy, thought Harris, shooting in the store! He felt the gun in his pocket, and crouched by a counter full of corn, wondering what the situation was. Maybe he should have asked Tree for some details, but then she might become frantic, as she did sometimes. He didn't know to handle it, since his own mother had been perfectly negligent. A man darted in next to him and squatted, catching his breath. "What is happening?' Harris asked, whispering just in case.

The chubby fellow was clutching a groceries and panting, but had a wide grin anyway. He said, "It's the Vores. They're outside and they have the place surrounded." Bless his heart, he thought this was the Alamo. Harris knew that the place couldn't have changed that much in the five minutes since he'd walked in. "They say that there's too many of their robots getting blasted in here, and since the town or Stalwarts won't establish order, they're going to shut the whole place down, or they won't be able to eat."

Incredible. "This is OUR place. We won it in the Storm! They have their own grocery store!" Technically, of course, no one had "their" grocery store. But the class lines were obvious. The Vores didn't frequent Stalwarts, and they didn't want to, if they could go to Destiny. You could tell that they only sent their bots in to harass Runnies, since they bought one or two items, the same things they could also get at Destiny, that would be weeks fresher as well. The Vores didn't want *Stalwarts*. They wanted everything. They could walk into Stalwarts like normal humans any time they wanted, and try to fit in with the usual crowd, or program their Vorebots to be less aggressive, but they never did. It was incumbent on the other customers to play nice with the robots. That was why they got shot.

Harris was furious now, thinking about the control the Vores put on everything. They were loud and intrusive, their cars vast and threatening. They ignored social pleasantries and forced everyone to accept their passive-aggressive immensity. No matter what they did, they took up more space than everyone else, and even if they weren't present, they still forced themselves into everything. Society would shape itself around whatever a Vore wanted, because the Vores moved the money.

The guy next to him laughed raucously. "I know, bro. Who do they think they are? I've never shot a robot. And one of them broke into my car. It had a virus or something." He patted Harris distractedly, getting ready to head closer for the doors. Harris wondered what he was doing in there anyway. What did he think was going to happen? Nobody was shooting now. You shouldn't shoot a Vorebot anyway; it was dangerous. The bullet was as likely to ricochet and hit an innocent bystander, then the security tapes had to deleted again. Harris felt the rush of adrenalin leaving his body and felt stoned again. He should go. What a silly idea to come in here. The fellow next to him stood up and walked quickly over to the registers, watchful but not rushing. When Harris stood up and raised his head, the store was quiet, since a lot of the customers had left in a hurry. And how would one know if a civil war broke out, right in front of them? He bent over and squat-ran toward the registers, feeling silly at his stance, but not wanting to get shot either. Never trust anyone with a gun. He ran his things through the checkout robot as fast as he could dig out his plastic cards and wave them at the machine. Even in a war, he was law-abiding. And not a moment too soon, because when he checked the escape route, there were a dozen robots wheeling in the front door. This was unexpected. It was early for them to come in for groceries, and this alone gave them a menacing air. They never came in groups. Harris pulled his bag close and tried to walk inconspicuously past the bots, as though they all did not possess as many eyes as a spider.

There was a Vore robot right in front of his feet, no doubt analyzing him with its spider eyes. Harris felt the not unpleasant rush of losing his cool. Enough of these cold spying trash cans, right under your feet all the time. They knew better. Everyone knew better, and nobody cared. "Cowabunga!" he screamed, and nailed the offensive bot with the grocery bag. It made a big satisfying smacking noise, and the robot tipped and skittered away, its alarm light flashing. Nice. They could talk too, but they rarely did. This was more care than the owners wanted to lavish on their machines, since it would require them speaking the appropriate sentences for the bots to memorize. A few "excuse mes" would probably have saved a lot of the bots from being attacked, but why bother? Harris hit the Vorebot again, leaving a smear of oil or dirt or something all over its shiny side. That smear was his groceries, and this pissed him off more. "You dick!" he screamed. He was starting to get an audience, so it was time to exit. This was so not in his nature. He left the wounded bot flashing and dashed out of the store, victorious. More Vorebots were starting to zip by on their way into the store, with their annoying slightly-too-fast roll.

He heard a bray of laughter, and the man he'd spoken to before towered over him. "Outstanding!" he boomed. Why was everyone yelling so much? "We're going to have a rumble here, man. Get ready for flying metal!" Harris hoped that he meant flying robot parts and not bullets, but it was hard to tell. Some of these customers were not here for the groceries this morning. How had Harris not noticed that the man was wearing a small pistol and a very large knife? "I'm a musician," he said weakly. But this was his store. He couldn't abandon it. He collected his dignity, now slightly wounded by a fight with a bot—it was beneath him, he'd always believed—and followed the big buy back inside.

The other man seemed to have inside information about the battle plan. He headed to the back of the store, where to Harris' surprise there were a few dozen Runnies lurking about, armed and ready to rumble, he guessed. They were dressed nondescriptly, but their pockets were bulging with guns, ammo, tasers. Harris recognized a few of them from Bartertown. He hoped they weren't taking any survival strategies from anything that he'd given them. It seemed more logical to watch the main entrance, where the enemy would enter.

"The beer cave, brother," one of the Runnies told him. "We guard the beer cave first, because if they set the place on fire, we can get the beer out the back." He looked resolute. Harris tried to look nonchalant, as though he carried weapons every day while waiting for certain death, one that could easily have been prevented if only someone had read The Art of War. But the other warriors welcomed him as one of them, so he emptied a beer while he was waiting for some more action.

"It's pretty quiet again," he observed, and two of the Runnies answered, "TOO QUIET!" then almost fell over themselves with laughter. How long had these people been here? Harris noticed a few empty beer cans sitting in a corner, then he noticed a few more. Then a trash can that was stuffed full, which was kind of odd, even for Stalwart's. There were rules about drinking in the store.

"How long have you guys been here?"

"Oh man," said a fellow with a cardboard box over his head, eye holes cut out, in a parody of the Vores. "Since this morning. It was on the internet last night, and we started getting ready." The internet. That explained it. Maybe he and Tree should pay more attention to—no, they shouldn't. No.

Hindered by their headquarters at the beer cave, the guys decided to spread out and attack Vorebots from ambush. They filled their pockets with more beers and fanned out. Harris stocked up before he took a position over by the toy section, properly segregated from the beer cave. Before he reached the safety of the bike section, he heard more gunshots, but coming from the back of the store this time, which meant that the Runnies had wasted no time in joining battle. It was not really his thing, despite the pistol. He was a token fighter here, and it should be obvious to anyone.

He found a toy saber on a shelf and got into a safe space behind a wall of bicycles. They were also spying on him, but at least they weren't on the side of the Vores. There was no reason to have tracking chips in bicycles, but they all did anyway. Harris opened a beer and poured part of it on the bikes in front of him, making them sizzle and short out. Stalwarts didn't even stock waterproof bikes. Someone was going to get electrocuted, and the bike would properly record it on their tracking chip. They sent millions of them over on the slow boats, through hurricanes and pirates and tsunamis, and they were all total crap. They never should have been made—with the sweat and tears of feral South Pacific children—let alone sent over here with only one decent part, and it was the tracking chip.

Harris took the saber, which was surprisingly heavy for a toy, and slapped some Vorebot models from a shelf. It was bad enough they had tiny headsets for toddlers, they also had Vorebot toys, so that even if a kid couldn't afford to get headsets, they could still learn to lust after their own little robots. This was all the Vore's fault, the way the entire world had become stupid and incomprehensible, the whole stupid mess. He thought his head was hammering from righteous anger, but then realized that it was a lot more gunshots. He put down the saber and trotted back behind the bikes, wishing that he could see the front door. What a dumb idea this was. He drained another beer to cut down on weight, and was about to head for the front of the store when he heard his phone give a little 'boop.' The hell—Tree was trying to reach him. Didn't she know he was at war?

Are you at Stawarts??

He hesitated a minute, then realized that a man in his situation didn't have time for chit-chat. He sent back quickly—I'm very busy—then put it away. She was going to be mad. He felt energized by the beer and bashing the toys, so he ran up to a vantage point where he could see the front. There were lines of Vorebots coming in now, and another straggly line of Runnies was across from them, mostly shooting at the bots, but also throwing things like cakes and potatoes. Tree would be proud. The ten-pound potato bags were fairly effective, but they still didn't kill the bot, just knocked it over for a few minutes, until its spider arms could right it. Shooting was risky, because they were more or less bulletproof. There were only a few tiny spots that weren't shielded from gunshots, but everyone enjoyed shooting at Vorebots more than anything, so they blasted away at the line of offenders anyway, creating a dangerous situation for anyone left in the store. A man was hit in the head by a bullet fired by his own brother, after it bounced off a Vorebot. Pictured in the hospital a week later, both brothers denied the true version of events and blamed the wound on illegal Vorebot modifications.

A bot blew up with a little 'wump' and a fake nuclear cloud, which was an impressive app, even for a Vorebot. Someone had gotten in a lucky shot. There were still so many of them gathered at the front door, blocking it completely, even if they weren't making any headway inside. They weren't really fighting, only acting as roadblocks and allowing themselves to be shot. The Vores themselves were nowhere in sight, those scumbags—hiding in their fortresses and waiting for their pets to do the hard work for them, whatever it was. Harris couldn't slip out without getting in the line of fire, so he might as well enjoy it. Another Runnie was hit by a ricochet, this time across the neck. It looked gruesome but the man got up, wrapped some paper towels around his neck, and kept firing.

It was all too much. It was enough to make Harris lose his rapport with his band of brothers, and even with the things he'd seen at Bartertown, he tried to respect everyone. He watched the chaos for a few minutes, making sure that his head was shielded from the ricochets. He decided to go back to the beer cave and restock, since no one was winning. It must be halftime. He dashed to the rear of the store, where the beer cave was being emptied by regular shoppers who thought maybe they could slip out with some free groceries while everyone was distracted. Harris waved his saber at them, glad that he'd stopped and picked it back up.

"Excuse me, but this is for the guardians of the store, you pathetic thieves." He approached them menacingly and they scattered. You couldn't blame them for wanting to take advantage, since the riot itself was a huge irresistible impulse. Society put too many temptations into place, told us to indulge them—-then was shocked when the whole place got trashed. It was suddenly crystal clear to him. Harris gathered another six-pack for himself, then went back to the toy section, where the noise seemed to be abating. They were either running out of bullets, or developing sense, so they must be out of bullets. There was a rank smell in the air, and then a lot of noise, yelling and running feet. Harris crouched next to the bikes again. He could see some smoke from the front of the store, then yelling and running footsteps as the Runnies came back toward him. How could they be losing, when the Vorebots weren't even defending themselves? Then he smelled it—the Vorebots had released skunk. They couldn't have mace, or bear spray, or anything weapon-like, but skunk smell wasn't regulated. It had slipped through the cracks, just as it was intended to. By the smell, several of the Vorebots had released their supply at once, and the Runnies had fled.

Harris laughed. He was one of those who were wired to find that deep musky stink not at all unpleasant, or even mildly nice. He took in a deep whiff. Skunks were cute and innocent. We put them in cartoons. Even a skunk was better than Vore culture, but they couldn't leave them alone either.

He realized that his butt was vibrating like a 20th-century exercise machine. Tree was bothering him again. He yanked his phone from its harness and saw that he had missed a couple of texts from her. What were they, married? He sighed and drank more beer, then looked at the last one. Harris more coming in.

How did she know? She wasn't outside, was she? Of course she was. She may even have taken the bus over, if Mara wouldn't oblige her. He checked the rest of the messages, which somehow he had missed in the heat of battle.

Mara says to get flour and sugar, cover the floor. they can't take dust!!

It clogs their fans sensors.

Flour. Of course. Mara was married to a smart guy, so he trusted her. Tree was too high-strung, and she might give him some bad information. Liquids didn't work on the bots, since they were hardened against water as well as any car, but they couldn't get dirty. Harris laughed again, breathing in the reek of forty or fifty skunks without a care as he ran over to the baking aisle.

"We have a new plan!" Some of the Runnies, eyes streaming and noses covered with cloth and towels, popped up from their hiding places and watched as he grabbed two big bags of flour, then ripped them open and poured them everywhere. "Dirt, comrades! We need filth!" A couple of the Runnies caught on immediately and stampeded the cooking aisle, hands covering their noses. Bags of flour went first, then the sugar, corn bread mix, and oatmeal. Then the cooking oils, because why not? The skunk smell was replaced by sweet kitcheny smells. Finally having something constructive to do, the Runnies roared for Vorebot annihilation as they emptied the shelves. A pallet of chocolate pudding cups was ransacked, the lids pulled off like hand grenades and sent flying. A couple of Runnies fell in the mess and almost shot each other.

The overhead fans came on, then the sprinklers, which only had a quarter of the water pressure they needed, so they fizzed and hissed water all over the store. The human combatants coughed and choked in the foodstorm as they were soaked and covered in white paste, their faces covered like bandits. But it was doing worse things to the Vorebots, who had been advancing confidently into the store after they released the skunk bomb. One by one, the robots' little alarm lights went on and they struggled to breathe—or at least Harris imagined they did for a second. Don't be stupid, he told himself, they're not alive and they don't breathe. They only have fans, mechanical fans. The bots became more and more bogged down and finally they all stopped moving. The store was still. The Runnies looked upon their works and were amazed. They had destroyed most of the grocery aisles, and a few other departments besides. But it was for a good cause, they reassured themselves, looking at their destruction.

The rude metal cans that had tormented Runnies since the day they were invented were dead. They were just another machine—one more tech toy that people prized more than life, but they were only one more gadget. They got tired. They gave up. They weren't *sentient*. They were an electronic shopping cart. As the Vorebots stalled out, coated a virginal white, they seemed harmless and dull, barely worth notice, let alone a panic. A few of them squeaked a little as they attempted to send information to clogged circuits. It was a bit unnerving, even if you hated them.

The filthy, sticky Runnies looked at each other. A spring rain sputtered down from the ceiling, cementing the cooking dust into clothing and crevices. The sodden mess bummed everyone out, no matter how complete their victory, so they tramped back to the beer cave to see if they could find something to cheer themselves up. It had been ransacked, but there were still a few cases, so they took everything that was left. It was going to be a while before they could get groceries again, but they still had their store. The cowardly Vores wouldn't even come in and try to retrieve their bots, but would go home and start pushing buttons for a new one. Harris and the other Runnies took turns beating on them as they passed, but the thrill was gone. The Vorebots were as dead as only an electronic toy plastered with flour in the rain could be. Some of the warriors were slightly embarrassed about the melee now, even though the majority of them were drunk, at least. It had seemed like a takeover was imminent. It had been on the internet. But it had been far too easy to put down, and now the people who lived in the parking lot would have to come in and clean it all up. The victors looted a few things they really liked, figuring that it was owed to them for saving Stalwarts. Most of it was wet anyway. Harris got some new groceries to take home to Tree.

Mara started the car at the puny charge of ninety-three percent and they left Destiny while the Vores were still doing their aimless merchandising all over the parking lot. They liked to use Destiny as a backdrop, since Destiny was a classy store. Tree had been watching a man with a camouflage headset review a cart full of hunting and camping gear, using all the hand gestures and over-the-top body movements demanded of his trade. This pack! This boot! This hat! He grinned and postured. As he reached the end of the parking lot, he dumped his entire cart into the even larger dumpster that announced DESTINY on it. He didn't actually use any of that gear, because the outdoors was too dirty for his electronics. He only reviewed it. He'd be paid well enough for his blurb that he could toss all of it, since he had another box of products waiting for him at home. The goods would remain in the dumpster until tonight, when any Runnie lucky enough to catch the episode on their drone camera would descend on the dumpster and take most of it for Bartertown.

Mara caught Tree's death glare at the entrepreneur and quipped, "Don't forget, he's conserving resources by working from home."

"We have to stop these people, for the good of the planet. You can see this too, right, Mara?"

"I'm not going to take you over there if you talk like that." Tree sent a text to Harris. Maybe he could attack something for her.

They were at Stalwart's in a minute, since it was only a few miles away. The parking lot was full of Vore vehicles, which was—weird. Mara felt a sense of unease herself. The Vores only went to Stalwarts to be invasive, the same reason they did a lot of other things. It wasn't their preferred store. She parked by the road, in case they needed to leave fast. Tree spotted Harris' empty truck at the other end of the parking lot. So he was inside. They scanned the lot for clues. There were a lot of Vorebots going inside—more than usual, probably. And minus their owners, so that was suspicious. The whole setup looked fishy, just as Tree said. There were way too many Vore vehicles in the parking lot, too many robots entering the store by themselves, and none of the Vores were exiting their vehicles to accompany them. They looked at each other. Mara asked, "Well? The battle is on. What do we do?"

"I don't know. But it's happening. We're witnesses to history!" Mara didn't look so impressed, but they settled in to witness anyway. The Vorebots continued to roll, and there were shots coming from inside the store. They couldn't hear them very well, but someone was definitely shooting. The bots slowed down a little and seemed to regroup, rolling around on their ball feet until they made a new kind of formation. Tree sent Harris another text, since he might be in danger.

Mara says to get flour and sugar, cover the floor. they can't take dust!!

It clogs their fans sensors.

There were more shots from inside the store. With no clue as to what was going on inside, Tree writhed in agony. Some of the bots were milling around at the entrance. Were they going to trip everyone with their spider arms? A last wave of bots rolled into the store. There must have been seventy of them in there now, but as yet, their owners hadn't made a move to get out of their vehicles. Tree watched the Vore cars, because that was odd in itself. The Vorebots now appeared to be having a little trouble, and several of them were stalled out in the doorway, or going around in circles, their judgment clouded by something. A few were shot and were trying to get back to their cars, blinking and wounded. The Runnies were winning. But why? They never won in Vorebot encounters, being hopelessly outbrained by the AI. And she knew they were guarding the beer cave again. Tree stared at an ominous-looking Vore hulk.

"Mara, these Vores are making me very nervous. They're waiting for something."

Mara agreed. "Where are the legal documents? They have to do a big ceremony where they produce the papers, otherwise I don't know how serious this is. They're too lazy to actually kill anyone." She sent several texts to Hani while they watched the inaction. A few Runnies came out of the store, looking rushed but not wounded.

"Do you see smoke? They didn't set it on fire, did they?" This was pretty boring for a war. The situation appeared to be at a stalemate. Tree waited for the Vores to exit their cars. The parking lot Runnies watched from their lawnchairs. And then the Vores opened their doors, and all of them left their vehicles at once. It sent a chill down Tree and Mara's spines, even if they knew that the Vores were idiots. Their giant heads got out with their tranquilizer guns, and Vores had the best of everything. They could have anything inside those darts. If they were having a good day, they might be packing heroin or tranquilizers, but if not, it could be rat poison.

"This is bad," Mara observed, swearing a little, which was unlike her. They slid down in the seat, lest they became a target of one of these loons. Mara sent a couple more texts. The Vores huddled, then appeared to be trying to set up some sort of military formation in the parking lot, while their precious bots were being killed in the store. Typical. Way to set priorities. None of them could grasp anything well, because of their fingernails. Then they needed to do hand-eye coordination exercises for a few minutes, where they tossed their weapons back and forth between each hand, getting their headsets synced up with them. Then they decided to compare guns and darts while posing for pictures. They didn't get to break out the real weapons very often, so this took a few minutes. It was worse than when they compared their masks with each other, and they did that constantly.

After that session, they tried to make some sort of marching formation again, but then one Vore accidentally stabbed another with a vomiting dart, and that started a fight. Vomiting darts were very unpleasant but only lasted a few minutes, fortunately for the girl. She struggled to remove her headset fast enough to barf her personalized, pre-biotic, probiotic breakfast all over the ground. It was close, because they really did not like to take those things off. Tree and Mara snorted. The parking lot Runnies wailed with laughter and started posting videos of her to the internet. The Vores began arguing about carelessness and taking this seriously, and Tree and Mara laughed more. But the Vores did finally get it together after a few of them took some pills, or at least they were all pointed in the same direction. It was starting to look worrying again. But Mara was nonplussed.

"We're cool. I'm bringing in the reinforcements." She pointed at the road. Tree saw a big blocky car coming their way that looked familiar. It was the PT car, the one Tree hadn't seen since Mara parked it behind their house. Hani drove up at a fast clip and parked close to them, smiling as widely as his wife usually did. She returned his grin with one of her own. Hani waved at Tree, then flipped on the PT screen.

SUNSTORM COMING TAKE COVER

The Vore vehicles responded so fast, Tree didn't realize what was happening right away: they all left. They started themselves and drove out of the parking lot in a formation far more orderly than their owners could ever master, since the vehicles had good AI, but the Vores kept interfering. The drivers were still standing in the parking lot with their dart guns when their vehicles all started driving away. A few of them were alert and managed to get back to their car before it got too far away, but thirty or forty Vores were left standing in parking lot with their mouths open, looking at the rapidly vanishing line of cars, then at their dart guns. They were mostly illegal and not something you wanted to be caught with, even at a dump like Stalwarts.

If any vehicle received warnings about an electrical storm, it was programmed to head for the nearest geographical place where it could hide. This was a life-saving feature for them, and the engineers had thought that it would be widely appreciated. Then to their shock, it was not. The app was still in there even though it wasn't used, because no one ever removed invasive technology, only added more. Most people had forgotten about it, but Hani hadn't. Mara and Hani smiled at each other across the parking lot as they watched the giant black vehicles pull out, a few Vores running after them, signaling to them with their headsets. But once the sunstorm warning came down, finding shelter was the default. Hani turned off the PT, and Mara jumped out of the Trotter and ran over to him, giving him a bear hug and a big kiss.

"I knew you could do it, honey. We can't let them get away with this."

Tree was confused, like the Vores, since it was dawning on them that they would have to walk home, or wait for their vehicles to come back, which could take a few hours. Naked without their security trucks, their four hundred-pound purses, and at the wrong store, they panicked. They ditched the dart guns with the parking lot Runnies, who were thrilled to be getting unknown drugs from the Vores, since they had the best stuff. Then they all trotted off down the road after each other, their sculpted calves flexing like nobody's business as they jogged toward the finer neighborhoods.

They'd been abandoned so fast, the Vores were also left without the binders of legal documents that they were going to use to overwhelm the Runnies, after they'd filled them full of drugged darts. It didn't particularly matter how the whole business went down, since the Vores were in the right. Once the Runnies were "served," almost anything was legal, even if the papers were on fire and served out of a cannon. But all of that was forgotten for the moment. The Vores could come back. They had time. They had lawyers.

When the battle-weary Runnies left the store, the Vores were already long gone. The battle of the parking lot was over too, even faster than the one inside. Robot war wasn't as interactive or as visual as regular war, Tree reflected. There weren't piles of bodies when someone took over a computer system. She was walking around the parking lot mulling this when she saw them. The soggy, rumpled Runnies looked like they'd been in some kind of a fight. Mara's advice must have worked. It looked like Mara and Hani had saved Stalwarts almost single-handedly—and then there was this crew. Harris was at the front of the pack, grinning like a fool. They looked as satisfied as people who had just destroyed most of a grocery store could be. Tree continued walking around the parking lot, not wanting to interrupt the victory party. It had only been a little over an hour since they left Destiny.

A citizen of the parking lot took the photo. He'd been lurking by the door for his chance to go in and salvage some of the Vorebots for parts. Instead, he snapped a picture of Harris as he exited the store—arms above his head, grinning like a champion. He had a toy guitar in one hand, and in the other, a bottle of the same beer he'd drunk in his commercial thirty years ago—the last brand left in the looted beer cave. Thirty years was a long time for a beer to be on top, after all. It was a repeat of the pose he'd struck when he ran out of the surf in his famous commercial, and someone made the connection. The still-sexy eyes, the good teeth, the bandanna around his neck, the pistol stuffed into his front pocket like—well, everyone knows what a pistol stuffed into your front pocket looks like. There were other warriors right next to Harris, laughing and grimy, raising their fists in victory, but none of them had ever been a rock star, or looked quite like that, at that moment. Harris was viral by the time he made his way home, but he'd turned his phone off. He was in no hurry to admit to Tree that they owed the whole show to a cooking tip from a woman. He hadn't fired a shot, or done much of anything, really, except steal some beer.

But that was how it was in war—you had to make decisions in the heat of the moment. Gathered with his fellow heroes in the front of the parking lot, he enjoyed the glow of victory for a few minutes, as they dared the Vores to come and try to retrieve their dead robots. None of them did, and the Runnies had the rare feeling of being top dog. A police car drove by slowly, and seeing that the situation didn't look much worse than it usually did, breathed a sigh of relief and kept driving.

Tree was still wandering around when she saw a white guy peeing on the side of the store. So uncivilized, these people. "Hey," she walked up on him. The guy jumped and stuffed himself back into his pants.

"Were you in the store? What happened? Did you do the flour thing?"

The man turned and grinned at her. "We WON. Those robots are all dead. They had no chance."

Tree felt like saying, "Do you know who I am?" Instead she said, "Yeah, that flour is good stuff. *Harris* knew, because I told him while he was in there."

"The *rock star* Harris? Oh wow, do you know him? He had that song, 'Compelling world.' You know him? '*Trust each other, lose our fear. (lose our fear, lose our fear),*'" he whispered dramatically. Tree had had quite enough of this already.

"Yeah, I know that song. You realize that the Vores were about to go in there and slaughter you, right? We were out here and saved you. *My friend* showed up and hijacked their vehicles."

The man was having none of this. "We won. We kicked their butts."

"You didn't even see the Vores. They had weapons, real weapons. And legal documents."

The white guy brushed some now-dry flour off his face and said, "I don't know what you're talking about, but that sounds like crap to me. You can't hijack the Voremobiles. You're one of those eco-warriors, aren't you? You probably don't even know Harris. He wouldn't need to go there, if you know what I mean."

"He *lives* in my HOUSE!" Tree was so right, she didn't even stop to bury the guy with her rightness, and stalked off. She wondered about the PT car for the first time. That might get Hani into some trouble, if anyone had recorded that. And what was he doing at Stalwarts in the middle of the day, anyway, when he should be at work? Tree circled back to where she'd left the PT car. Both of them were still sitting in it, looking like soulmates.

"Hani, do we need to call you a lawyer or something? Because this seems kind of impulsive of you. Almost an irresistible impulse, and you don't seem the type."

Hani didn't look too worried, since Mara was sitting in his lap, but maybe he would be later. He'd given his students some math problems that were accessed on their headsets, so they probably didn't even realize he was gone. The PT car was an anachronism, but not so unusual that anyone would make note of it in the parking lot. He'd only left the sign on for a few seconds—just long enough for the AI to see it, so the Vores themselves probably hadn't, and would be too embarrassed to make much of a scene. A glitch in the software or something. You put up with that sort of thing, for the convenience.

After a little more socializing, Hani pushed Mara off his lap and drove the hero car back up the hill. He'd saved a bunch of Runnies, and nobody would ever know except Tree and Mara.

She was mistaken though, because of the power of the internet. Because of the power of that photo of Harris and his battle-floured friends. Tree went home and put her feet in the pool while she thought about things. Hani should get credit for his role in saving Stalwarts, but more than likely his actions were kind of sketchy with the University. Especially since he'd left his classroom and slipped out with a grad student who'd agreed to run him home right then. His students forgot to leave once they got their headsets on, and were still there two hours later when Hani got back. He had to give them all A's for the day, and now they would never stop trying to blackmail him.

Harris got home later and after a shower, came to regale her with tales of their heroics. He may have made it sound a little more dangerous than it had been, but since Tree knew about the flour, he couldn't lie too much.

"Yeah, it stopped them right away. I almost felt bad for them. They started squeaking and whining. It was like they couldn't breathe."

"No, Harris, forget the bots," Tree told him, uncomfortably recalling the Vore vehicles that thought they were going to die. "You can't start having feelings for them. None of you guys knew about the Vores outside. They were going in this time, and it was serious. They had real weapons. And Hani stopped them."

"Hani? Isn't he at work?" It was so odd to find someone who had a full-time job now, no one could remember how it worked.

"No. Well, he was, but he came to Stalwarts and saved us. He saved Stalwarts, and nobody can know about it." She filled him in on the PT car and the ethical dilemma. "I mean, you guys were great. But Hani stopped the Vores in the parking lot. It was so funny, Harris. It must be all over the internet."

They checked, and the usually balky internet was on fire. It took them only a minute or so to find videos of the Battle. There must have been seventy dead Vorebots inside the store. Most of the place was soggy and covered with white mud. A few sprinklers still dribbled into buckets. The parking lot Runnies were already inside cleaning though, giving big thumbs up as they swept up flour and took cartons of ruined goods out to the parking lot, plus anything else they wanted. The lawn chair section was wiped out, again. Where did all those chairs go? The place would be open again in no time, but with shortages. Then Tree found the photo of Harris coming out of the store, combined with a shot from his commercial, with his tiny swimming trunks, his guitar, and his big white smile. He was right—he had been hot. Why hadn't they slept together in college?

"Oh no," Harris said, looking over her shoulder. He didn't want to be on the internet. Did he? Tree smacked him in the shoulder. "Harris! You're a meme! Why didn't you tell me about this rock star stuff?"

She hadn't forgotten, had she? Because he wasn't going through it again. He was sober now. They searched for evidence of the PT car using its sign, but so far there was nothing posted. There were several videos of the Vore girl throwing up, naturally. She'd put on a good show for a few minutes. Tree felt a little let down. It had been so anticlimatic, even though it appeared that her side had won—against the Vores. They should be celebrating, and yet, it was all kind of meaningless. If Stalwarts had fallen, surely another store would have come along to feed them, wouldn't it? No one, not even Tree, could imagine running out of the basics they would always need, even if it kept happening. Had they overreacted?

But it didn't matter. Stalwarts was prepared to make it all legitimate, and make Harris a real hero. They were going to own it just as they had the original riots—after they changed most of the story for their own purposes. All they had to do was put a few rumors on the internet and watch them go. Harris surfed for a few more minutes and felt his private life being drained from him by a viral infection. He was already getting texts from complete strangers; how did they do that? He tried to remember how much of him was available on the 'net, and there was a disturbing amount. He should have been paranoid like Tree. At least the first time around, he'd been a more than willing participant in the exploitation and the fantasy. "I don't know how I feel about this," he said finally.

"America has spoken, Harris. You have to do whatever the internet tells you to do, or they'll come for you." They probably would too. The little weirdos would fly drones over her house and spy on them, sitting there with their feet in the pool. Scandalous! Harris might put up with it and play a song for them, but Tree had a gun too, and she'd shoot a drone for looking at her. It was Harris' own fault anyway, for still being so hot at his age.

Harris was right. In a peak consumer society, there was no right or wrong, and nobody was responsible for anything. Everything we did today was an exercise of our freedom, so there were no boundaries, no wrong moves. If real estate bubbles, predatory loans, superyachts and twelve-bathroom homes were acceptable or even desirable, then so was being a bank robber, an eco-terrorist, or a wildlife poacher. The only real sin was in not exercising your full freedom of choice, even if you needed to invade someone else's space to do it. Even if you were a corporation. Even if you needed to engage in fraud, create tools that would bankrupt society, or dump your boyfriend because he didn't have enough money, everyone needed to reach their full consumer potential. It was the promise of the American Dream.

The destitute, drug-addicted, and economic misfits were welcome here too—as examples of those who had also exercised their full consumer choices, but poorly. In the great yin/yang of The Economy, both sides were needed. The wiser souls needed the misfits as examples of what they should insulate themselves against. For this reason, the poor shouldn't be given too much, because it would throw out the natural balance. There could be no other reason for the poors' ugliness than their own choices. A system this verdant had more than enough for everyone.

They looked at more videos from the day. There was one of Harris sitting on a bike in the back of the store, playing a toy guitar and bellowing,

"Ninety-nine bots in our store today, ninety-nine bots to be killed!
We chased 'em down and dusted their crown,
Ninety-eight bots to be killed today!"

The chubby guy who had gotten Harris into it was leading the conga line as they sang and bumped around the toy section. They all had toy guns and real guns and big plastic knives. At least three of the warriors now had boxes over their heads, so they kept running into each other.

"What discipline." commented Tree. "Those guys are real survivalists, right?"

"I'm really glad you texted me about the flour, Tree. They had no plan," Harris confessed, since everything was going to turn out all right anyway, and Tree wouldn't blab except to Mara, who already knew. "We could have put on a much better show if those guys hadn't been guarding the beer cave for hours already. No one had any idea how to stop the bots. Most of them were just there for the beer, and they kept shooting, even though people were getting wounded. We could have been hurt, couldn't we?"

"Or been very, very sued. Or thrown up a lot. Nobody knows, so it's a good thing Hani showed up. It didn't look like much, but it could have been a real riot, and real dead people." They stopped looking at their phones and went to bed.

Every Successful Species has to Find a Niche

· · · ·

The Battle of Stalwarts
The rumors spread across the land of lofty legal readings,
To rob us of our grocery store by secret Vore proceedings.
Runnies came from near and far to save our favorite mart,
Where we not only buy our food, we sometimes lose our hearts.
Freedom! we cried, and it rang throughout the valleys,
Our way was clear, the die was cast, and at our store we rallied.
The fierce Runnies held the store,
While Vorebots lost their traction.
Lurking in the underbrush,
Vores waited for their action.
Then from the college on the hill there came a man of reason,
A man of rationality—a man for every season.
He made the call, Vores rued the day,
Math skills helped him save the day.
From the wags of Bartertown, to desks of learned scholars,
The story of the man of math still echoes through the hollers.
Through the night he rides alone with flags of flashing lights,
He knows pi to 80 digits, from those endless sleepless nights.
To honor him we learn to count, and this we'll always know:
*Stalwart's is **our** parking lot, and where we'll always go!*
(Repeat last line——encourage conga line, pass out souvenir flags)

"I know what you're going to say, OK, and let me head it off by saying that I didn't write that. z It was more like—a committee. A committee of sponsors. Stalwarts, obviously, and the math department at the university, and obviously me."

"The math department? How did they get involved in this? I thought Hani wasn't supposed to have that car."

"Turns out they knew about it, since there is a GPS tracker in the PT car, and it's their car. Also turns out that the math department doesn't like Vores much, and when they saw those videos, they knew what had happened. They'd been working on sunspot protection for years, and their messaging could go right through all the firewalls. That's why we have all those bomb shelters for cars—the guys at the college asked for them."

"Is that what those are? We have bomb shelters for cars, but not for us? Good thinking."

"We can use them too, since you're in your car, right? Hani told me all about it. It was a great safety feature, but no one liked losing control of their cars, even if they weren't driving them. Those guys were very proud of their tech, even if it had to be withdrawn. They know about you and Mara harassing the Vore cars too, by the way."

"Ooh. Is that bad? That was funny too."

"Let's just say that it's a good thing that a certain faculty wife really liked her blind horses. She said that they were even better for use as therapy horses, because the people could relate to them better.

"That's what I told Mara. Handicapped horses have more empathy."

"I think they already have something set up for next year—bigger trailer, more horses. Anyway, they were going to discipline Hani for taking off like that, but when the math department saw the videos, they were laughing so hard, they couldn't do it. He did leave an assignment. And Stalwarts is furious about the stealth lawsuit, so they're saying that if the Vores want a culture war, they can have one. The department is really suffering since all the headsets came in. They graduated two hundred students a month ago, and not one of them can do math well enough to become an astronaut. From the *Astronaut College.* They saw the picture of me on the internet, and somebody had an idea to partner with Stalwarts. Hani was all for it. He helped me write the song."

"I can tell. That'll be a surprise to Mara, that Hani is a van man. And the endless sleepless nights. And here she thought they were happily married. You probably got dragged into this so that he wouldn't lose his job."

"Tree, it's hard to make up long songs that tell a story. People think that you just rhyme words, but there's meter and things to consider too. They wanted it to be really American. Then they made me do the music too, since I'm a musician. I was there for *hours*. I like songs with repeating lines better."

"I can't believe you're such a sellout. So are you rich again?"

"I am still rich. And now I am richer."

"You're going to get those solar panels now?"

"Four of them, not two. We're going to be able to play records and wash clothes at the same time."

Tree didn't care if he was a sell-out if he got the solar panels. Reliable electricity was going away month by month, but they kept getting charged for it anyway. Tree liked to think that anarchists were cutting down the lines to safe humanity from themselves, but it wasn't even that logical. Squirrels in Washington had chewed up some wires and started a fire so big, most of their remaining habitat had burned to the ground, proving that they weren't smarter than humans after all. Take that, Sierra Club! But no one wanted to be a firefighter anymore. Smoke-jumpers born with too many thrill-seeking genes found other pursuits after they saw a few fire tornadoes. No one was going to parachute into one of those. It was too late for fighting wildfires, like it was too late for a lot of things.

Tree looked at the poster again. It was god-awful—bright and summery-looking, not like the bland field of concrete and blowing debris that was Stalwarts most of the time. Tall, sleek-looking humans with full heads of hair stood in the parking lot, math problems whizzing around their heads as Vorebots fled the store, covered in white splotches. In the background loomed the bulk of Stalwarts, more respectable-looking than Tree had ever seen it. The parking lot was clean and empty, no Runnie camps to be seen, while some big black shapes were escaping down the road. It all had little resemblance to reality, but it was advertising, so that wasn't surprising. Besides, what was wrong with making fun of Vores, or learning math? Then she saw the text on the side.

TOUR DATES October 4-31

Final Show at the **Haunted Stalwarts** in Miami!

Enter to win!

"You're leaving? You're leaving me to go to Miami?" How long had he been here anyway? Five or six years? She'd rarely spent a night alone in her house since he moved in. Tree was surprised at how panicky she felt at the thought of him leaving her alone. She used to have dogs.

"It's only for a month. I have to do this, Tree. It's for my old age." And for the posters they'd made of him leading the troops in Stalwarts. And for the paycheck. He might even buy six solar panels and a new guitar. He was kind of rusty, but he wasn't fossilized yet.

"You know if you go to Miami, you have to walk around on boardwalks, or the alligators will eat you? The people there talk so pretty, no one will notice you singing. All of Bourbon Street moved there after New Orleans flooded out, and they party all day long. The parrots fly in to hear the music and roost right on their shoulders. Once they get going, nobody is going to hear you at all."

"I know! They love live music! We have three shows there. It's going to be an easy gig, even if we do have to play in Texas. Miami also has the only Stalwarts on a barge, for the boat people. It's really popular. For the Haunted Stalwarts they're bringing in real dead Vorebots. I can't wait to see it. It'll be good for me, Tree." He didn't explain why, but clearly he was thrilled to get away from her, even for this trashy nonsense.

After she'd registered her disapproval, weak though it may have been, Tree was free to be envious. She'd like to go to Miami and see the parrots too, and watch Harris sing. She knew he could could sing a tune, but could he really perform? She could check on the internet, but by that time it could have been altered. At least she'd witnessed the spectacle at Stalwarts with her own eyes, because what she had seen there was not the same story that was out in the world after three weeks of hype. That "Ninety-nine Vorebots" video had almost five million views. Five million people, minimum, who could see with their authentic internet eyes that Harris hadn't led any troops except in conga dancing. No one even understood the part in the song about the math man. The crew inside the store saw none of it, and since it hadn't been recorded, it had already vanished into history, until the university decided to bring it back.

Did they really all support Stalwarts anyway? It wasn't as though they had much of a choice. The store had been trashed for weeks, even with the parking lot crew working hard, or maybe not, but no one was going to replace them, or supervise them either. Now half the inventory was behind the big locked door, at least for a while. One day Tree wanted to make some cookies and went in for sugar and waited for hours. Perversely, she'd *known* that it would take her hours, and had still decided to come in, knowing that she would make no cookies that day. She pondered this while she stood in line. It was fine, though, because she sat down with a woman who had a ferret in her cart and they fed it carrots until it ran all over the store. It was still better than going to Destiny, the place where things ran like clockwork and were cold, boring, and predictable. She hoped that the Vores didn't put a hit on Harris, the public face of Vore ridicule.

Harris had to be gentrified before his tour, since he had become too common for American consumption. A guy came out to the house one day and gave Harris a trim and put highlights in his hair. Then he massaged his face with oils, and offered some paralyzing agents and collagen "to smooth out your cheeks," but Harris demurred. The guy also said that he'd do a massage, but Harris told him that he'd do some yoga instead, so that he'd be limber enough to jump around on stage. Tree could show him.

"All right then, I'm done," the disappointed hairdresser pouted and put his things away. He gave Harris some jeans made from the finest cashmere wool, and a sweatshirt with the college logo on it. The jeans fit him like a second skin and were as light as a spiderweb. Tree wanted a pair.

"Yes, I know," said the hairdresser. "That's the whole idea." Harris took them off to save them for the tour, and Tree put them around her neck like a scarf. They were amazing. The stylist fluffed Harris' hair up again and gave him some new earrings, then departed. Harris shook his head around and roared. Tree hadn't realized that big hair was back either. Was that glitter? She might have to have a word about that, later.

Harris looked too fine to sit down in the house, so they went out for beers. In the dark bar, he looked twenty-one again. A few Vores came by and gave him poker chips, since they remembered him as that clever Runnie who could play the guitar. Except for them, it was just like old times.

"Did he put makeup on you? You look amazing. And you can really carry the eyeliner. Some guys can't."

"It's not *makeup*. It's essential oils."

'Oh yes, of course. Essential skin-colored oils."

A few days later Tree took him down to the highway to meet the bus. It was bigger than Tree's house and looked like it could stop a freight train. STALWARTS shouted the side of it, as well as the three flags flying off the top. She'd taken a picture for infamy.

"Not a word," Harris warned her as she snickered. "Don't forget if that if we hadn't saved it, you'd be eating potatoes and snow cones for the rest of your life." Oh, who was this "we"—Hani and Mara? Tree hadn't even known that Stalwarts had their own flag, but apparently they did too. Harris piled on the bus with his all-girl backup band, The Raging Pussies, and was gone.

Tree felt a pang. She finally made a friend, and he becomes famous at sixty? He'd already *been* famous, and he hadn't done anything to be famous *for,* then or now. As long as capitalism survived, this empire of fraud and deception would thrive. She should send that to Harris, maybe he could write a song. Do some good for once.

She drove by Mara's on the way home, but the Trotter was gone too, so she went home and put her feet in the pool, her torso wrapped in a blanket. Such luxury. If Harris bought some more solar panels, maybe they could put some more insulation in the house. Pile books to the ceiling like Mara and Hani did. Some prairie dogs came and begged for treats, so she gave them crackers she'd picked up at Bartertown, since they were terrible. At least the tiny dogs were predictable. They loved anything she gave them.

* * * *

She needed to get down to Bartertown with the blue boxes before it got too cold, so she scheduled a day with Mara when the sun was supposed to be shining. They did a sweep of their houses and found the piles of things they did not want to look at through the winter. Tree needed something good to trade for charging those boxes, even if she figured that she'd be super-charming and he wouldn't notice what she'd brought so much. She usually had to go to the library to charge up, where she had to hang out for hours, trying to keep the clunky batteries hidden as they borrowed electricity from the town. Tree had some heavy-duty boxes, as big as cats. The library was fairly tolerant of people doing this, but still. So it would be foolish of her to not take advantage of solar panels at Bartertown. She wasn't going to dither around and watch TV all day just because Harris was gone. She had things to do. She also had a prize from Destiny that she needed to show off—several fold-up electric carts of some sort, but modeled with holes and fittings to carry a Vorebot around. Because the Vorebots themselves were not also tireless carts that carried things....

"I guess they didn't sell at all, because even the Vores have some sense left," Tree concluded, showing off one of the military-grade carts to Mara. They were camouflage, naturally, in case the Vorebot needed to hide from incoming fire. They were quality wagons, since they could carry the weight of a bot and had been ludicrously expensive, to go with the other ludicrously expensive Vore fashions, until they were canceled simply by tossing them in a dumpster. Presto-chango, now you're worth nothing—that was how the free market worked. So now Tree had six of them, which would be worth a fortune at Bartertown every day. And people tried to say that capitalism was a rational way of doing things. She'd promised that she would get Harris something exceptional with one of them, since he'd come down to help her get them out of the dumpster, where she was guarding them from some hostile Runnie drones.

She drove three of them down to Mara's, all folded together in a very fashionable way. There was no good reason to have multiple robot strollers, let alone one, but it didn't matter, as long as it was cool. They were too—just as cunning as they could be, all nested together like kittens. There were straps so they could be fastened to the back of a Voremobile. On top of this fashion statement Tree laid a big duffel bag of sewed up clothes, the blue boxes, a lemon cake, some books and a sleeping bag, then rode it down to Mara's and went in. It was crispy outside, but cozy in the house, as usual. Tree sat on the couch and was quickly covered with cats. Mara had a tote full of edibles again, which wouldn't take her long to to get rid of. Tree spotted something unusual.

"Is this cat hair I see? And some cat prints on your windowsill? Did the robot move out?"

"I guess he did. We sent it back to the school. Making room."

"Well, that's good, because it's kind of weird, even if it did all those things."

"We had to give back the PT car too. It's like they don't trust us or something. But Hani got a raise anyway. They said that they appreciated him trying to teach those idiots."

"Is that what they said?"

"Almost a direct quote, according to Hani. Some of the colleges are starting a lobbying effort to get the math standards lowered for astronauts. That last eval by the Space Force was pretty devastating. The Indians are good at math, and they're always up at the space station. Plus the AI does a lot of the work up there now, so the requirement doesn't need to be so rigorous."

They set off with their fashionable carts. Tree was definitely keeping one of them for her Bartertown shopping. It was by far the nicest thing she'd had to help with labor. Mara seemed a little distracted and not as lively as she usually was. Halfway down the hill, she stopped to rest on a rock, then suddenly leaned over and neatly threw up her breakfast. Tree was startled. Mara never had a twinge of poor health.

"Is it the microplastics? Did they get you too?"

"Micro-something." Mara wiped her mouth and grinned from ear to ear. "I'm pregnant."

Tree hit the snow cone stand first thing, when Fiona had the best flavors. With her fancy cart, Tree could lounge around like one of the elite, bringing her table with her. After she picked up a strawberry snow cone, her favorite, she followed Mara to a table, then helped her spread her wares out.

"Be super chill and zen, Mara, for the baby. There's all kinds of hazards out there now."

A woman at a nearby table looked like she was about to burst into tears when she overheard this.

"Stop it, Tree, keep it down. It's not nice to do that. And I still have months." Mara did look relieved to sit down on some ratty chair though. Tree felt great though, thanks to whatever Fiona had put in her snow cone. She'd paid way too much for it though.

"You keep it down, Mara—hey, do you get it? Keep it down." She made a barfing gesture, and Mara laughed despite herself.

"It's going to be so exciting. You must be so excited." Tree was in awe of being close to someone who was having a natural baby. It was even more miracle-of-life than it used to be, and women who had babies were followed around in the streets, so that other women could get a glimpse of the miracle. For that reason, the Vores tended to keep their babies locked up somewhere so that no one could see them without permission, making real babies even rarer, and real Vore children even weirder.

Tree borrowed Mara's smile and left her to barter while she wheeled her fine carts around, attracting the attention of other traders who really wanted one, even though Tree was taking up most of the walking space with her ostentatious electronics, very Vore-fash. She drummed up some interest but wasn't prepared to part with one yet. This was the most valuable merchandise she'd had in years. She scanned the surroundings and found Terry's big solar setup in a far corner, close to the construction end of 'Town. It was noisy over there and attracted big guys who stood around in circles and complained about how hard it was to do anything now, as they hauled merchandise in and out like teams of Clydesdales. Terry looked bored instead of talking someone's ear off, even though four people were leafing through his pornos. He must need some more cigarettes to wake up. Tree brushed her hair back and turned the corner with her spiffy rig. She hid behind the wagon and rolled it up to Terry's layout, then parked beside his table. She did have a mission here after all, a perfectly normal errand.

"Hi!" she said brightly, then, out of social skills, she busied herself pulling the blue boxes out of her bag. He was watching her, she could tell. She concentrated on her task. Once the boxes were sitting on top of her gear, she didn't have to speak anymore, because he could tell why she was there, it was obvious. She had to anyway, because he was obtuse.

"I need to charge my boxes," she gestured at them.

"I can do that," deadpanned Terry, staring at her. Was he making a lewd joke, and not even a good one? Or was he just answering her, like a normal human being? Oh the world. It was so confusing.

"Yes. I uh, I brought you the cake. I brought you a lemon cake, like you wanted. To charge our boxes. For the winter. Is that enough? I mean, you are getting the sun for free."

"I'd take one of those wagons, " Terry said, a man through and through. She plugged in her boxes and handed him the cake. It did look good. It was one of her better efforts. She'd squeezed real lemons, put the little curls on top. Zesty. She had cookbooks from a hundred years ago and most recipes still worked if you could get the ingredients. Because original was better.

"These wagons are for—well, I don't know what, but we are going to get something good for them." And if Terry wanted one he could go buy one for full price, whatever it was. Not that he'd check. He'd just point at it and wait for it to be delivered.

"You better sit down. I doubt you can last until those batteries are charged." He gave her a chair, pretty decrepit but it still worked. He had at least four more boxes of porn magazines under the table, even after months of trading.

Terry saw her gaze. "I made some good investments in the 90s, when I saw where the internet was going. You just can't replace quality porn magazines with digital."

In the 90s? "Your father started a porn publishing empire?"

"The best quality international porn, some of it quite rare. Of course no one appreciates that now. This one is from Italy." He handed her a glossy rag.

"Well," said Tree, leafing through it. "I see. Yes, this is quite interesting." It was to most of the Bartertown crowd, though, and Terry's table had constant traffic. Tree put the magazine back on the pile and before she knew it, she had a lapful of beer, a lamp, a bag of apples, three jars of peanut butter, and some golf clubs. The magazines kept leaving. Terry told a couple of prospective traders that classic porn magazines were never going to go away, like Star Wars. He had a porno of Star Wars, by the way, printed in Russia in 2012. They gave him a winter coat for it, and Terry gave it to Tree.

"I'm warm enough, thank you," Tree piled the coat under the table. During a lull in the festivities, she couldn't resist.

"Terry," she tried his name, and he turned toward her: Mr. Fabulousborker at your service. She was shocked when their eyes met accidentally. Whoa baby, put your sunglasses on. Only lovers looked directly at each other now. "Do you—do you know the Vores?"

"Of course I know the Vores. Everyone knows the Vores." He was so useless. He knew what she wanted.

"Do you think—are they good people? Don't you think that stuff is weird and not good for us?" She didn't feel like getting into the technical details. He either got it or he didn't, and surely he did. Don't be stupid too, she begged him.

"They are idiots," Terry said succinctly, taking his cigarette out of his mouth to enunciate clearly. He grabbed a kid's phone and plugged it into the solar setup, then handed him a rather tame nudie magazine, much to Tree's relief. Why, he wasn't even collecting anything from the kid. Maybe he did have a soul.

"I know!" she said excitedly. "They don't have any situational awareness!" Then, embarrassed at her outburst, she got up and rearranged her wagon full of stuff. She needed to go trade some things—but now they had made a connection, so she needed to press her advantage.

Mara came by when she got rid of her baked goods, but Tree looked fairly relaxed for a woman who'd planned an entire day of enterprise. Her batteries weren't all the way charged, she explained, so she couldn't leave yet. Tree tried to show her some good cartoons from the pornos, but Mara didn't seem very interested. What a prude.

"I see," she said significantly, looking at Tree, at Terry, the empty beer cans on the ground next to them. Then she looked at the solar array, as though Tree was lying to her. It was still working, even if it was getting dim over there. "You're not quite charged up yet." So both of them could make terrible jokes.

"Mara saved Stalwarts," Tree told the crowd in general. Terry looked impressed, as though he cared. He didn't shop there. He was only responding to Mara's attractiveness, like they all did. If she had a pretty baby, people would follow her around day and night. A few of the traders applauded, since they loved The Ballard of Stalwarts, even if they didn't remember her being in the song. One of them began recording her. Mara colored.

"Fine, I'm leaving then. You get me know how the charging goes." Tree gave her a Vorebot cart to help her home in her delicate condition. She had an impressive haul, as usual. Was that a DVD player? Tree would be borrowing that. She opened another beer, signaling that she was resigned to sitting there until the sun went down. She had to pick up the slack since Harris was on tour, just as she'd been telling Terry. The fact that they were her batteries and her house didn't faze her. They'd had some sort of emotional contract, and Harris had broken it. Now she was vulnerable to day drinking and loitering at Bartertown, something she didn't do unless it was a really nice day and the snow cones were excellent.

It was getting colder too. Tree hunched up in her nice coat. The batteries were close to finished. A few of the hyenas were starting to show up, waiting for the exodus of traders and their jettisoning of valuable goods. They seemed to know Terry, and no wonder, since they all needed their phones charged daily. They drifted over and plugged in their phones, then pawed through the rather mundane collection of nudie books. Terry had switched them up for the hyenas. No Star Wars porn for them. Some of them went behind the table and started picking up boxes and loose things around the solar array. Of course—Terry didn't haul all that stuff in and out every day. He hired someone to do it for him. He was practicing golf swings with his new clubs, threatening to take out a few of his workers.

"I should have guessed." Tree drained her beer. She piled up the assortment of goods Terry had amassed during the day. Cowboy boots, some sheets, something that looked like a lobster trap. So far from home. And what was that man doing here, speaking of far from home? Gambling debts? Hiding from the Chinese gangs? All those rich guys got mixed up with them, even though they swore that they didn't. Then their bodies were found covered with melted plastic. The Chinese had a lot of microplastic poisoning, much worse than Tree's, and they weren't too fond of the people who had covered the world with it, even if they had a hand in it.

"Those kids are great workers," Terry told her. "I can't believe how strong they are, since all they eat is ultra-processed foods." He shook his head in admiration, blowing a smoke ring. He'd uncovered another pile of sweets and cookies and had handed them out to the hyenas when they showed up. Tree's mouth watered, but she controlled herself. You couldn't even find that stuff at Stalwarts.

The kids began picking up all of his gear while they crammed sugar concoctions in their mouths, since the sun was clearly going down now and the solar business was over. After loading, five or six of the urchins got around the wagon, which was not electrified at all, and hauled the load off, as though a man like Terry couldn't afford the best motorized cart to haul his junk around. But he was a job creator.

Tree packed up her batteries and wiped some lemon cake off. She needed to be more careful with her precious coat. Terry watched her grooming, then came close to her to get a better look.

"Is this a Blue Blur? You don't see those often. You don't find anything much nicer than a Blue Blur." He fingered a sleeve. Of course he knew about the Blue Blurs. He'd probably gotten ten of them for his mistresses. "Maybe you do have some taste after all."

"Maybe I do," Tree retorted, standing too close to him. She needed to go. She couldn't really hang around and discuss the finer points of inherited wealth, or rapacious capitalism. They hardly knew each other. After cleaning up the beer cans and gathering her stuff together, she turned back to Terry, having run out of excuses.

"I'm heading out. Thank you. I'm ready for winter."

"I'll see you tomorrow," Terry responded breezily, his back to her.

"What? I don't know if I'm coming tomorrow," the words came out before she could think of better words, because of course she could come back. No one needed a reason to hang out at Bartertown. But she'd worn her fur today.

"I have to do inventory. You know how to do that, right?" They assumed so much, these people. They'd shared a few beers and made eye contact once or twice, and now she was his secretary?

"Is it a spreadsheet?"

"It is a spreadsheet. A big one."

Tree was soothed thinking about all of those logical little boxes, even if she was clueless as to how bartering could be turned into numbers. He probably had a system. His kind didn't know how to value things unless they had a dollar sign attached to them.

"How in the world—yes, I can do that. I used to do a lot of spreadsheets." Tree was extremely curious to see how this man did his books. And how had he known of her fondness for spreadsheets? She would probably be participating in tax fraud or very creative accounting, at least. But what else did she have to do? Harris was gone. Mara was going to spend the next several months dusting and turning her home into a nest. Maybe Terry knew some things that would help her subvert the dominant paradigm. If he was a criminal, would that be a subversion of the dominant paradigm, or was criminality actually the dominant paradigm? He'd have an opinion about that, instead of saying, what are you talking about, woman? like most people did. They could debate it.

"Well, I guess I can. Come back." In fact she'd traded almost nothing today, and had to haul it all back home. Porn magazines were more interesting that whatever it was she'd brought. She couldn't compete.

"I guess I'll see you tomorrow then. We can do spreadsheets." She was even more casual than Terry. He was very busy packing his boxes up and just kind of waved at her. She walked out of there like a racehorse, feeling a warmth in her blood that was no doubt due to her superior choice of outerwear. On the way home, the electric cart humming up the hill with no effort at all, Tree stopped to talk to the deer. They were sitting closer together now, their breath fogging in the cold. Soon they'd move downtown to forage for lawns and treats all winter. Tree squatted down for a few minutes, snug in her Blue Blur, and told them about Mara's natural baby. They seemed really happy for her.